The Man Who Sold
Air in the Holy Land

The
Man Who
Sold Air
in the
Holy Land

STORIES

OMER FRIEDLANDER

RANDOM HOUSE
NEW YORK

Copyright © 2022 by Omer Friedlander

All rights reserved.

Published in the United States by Random House, an imprint and division of Penguin Random House LLC, New York.

RANDOM HOUSE and the HOUSE colophon are registered trademarks of Penguin Random House LLC.

The following stories were previously published in substantially different form: "Alte Sachen" in *The Chicago Tribune;* "The Man Who Sold Air in the Holy Land" in *Moment Magazine;* "The Sand Collector" in *Winning Writers;* "Scheherazade and Radio Station 97.2 FM" in *Sonora Review;* "Jellyfish in Gaza" in *The Baltimore Review;* and "Walking Shiv'ah," titled as "Aleph Friedman Killed," in *Lunch Ticket.*

Grateful acknowledgment is made to the following for permission to reprint previously published material:
HarperCollins Publishers: Excerpt from "Eyes" from *The Great Tranquility* by Yehuda Amichai, copyright © 1982 by Yehuda Amichai. Used by permission of HarperCollins Publishers.
University of California Press: Excerpt from "God Full of Mercy" from *The Selected Poetry of Yehuda Amichai* edited and translated from the Hebrew by Chana Block and Stephen Mitchell, copyright © 1986, 1996, 2013 by Chana Bloch and Stephen Mitchell. Used by permission of University of California Press.

Library of Congress Cataloging-in-Publication Data
Names: Friedlander, Omer, author.
Title: The man who sold air in the holy land : stories / Omer Friedlander.
Description: First edition. | New York : Random House, [2022]
Identifiers: LCCN 2021033335 (print) | LCCN 2021033336 (ebook) |
ISBN 9780593242971 (hardcover ; acid-free paper) |
ISBN 9780593242988 (ebook)
Subjects: LCGFT: Short stories.
Classification: LCC PS3606.R55527 M36 2022 (print)
| LCC PS3606.R55527 (ebook) | DDC 813/.6—dc23
LC record available at https://lccn.loc.gov/2021033335
LC ebook record available at https://lccn.loc.gov/2021033336

Printed in the United States of America on acid-free paper

randomhousebooks.com

2 4 6 8 9 7 5 3 1

First Edition

Book design by Jo Anne Metsch

To Ima, Aba, and Elam

Contents

The Man Who Sold
Air in the Holy Land

Jaffa Oranges

We are a fruitful, many-branched, and sprawling family, ranging from Jaffa to Haifa, and our business is oranges. I will be eighty-seven at the turn of the new millennium, and I own one of the last true *shamouti* orange groves, where the fruit is sweet and the peel is thick. My four children—three sons and a daughter—work in finance and law, and my grandchildren—all nine of them—can't tell the difference between a *shamouti* and a mandarin. From time to time, they come visit the grove in HaSharon, help pick the fruit, wrap it individually in waxed paper, and pack it in crates, which are later sold in the farmers market. I'm always reminded of a poem by Yehuda Amichai when I think of my children and my grandchildren. It's called "Eyes," and I know it by heart. *My eldest son's eyes are like black figs for he was born at the end of the summer. And my youngest son's eyes are clear like orange slices, for he was born in their season. And the eyes of my little daughter are round like the first grapes. And all are sweet in my worry. And the eyes of the Lord roam the earth and my eyes are always looking round my house. God's in the eye business and the fruit business. I'm in the worry business.*

When I stumble across the young woman wandering around the grove, I'm preparing for the spring. Since dawn, I've been clearing out the unripe fruit clogging the irrigation canals. I'm wearing my *tembel* hat, its brim hardly covering my large ears, which stick out. My movements are slower than they used to be, my bones ache. The woman, wearing a button-down blouse, billowing beige pants, and sandals, is accompanied by one of my workers, an Arab man who guards the grove, whose hands are always clean and spotless, fingernails clipped and neat. The woman does not seem surprised to see me. In fact, she's been looking for me. She is starkly beautiful with radiant olive skin, dark, tumbling curls, and black eyes under unusually large lids. She tells me she is the granddaughter of my childhood friend Khalil Haddad, a Palestinian whose father owned one of the largest orange groves in Jaffa during the British Mandate.

I can see the resemblance immediately in her eyes. He had the very same ones, dark as coal, heavy-lidded. I try to control my breathing, as we walk through the grove, the light golden on the plump fruit. Her hands cradle the oranges, she presses her ear to them, as if they might whisper a secret. What does she know? What has Khalil told her? My heartbeat is rapid, my hands shake. I have not spoken Khalil's name aloud for years and years. None of my children or grandchildren know his name. The soft grass is spotted with fallen fruit, buzzing bees flit from purple lemon flowers to white lime flowers. Lilah explains that Khalil told her about me—his devoted childhood friend, his only Jewish friend—countless times. When her grandfather died several months before, she decided to come here to ask me about him. She loved him very much, but she feels like she doesn't know much about his past in Palestine before he lived in London, before the war, before al-Nakba.

"It wasn't an easy trip for me," Lilah says.

Despite her British passport, she tells me that she was interrogated by the border control officers for hours at the airport.

"And what did you tell them? That you were just going to talk to an old man about his oranges?"

"It doesn't matter what I told them. I am Palestinian, so they were suspicious."

I never saw Khalil after he departed with his family. So many Palestinians fled by sea and land, after the heavy bombardment of Jaffa. The port was overwhelmed with refugees crowding small boats. The Haddad family, like the other orange growers, dismantled their water pumps and deserted their grove, carrying with them only a small portion of their belongings in handcarts. Jaffa was burning, the trees in the orchard were burning, the oranges were burning, and the flames spiraled up into the sky, and for days, ash floated in the air, blanketing the abandoned city in a haze. I don't like to think back to those moments.

"Khalil and I packed the oranges together into crates in your great-grandfather's orchard. We wrapped each orange individually in waxed paper."

I pick an orange and withdraw a pocketknife, flick the blade open. The blade glints in the sun, and I see my own face reflected in it, splotched with cancer spots and a sprinkling of veins like the rootstock of a tree. Without noticing, I've grown old. Rot sets quickly in an orange, infecting the entire fruit. The trick is to squeeze it firmly and listen to its sound. You can tell by the fermented smell that it's spoiled. But the orange in the palm of my hand is young, unblemished. I dissect it, peeling the thick skin in one long curly slab, and offer her the naked fruit coated in porous, bitter white tissue.

She eats a segment, juice spilling down her chin, and spits out a pip. "I thought Jaffa oranges were meant to be seedless," she said.

At the time, for a Jew like me to be friends with a Palestinian like Khalil wasn't so strange. Under Ottoman rule, Jews and Palestinians carted sand together to make cement, toiled in orange groves and vineyards, tinkered in metalwork factories, ran seaside brothels, and oversaw the Bride of the Sea's crown jewel, Jaffa harbor's booming export business, fleets of cargo vessels sailing around the world, carrying citrus fruit. When Palestine changed hands, from the Ottomans to the British, my life remained mostly unchanged.

As a child, I spent most of my time in the packinghouse with Khalil, wrapping oranges and packing them in crates. It was a good job, monotonous but not difficult. Every morning I walked with Khalil to the packinghouse, past the newspaper vendor selling copies of *Falastin,* and Abouelafia's bakery, where filo pastries were baking in large stone ovens, stopping by Abu Ahmad's, the tiny sweetshop, our favorite spot for halvah for many years before it burned down. Camels ambled lazily through Clock Square, their hooves clicking on the cobblestones. Khalil's father and the other landowners sat under the shade of palm trees in elegant white suits, drinking coffee from small glasses.

"Tell me about my grandfather," Lilah says. Her voice is excited, like a little girl waiting to open a present. Her eyes—Khalil's eyes—gleam.

"Well, he was mischievous."

When we were nine, I tell her, Khalil decided to steal a camel, and he enlisted my help. The camel belonged to a rival landowner named Nabil, a crook renowned for his temper, who humiliated his workers. Once Nabil struck a Bedouin girl who stumbled over the hem of her dress and dropped the fruit that she carried in a basket on her head. For this, Khalil wanted to punish him.

That night, barefoot, we scaled the tall walls surrounding Nabil's grove. The air smelled of salt and fish from the sea, citrus and orange blossoms from the land. I cut the soft flesh of my foot on a sharp brick edge, bleeding into the wall, and Khalil, already at the top, his legs swinging on either side, reached out his hand to hoist me up. The grove was pitch-black, grass long and thick, trees alive with chirping and rustling, startled birds taking flight.

Most of Nabil's camels were tied by the warehouse and packinghouse on the first floor. But there was one camel he prized above all, a dark-furred racing beast he kept separately. She was nicknamed Midnight, *Muntasaf al-Layl*. Her coat was pitch-black. We found her sitting elegantly on her own, tied to the well, aloof and mysterious. Untying her, we loosened the coarse rope around her neck, pulled and pulled, tugging with all our strength, but no matter what we did, we couldn't make the proud beast follow our orders. She simply sat there, her long curved neck unmoving, blinking slowly at us. We yanked the rope, clucked and cursed her. Finally, Khalil stomped the ground in frustration, and she reared up, straightening her legs. She charged us, her fierce jaw snapping, drooling fat lips, crooked teeth snarling. We backed away, but she lunged at us, making a high-pitched bleating sound, then moaned loudly.

Suddenly Nabil was beside us, dressed in his nightgown, a sheer silk robe spilling to the floor, dragging behind him on the grass. He wore nothing underneath his gown, and I could make out the shape of his body, the bulge of his belly, through the thin fabric. I thought Nabil, his face contorted in anger, would strangle us to death.

"What stopped him from strangling you?" asked Lilah.

"Khalil stopped him. Simply because of who he was, he could get away with a lot more than me. His father was an important man in Jaffa."

Despite Khalil's family status, Nabil did take his revenge on us by dropping us into the bottom of the well. He seized our wrists, lowered us into the dark, and left us sitting in the well all night. The stone walls closed in around me, cold and wet. I couldn't sleep, the ceaseless dripping made it impossible. I was terrified, but I didn't want to cry in front of Khalil, who was braver than me. He kept inventing escape plans to pass the time, concocting scenarios to punish Nabil in different ways. Dangling him over a sea of carnivorous fish, feeding him to a giant squid, stuffing him inside an enormous glass bottle to float for eternity. We passed the time this way, imagining the worst possible outcomes for our captor, and eventually, in the early morning, one of the workers, a kindhearted fruit picker, who also worked on the Haddad orchard, rescued us. We promised never to tell anyone about the incident, and I have never spoken of it, not until today.

Even though we had already been punished, we were terrified Nabil might strike the Haddad orchard. He never did, and soon enough we all had bigger things to worry about. The Jewish Communist Party printed flyers in Yiddish and Arabic calling on Zionist workers to topple the British occupiers, and organized a May Day parade through Manshiyya, a mixed Jewish-Arab neighborhood, waving red flags with pictures of Karl Marx. Soon they clashed with a rival Jewish Labor Party protest, and fighting erupted between the protesters and the British police. Believing that they were under attack, the Arabs began chasing Jews with wooden clubs, breaking into homes, stabbing pillowcases, scattering the feathery down across the alleyways. And the Jews took revenge, rampaging the Arab-owned businesses, smashing glass windows, ripping lace curtains, beating store owners with iron rods, and leaving trails of blood along the cold stone floors.

"The May Day riots were the beginning of the end of the cooperation between Jews and Arabs," I said. "Khalil and I were too young to understand the tensions that were developing, but they were very real."

"So, besides packing oranges, what did you do all day?"

We liked to trick arrogant men. Khalil went to a British school in Jaffa and knew the name of every street in London before he ever set foot in it. "He had an extraordinary memory, your grandfather." He made a bet with a local tradesman, Abdullah, for a bag of British caramels. Abdullah was convinced he knew London better than anyone in Palestine. He even affected a British accent, sometimes, when he spoke English. We heard rumors that he ate sandwiches made with buttered bread and thinly sliced cucumber. He was always sucking up to the British soldiers, getting cozy with the colonizers. We wanted those sweets more than anything in the world at the time. We were maybe thirteen years old. The bet was each time Khalil guessed a street correctly in London, we got a candy. The tradesman, having come from London, had a city map with him. One by one, Khalil named the streets correctly, mentioning their intersections and crossroads, even adding their proximity to important monuments. By the end of it, Abdullah was furious, and we had a burlap sack full of sweets.

Lilah laughs, and I find myself smiling at the memory. I miss my friend Khalil. We loved those sweets. We ate so many of them, we were sick the next day. If I think only of those early times, I can still convince myself I deserve his friendship.

"He did have a phenomenal memory," Lilah says. "He never forgot a single birthday. He remembered all my friends' names when I was growing up, and their parents' names, too."

"He was also quite the ladies' man."

Usually girls approached him. I remember countless times they gravitated toward him, as if by magic. All he had to do was breathe next to them, and they would start talking to him. He had an aristocratic, aquiline nose and those remarkable eyes, dark as coal, heavy-lidded. When he was twenty, he started dressing like his father in elegant suits. He also took to smoking a pipe. On anyone else, this affectation might have looked ridiculous, but Khalil had the confidence to do whatever he liked. He became the accountant for his father's business. His incredible memory and knack for numbers gave him an advantage over most of the older men. He impressed girls with his knowledge. *Give me a math equation to solve,* he told them. They would tell him to multiply ten thousand three hundred and fifty-four by five thousand six hundred and thirty-one, and he would whip out the answer almost immediately, performing all the calculations in his head. I was never good with numbers, they got all jumbled in my mind. For Khalil, it was effortless.

"No one else in my family inherited that particular skill," Lilah says.

"He was very inventive with his talent."

He caught a man stealing once. It was one of the export men, I forget his name now, who worked at the docks and was in charge of shipping the crates of oranges to their destination, in Europe or America. At the time, hundreds of thousands of orange crates were shipped from Palestine, of which tens of thousands belonged to the Haddad family. Khalil knew the number of crates his family shipped down to the last orange. The export man swindled them out of a few crates, each weighing sixty kilos and containing about five hundred oranges. It wasn't out of the ordinary. Out of thousands and thousands of orange crates, who would notice a few missing? Khalil did. Instead of making the man pay the family back for every single orange, he cut a deal. The export man would give him an item from each shipment he sent. His ships transported cases of corks, barrels of olive oil, bottles of wine, soap, and jewels. Khalil gave away most of these items he received, either to the poor or to the girl he was seeing at the time. I remember he gave me an oval cake of lavender soap and made some dirty joke about it. The soap wasn't particularly expensive, but I kept it as if it were made of solid gold. A gift from Khalil meant something to me. I treasured that soap, although I would never have admitted it to him at the time, but with everything going on around us, our friendship couldn't last.

"Did you grow apart?"

"We did, slowly."

Our friendship began to unravel, I tell her, when the Arab National Committee called a general strike and an anti-Jewish boycott in Jaffa, and I lost my job. Khalil's father fired me from the orange grove, along with the rest of the Jews. "The Arab landowners, including your great-grandfather, possessed most of the orange groves around Jaffa at the time, and they were worried about losing the citrus business. They were afraid it would all go to the Jews, who used to be their partners." After the strike was called, there was rioting throughout the country. The Arab rioters evaded the British by barricading roads with shards of glass and nails, hiding in the maze of Old City alleyways. The rioters knew Jaffa better than anyone, and the British understood they didn't stand a chance, so they demolished hundreds of homes. Thousands of Arab residents were given a day's notice to evacuate, and soon all that was left was ruins.

Hoping to save our friendship, Khalil convinced me to sneak into the extravagant Alhambra Cinema and Theater, for a performance by none other than the Voice of Egypt herself, the Star of the East, Umm Kulthum. I was so nervous, sweating profusely. The chairs were all red velvet, the floors polished marble. I felt out of place, with my rough, calloused farmer's hands, my shabby clothing. Khalil seemed at home anywhere, smiling calmly at the shifty-eyed guards at the theater's entrance, at the women in elegant dresses and pearls, the men in dark waistcoats, while I was constantly thinking of being found out, exposed as a fraud. I wish he had intervened on my behalf, defended me in some way, but he let the guards escort me out of the theater and toss me out onto the street.

"They caught you?"

"Oh yes, they threw me out. But not Khalil, they never suspected him. He was a smooth talker."

The last time we spoke was at the port. It was the beginning of November. I had gotten a job at the docks with the new Zionist shipping company, unloading crates from cargo ships. Khalil was wandering around the docks, making sure a shipment of his family's orange crates was properly stowed away in one of the transport vessels, and he spotted me. I had finished my shift and was getting ready to leave after a long day's work. He was dressed in one of his father's elegant white suits, while I wore my khaki shirt, soaked with sweat. We were very polite with each other, shaking hands with cold formality, where only a few months before we would have joked and hugged each other.

We sat down on the promenade wall, looking out toward the water, at the businessmen strolling with their young wives, and farther, to the docks, at the bustle and chaos of the dockworkers unloading sacks of cement, the porters carrying crates of oranges. Khalil withdrew his pipe, stuffed it with tobacco, and lit it, puffing away. Teasingly, he asked me if I missed the Haddad family oranges. I told him I'd had enough oranges for a lifetime. I was sick of them.

"Three weeks later, as you know, the UN Special Committee on Palestine recommended the Partition Plan," I say.

A truck loaded with explosives concealed under a layer of oranges was detonated outside the Saraya. Barrels and metal drums filled with gunpowder fitted between old rubber tires were lit and rolled down crowded *shuks* and cafés, killing many innocent people. Remember Nabil, whose camel we tried to steal when we were children? He was killed in one such explosion, while sipping his morning coffee. It was only pure coincidence that Khalil's father was not there at the time, since it was a regular spot for landowners and orange growers.

Lilah and I walk past the Arab orange pickers, working in pairs. One climbs the wooden ladder leaning against the tree, to pick the fruit from above, while the other wades into the thicket to collect the oranges below. They are careful with the sharp shears when they cut the fruit from the branch, slicing it with precision. I watch as an orange tumbles into the open palm of a fruit picker's outstretched hand, like a decapitated head, and is then carefully dropped into the jute-lined basket.

"And nothing remains of my family's orange grove?" Lilah asks.

"All the orchards in Jaffa are long gone."

I cannot tell her the truth, the reason that my grandchildren know nothing about Khalil. I cannot tell her I did a terrible, shameful thing at the end. He didn't even know it was me. It could have been any soldier who did it. Why burden Lilah with such stories? Nothing has to change. And yet I feel the need to tell her. Maybe it has to do with her eyes, which so resemble his, or the way she is standing now, leaning against the tree, absentmindedly stroking the grayish-brown bark, picking a dark green leaf and twirling it between two fingers, just as Khalil used to do. I want to confess a secret that I have hidden away for too long, but I cannot bring myself to say it.

Instead, breathlessly, I tell Lilah the story of the hookah bar, afraid that she will insist on asking again about the orange grove. But she doesn't seem to mind the change of subject. Perhaps she thinks I am old and confused, forgetful. "Do you know," I say, "that your grandfather fell in love with a dancer?" I tell her of the time Khalil took me to Al-Bustan, a bar in Jaffa, dimly lit by oil lamps, whose floors were carpeted. The men sat on the ground, their legs crossed, eyes half-closed, smoking from narghile pipes. We joined them on the floor, and the waiter brought us a pipe, lit the coal, and burned it white-hot.

The entertainment started: a woman danced with silver bracelets around her slim wrist, dress flickering in the lamp-light, her exposed belly's musculature rippling in time with the beat of a drum and the harmonizing of an oud. When she whirled by us, her legs slender and lithe, I could smell her musky perfume, a hint of jasmine. And then she was on the floor, lying on her back. A man placed two wineglasses on her belly, one full, the other empty. She balanced the glasses and contorted her belly in such a way as to pour the wine from the full glass to the empty one, without spilling a single drop.

I looked at Lilah, adding that Khalil never stopped talking about that moment, for years and years.

"So he fell in love with a parlor trick."

"Something like that," I say. "But it wasn't so simple. Were you very close with your grandfather, Lilah?"

"Not as close as you were, it seems." She laughs, but there

is hurt in her voice, too, perhaps some bitterness. "Working together all those years in the orange grove."

She returns to the same subject, again and again, the grove. There is no escape. *Let it rest in the past. Let it go.* I don't want to talk about the oranges. I'm tired and I want to sleep in my bed and forget about this visit. I want to see my grandchildren, to spoil them with Strauss banana and toffee ice cream, take them to Lev Cinema to watch *Ice Age* and share huge tubs of buttery popcorn and Coca-Cola in glass bottles. Thinking about Khalil, the pain is too much to bear. It's getting late. The shadows are lengthening across the grass. Soon the workers will leave for the day, and I'll be all alone in my *pardes,* my orange grove. I wish Lilah had never come here.

"The oranges saddened him," Lilah says. "Once when we were visiting relatives in Paris, sitting in a brasserie in Montparnasse, eating bloody steak frites with sharp mustard and crisp endive salads and drinking red wine, he started talking about the oranges. For an hour, he talked about the oranges, and everyone stopped eating. They put their knives and forks down and listened. He loved the oranges so much that what we were eating was tasteless in comparison. It felt like eating cardboard next to his memory of those oranges."

I feel my throat constrict. I can just imagine him speaking about the oranges, cradling air, and pretending it was the most delicious fruit. Those oranges are gone. *Habibi,* you are gone, too.

"Tell me, was Khalil still handsome as an older man?"

"He was elegant," Lilah says, "with flowing silver hair, and a youthful gleam in his eyes. He liked playing jokes on people— that never went away."

Lilah reaches into her bag and retrieves a piece of yellowing paper in a transparent plastic sleeve. It's an old ticket for the Alhambra Theater. The theater is long gone by now, of course. It is gathering dust, its ornate building overflowing with trash, desecrated with graffiti. She tells me Khalil wanted me to have the ticket, that he kept it all these years. In fact, before he passed away, he told her the story of how we both sneaked in to watch Umm Kulthum and how I got kicked out because my clothes weren't fancy enough. He felt bad about it. He went back to the theater later, properly, with a ticket and all, and he saved it. He wanted to give it to me, to apologize. *Khalil, I don't deserve your apology. It's me who has to apologize. You should never forgive me, even if you were still alive to hear my confession.*

I cannot look her in the eye. I stare at my hands instead, at the thick blue veins, the crescents of my fingernails trimmed to the quick. Those hands picked so many oranges in a lifetime. I picked oranges from the Haddad family orchard in Palestine, and then I picked oranges in Israel, in my own small eight-*dunam* orchard in HaSharon. I can feel Lilah's hand on my back, a gentle pressure. She must think I am overcome with emotion, with nostalgia and fondness for my old friend. For so long I never even said his name aloud. Sometimes I whisper it when no one is there. *Khalil, Khalil.* I whisper his name to my oranges, asking for their forgiveness. So many wars, so much blood shed over this land. How much does a grove of orange trees weigh in the grand scheme of things, compared to the weight of the dead in the Six-Day War, the Yom Kippur War, all the other countless deaths in the short history of our nation?

"He wanted you to have it," she says. She places the ticket in the palm of my hand.

I look at her for a moment. She is standing under an orange tree with her arms crossed against her chest. Dappled golden light filters through the gaps in the leaves, fluttering shadows play across her features. She blinks rapidly several times, as if something were caught in her eye. I can tell that it isn't easy for her to part with the ticket. Maybe it was one of the only keepsakes her grandfather kept from his time in Palestine.

The ticket is the length of my palm, faded at the edges. Hall 1, Row 12, Seat 7. It cost three hundred prutoth cents. KEEP FOR CONTROL is stamped in blue ink. I turn it around, and there's a note on the back in Khalil's flowery handwriting: *Abu Ahmad's Halvah Sweets.*

"Does the note mean anything to you?" Lilah asks.

It means Khalil had the final laugh. Abu Ahmad's Halvah Sweetshop was one of our favorite shops growing up, a tiny kiosk of the most delicious candies. Rows of crumbly, marbled sesame halvah sweetened with honey, filled with pistachio nuts. We would go to Abu Ahmad's every day before work to buy a wedge of halvah, licking our fingers all the way to the packinghouse. The shop burned to the ground, an arson attack, but the culprit was never found. For years, we were obsessed with finding out who did it. Khalil always liked playing tricks on people, and here was his final trick. He knew I burned down his family's orange grove, he has always known, and he sent his granddaughter here to tell me, all these years later. Or perhaps the note wasn't a trick. After all, how could he know I set fire to his family's orange grove? Maybe he just remembered our favorite sweetshop. All that time we spent together

eating halvah at Abu Ahmad's, when we were children working at the packinghouse, wrapping oranges in waxed paper,
one by one, before our friendship was ruined.

"It's the name of a sweetshop we loved," I tell Lilah. "It had
the best halvah in the Middle East."

I never tell Lilah about the night Khalil and his family fled
Jaffa, the orange grove going up in flames around them. For a
long time, in my mind, oranges smelled like death. They reminded me of ash and rotting earth, hacked trees burned to
cinders and the fallen bodies of fruit, scorched black. The orchard was burning, the orchard was burning, and on the horizon, the ships were sailing away. I was a young soldier at the
time, we were establishing a new country, a homeland for the
Jewish people. I was throwing flaming rags onto the trees of
the orange grove with the rest of the soldiers. I was obliterat-
ing the orchard I helped grow and cultivate for years. I wish I
could finally confess, but I'm silent. I cannot say it. I want to
say: *I destroyed your family's orchard, Lilah. I betrayed Khalil.
I burned the orchard down. It was me, your grandfather's
childhood friend.* But I look at her young face and dark, heavy-
lidded eyes and don't say a thing.

Alte Sachen

W e were known as Alte Sachen, the haulers of Old Things, the last of a dying breed who wandered down dark, deserted alleyways, calling out for leftovers and collecting junk. Finned monsters lurked in the back of our cherry-red Volkswagen truck; furniture and scrap metal that looked prehistoric, crawling with rust, splintered, peeling, many-toothed. My favorite hauls were old radios—a crystal receiver, a foxhole with a cat's whisker detector, Bakelite plastic sets, and farm radios that ran on tractor batteries. Transistor radios were the most common. The rarest find was an expensive cathedral-style wooden console, or a tall and narrow tombstone set. Today the haul was weak, it was slim pickings. We got two tables—one of them missing a leg, the other coffee-stained—a peeling eggshell fridge, and a Singer sewing machine with a damaged motor. At the end of the day, we either melted down the metal and sold it by weight, traded in spare parts, or fixed broken furniture and appliances and sold them for a profit.

We lived in Tsfat, on the mountaintops of the Galilee, our ancient city of blue-domed synagogues and wandering Kabbalah golems, earthquakes and wildfires, narrow cobblestoned lanes crammed with shops selling cheap and holy trinkets. Gaudy Rebbe Lubavitch paintings hung in the storefront windows of gallery shops. Black and white penguins, those Ultra-Orthodox Haredim, schlepped around from one prayer to the next, bundled in their heavy coats, *tzitzit* tassels and *pe'ot* curls bouncing, dark fur *shtreimel* hats on Shabbat. There were no bars or clubs, no parties, not even a single movie theater. Once a year a three-day klezmer festival was hosted in the Old Artists' Quarter, musicians played their Yiddish tunes from the rooftops, laughing and weeping with their violins, cimbaloms, and clarinets, and when it was over, the city returned to its usual state of slumber. Every night, I paraded the empty streets, waiting for the day Tsfat would become the new Tel Aviv, a city that never sleeps.

We sat in the stuffy carcass of the truck on sticky leather seats, roasting on the spit of the midafternoon sun. For now, things were slow.

"Switch it on," I said.

My younger brother, Shoni, turned on the portable cassette player resting on the dashboard, hooked up to a megaphone mounted on the roof of the truck. It was his one task, at the age of eight, while I drove and carried the junk left out on the street back to the truck. We listened to a loop of our father's voice on the recording, distorted, mechanical, crying out from the megaphone: *We take it all, Alte Sachen, Alte Sachen! Beds, cabinets, desks, chairs, fridges, gas stoves, sewing machines, sofas, carpets, Alte Sachen, Alte Sachen!* I liked hearing his voice, it soothed me. The repetition of the chant, the steady rhythm of *Alte Sachen* followed me like a prayer for the road. In between, when Aba called out *chairs* and *fridges*, there was a pause, silence for less than a second, but in that break in speech I heard my father breathing. I kept waiting for that breath, fearing that maybe the next time the recording looped, it wouldn't come. I listened for my father's breath as we drove down the city streets. *Chairs.* Breath. *Fridges.*

Aba died last year on Purim, when Shoni was dressed as a panda bear. He wore a white T-shirt, dark pants, and a panda mask, some junk Aba had picked up one day, cheaper than buying a costume for Purim. After Aba died, Shoni refused to take it off, and now he sat next to me wearing his white plastic mask with black spots over the eyes and two round ears at the top of his head. He even went to bed with it. We slept in the same small room, on bunk beds. Every year Aba had promised we would each have our own room, but we never got one. Shoni slept in the bottom bunk with the cassette player cradled in his arms like a robot baby. Even though I left a little light on for him, to chase away the demons that came at night, he still woke up screaming and sweating from bad dreams.

Aba had always liked saying we'd get the best hauls from Holocaust survivors. They always kept everything, he'd say, and when they died, their kids threw it all away. Shoni and I used to look at the newspaper obituaries every morning with Aba, to see who had died that day. We charted a route through the city based on the deaths. Sometimes the obituary mentioned if the deceased was a survivor. We used to draw a yellow Star of David next to the survivors' homes as a little joke, but Aba got angry and said we had to treat them with respect. *Their own children probably threw away their things,* he said, *but we collect them, we fix them up, we make them beautiful again. It's our sacred duty. We aren't vultures or thieves.* So after Aba died, Shoni and I just drew regular stars on the map.

I lit a cigarette, a new habit I was developing that I thought would help me with girls. We waited on the empty cobblestoned corner of Ha'Ari Street, the truck parked next to a house with stained-glass windows patterned with Stars of David, megaphone blasting out our father's voice, too hot to move and too hot to stay. When I was really young, before Shoni was even born, we had a cart pulled by a horse, and Aba would let me feed him carrots out of the palm of my hand. We would go around the city in our horse-drawn cart, and I would sit on Aba's lap, and he would tell me stories by Mendele Mocher Sforim. Then the Knesset banned the use of animal-drawn vehicles, and we had to switch to a motor. On the wall next to his bed, Shoni put up a newspaper clipping Aba gave him, faded now, of a story that had run at the time, showing a cart pulled by a pale, bony horse with a mane of gray hair, Aba sitting with a cigarette in one hand, the reins in the other, me on his lap. The headline read, THE END OF AN ERA: LAST OF ALTE-SACHEN SWITCHES HORSE FOR MOTOR VEHICLE. I found it embarrassing and wanted to rip it up, but Shoni liked it.

"Tuesdays are always slow," I said.

Just as I was about to pull out, a girl came running out of the house holding a chair. She hugged the worn chair to her

chest, her arms wrapped around it. She wore a white button-
down shirt and a long, dark velvet skirt, the way most God-
fearing religious girls do. But something about her was
different. She had wild, immodestly untamed curly hair, as if
she were *mufra'at,* badly behaved. Beads of sweat dotted her
upper lip.

She stood by the truck until I came out and took the chair
from her with a grunt, throwing it in with the rest of the junk.

"Who's that?" She pointed at Shoni in the truck, looking
out blankly through his mask.

"My little brother."

"Are you also part panda?"

"Same mom, different dad."

"I see." She laughed. "So, can you take me away in your
truck, too?"

"We don't take people."

She leaned against the side of the truck and considered this
for a moment, drumming her fingers on the Volkswagen's peeling red paint. "Not even trash like me?"

She ran back to her house, twisting her head to look at me
as she did. I couldn't stop thinking about her as we made the
rounds, and I wondered if I should return and park on her
street and wait to see if she would come out again if we played
the Alte Sachen recording. There was a dead survivor's house
to check out on the other side of town, however, so we didn't
stay.

By the time I was fifteen, I could do all the heavy lifting Aba
did. I carried refrigerators with him, sofas, cabinets. My size
came from Aba, who was three-quarters Iraqi. My mother was
Russian, as unwavering as her snow-piercing ancestors, Baltic

Sea merchants from St. Petersburg. Shoni took on Ima's pale
features, like a tiny babushka doll, with dark, expressive eyebrows hooked like a bird's beak. He never helped out with
anything. He just sat in the truck in silence. Every once in a
while, he would say something weird, like did you know in
Japan they sold Hercules beetles in vending machines?

I was seventeen now, and the army didn't want me. Trouble
adjusting, they called it. I think they just didn't want a junk
collector with a dead father for a soldier. In any case, I was off
the hook, completely free to continue collecting junk for the
rest of my life. I didn't feel lucky, just numb. After we got back
home, I started working on the dilapidated chair we picked up
from the religious girl, stripping the layers of rotten wood, applying wax remover with a steel wool pad, and cleaning away
stains—thinking of her upper lip, shining with sweat, how soft
her hair must be when you ran your fingers through it. Later
I'd use a sanding block and glass paper to smooth over the
wood fibers, then add a layer of mahogany dye and a coat of
polish with a cloth. It was a nice haul and would probably be
worth a good sum once I finished fixing it up.

We lived by the coffee factory; the smell of ground beans
filtered through the windows and seeped into the walls, soak-
ing our beds and filling our nostrils day and night. Newspaper
clippings covered the walls of our room. Shoni cut out articles
about the afterlife and reincarnation and pasted them up on
the wall with duct tape. In some Druze village, a child woke up
one day speaking fluent French. He had grown up speaking
only Arabic, his parents told the reporter. He never saw any
French television. They didn't even own a TV set. The reporter
had confirmed this with a house visit, the article said. The par-

ents believed their child was the reincarnated spirit of some Frenchman who had died on the day their son was born. Shoni took this as proof that Aba had taken the shape of some child, or even an animal.

"What if he's in the horse?" Shoni asked. He was looking at the clipping of Aba, the last of the Alte Sachen to switch to a motorized vehicle.

I told him that was impossible. I remembered the day we sold the horse to an Arab in a nearby village. It was impossible, I explained, because Aba's spirit would have had to travel to a body born on the exact same day he died, at the exact same time even.

Shoni nodded, as if this made perfect sense.

"What about an object?" I asked, just to mess with him. "He could be in the cassette player."

We had Aba's voice on tape, caught like a fly buzzing around in a sealed jar. We heard him every day, reciting the *Alte Sachen* call, as if he were right beside us in the truck. After I told him that Aba's spirit could have traveled to the cassette player, Shoni kept the machine by his side at all times. When we were in the truck, making the rounds, he was the only one allowed to switch the recording on and off, to hold Aba's reincarnated voice in his hands. He was careful with the cassette player, handling it as if it were made of porcelain instead of plastic.

In life, Aba's voice had not been soothing or predictable like the voice on the recording. Sometimes he used it to entertain, telling wild stories, outlandish tales, but other times he cut everyone around him, his words jagged and rough. Most nights he came home smelling of beer. He was suspicious of everybody. Insurance companies and phone companies, grocery stores and fuel dispensers, the ticketing man at the movie theater. Everyone was out to cheat him. He railed against authority. Aba had been drafted in '73, right after the Yom Kippur War ended. He was never the same after the army. He joined a unit that was entirely wiped out in the war, a platoon of ghosts, unfortunate boys only a year or two older than him at school, all gone.

Aba grew up in the agricultural village of Birya, in the northern suburbs of Tsfat, by a sprawling forest of pine trees and hawthorn bushes, surrounded by the graves of the greatest sages and Kabbalists. Most of all he liked visiting the pale blue tombstone of Rabbi Itzhak ben Shlomo Luria. Between forest and graveyard, he developed his habit of collecting shiny little things. The wings of a marbled skipper butterfly, the cold body of a glass lizard, the glossy eggs of a sunbird. He kept everything he found, building an enormous nest in his backyard, like a human magpie. On our parents' wedding day, Aba gave our mother earrings made out of the wings of a marbled skipper and recited the blessing of the Sabbath bride: *Let us invite the Shechinah with a newly laid table, and with a well-lit menorah that casts light on all heads.*

On a humid August day, the summer vacation after Aba died, Ima wore her butterfly-wing earrings and decided to take us to an exhibit at the zoo. To let us out of our cages for a short while. We saw slow-crawling turtles, their shells shining like shields, the sudden leap of spotted tree frogs, the bright plumage of rare birds in flight. Ima pointed out the carp swirling in the water. She told us Aba was a fish, that he was swimming around and keeping an eye out for us. We could come here, she said, and talk to him if we wanted to. The fish rose up to snatch a scrap of bread, thrown in by my brother, and then they were gone, leaving behind nothing but a few vanishing ripples. Ima had seen the newspaper clippings and was playing along with Shoni's fantasies.

But it was a bad idea; when she wasn't looking, Shoni leaped up over the glass railing of the exhibit and liberated the fish, which squirmed in his arms, flapping around and jerking wildly, scales glinting in the afternoon light. Once Ima explained to the zookeepers and security guards that our father had died in March, we left the zoo and never came back. She stopped making up stories about Aba. He was dead and that was that. But there was no dead, not for Shoni.

Even when he was alive, Aba had not wasted his time with the living. When the Exhibition of the Dead came to Jerusalem two years ago, filling the Israel Museum with life-size models of the human body, he had taken us. He loved collections, and what could be better than a collection of dead people, bones and ligaments and peeled skin revealing a bleached spine, rubbery gray liver, the anemone of the brain.

At the museum, Shoni declared he would donate his body to science. He wanted to be exhibited in a display case, in some far-off European city, like Stockholm or Strasbourg, sliced open to reveal the red wound of his liver, shrunken kidneys dry as ginger root, under the subheading ISRAELI SPECIMEN. Some pale Swedish woman would tap on the glass, watch the boy trapped in amber, floating in formaldehyde, stuck in limbo. Shoni tried to make Aba promise, but he refused. Afterward Shoni claimed he wanted to be frozen like Walt Disney. The man's a Nazi, Aba said, waving his hand in the air dismissively, as if he were swatting an insect. Shoni's shoulders slumped—maybe he realized we would never get to watch *The Lion King* again. And that was that, we never mentioned Walt Disney again.

When we got back to Tsfat after visiting the exhibition, Aba decided to take us out for ice cream at Kadosh Dairy. He lit a cigarette and kept it in his mouth as he walked, smoke trailing from his nostrils, down Ma'alot HaGardom, the Great Stairs that divide the Old City from the Artists' Quarter. We walked past HaMeiri's Cheese, our footsteps echoing in the empty streets accompanied by the rising and falling sounds of prayer from Abuhav Synagogue, and all that was left of his cigarette was a column of ash, swept away in the wind.

Sitting on the stone steps outside Kadosh Dairy, Aba lit another cigarette, and Shoni asked if we were also trapped in a glass container, a huge one, like the figures in the exhibit, and we didn't even know it. Aba said it was possible, nodding slowly.

I said, *That's a stupid thing to say.*

Anything's possible, Aba replied, rubbing at the dark circles under his eyes, and he shivered, saying that a ghost from one of the flayed bodies out on display had sneaked into his lemon sorbet. Shoni looked closely at his own ice cream cone.

I returned to Ha'Ari Street, to the house with the stained-glass windows, and brought the girl's chair. Fixed, painted, and polished. I sat on the gleaming throne, lit a cigarette, and called out, *Alte Sachen, Alte Sachen!* The street was empty, and my voice echoed in the silence. I called out again, louder, and waited.

I was wondering whether I should just leave the chair next to her house and hope no one took it, when the girl came out, once again as if in a rush, her long dark skirt swishing behind her. "But I don't have anything for you," she said.

"I came to give you something."

She admired the chair, tracing her fingers on the smooth, newly painted wood, and whistled low and steady. She took my cigarette and inhaled deeply. "You're the first Alte Sachen I've met who gives stuff back."

She invited me to a party at an abandoned house in HaEm Garden that night. I'd never been out with an Orthodox girl before, and I wondered what she meant by party. She never told me her name, so I decided to call her Chair Girl. I was planning to go after dinner. After Ima made us pasta, she fell asleep on the sofa. She woke up an hour later, slipped on her one good dress, and put lipstick on—bright red against her pale skin—and told me she was going out to a friend's place in Rosh Pina and would be back very late. *Watch Shoni,* she told me. Bored and restless, I kept thinking of Chair Girl—her fingers tracing the smooth wood, her lips on my cigarette. I was glad I gave back her chair, although we could have used the money. I wanted to go to the party to see her, but now I was stuck with Shoni, who was sitting on the floor, cutting up gunpowder pellets from cap-gun ammunition to make a homemade firecracker. I called Boaz and invited him over to hang out at home, since I couldn't leave.

Boaz arrived, wearing a black silk shirt and a diamond earring. He had been my best friend for as long as I could remember. A self-proclaimed prophet with the sculpted cheekbones of a pharaoh, he could tell you when a night out would be good, and usually he was right. He said it had something to do with the moon's position in the sky, its fullness and brightness, the halo encircling it, or some other piece of crap that made girls lose it. I admired the ease with which Boaz navigated the alien world of girls. Whenever we met them, he kept touching their wrists or their bare shoulders, hugging them close in a way that brought his lips and silver tongue to their ear.

I told him about Chair Girl and the party she had invited me to at HaEm Garden.

"My soul," Boaz said, "tonight is the night."

"I can't," I told him. "I have to watch Shoni."

The Panda looked up for a moment, then went back to sorting out his explosives.

"Bring the little bear. We might need him, I've got a feeling."

"No way."

"He's a total chick magnet, man."

We went to HaEm Garden in the southern industrial zone of the city and saw the abandoned house, dirty limestone overgrown with dying grapevines, next to a toppled telephone pole, its wires strangled in the wild grass. The roof was damaged from a Katyusha rocket, one of hundreds fired by Hezbollah during the Second Lebanon War. The door was half open, dirty mattresses were scattered on the floor, smelling of urine and sour alcohol, shards of glass swept to the sides, old newspapers crumpled yellow with age crunched under my feet. Guys in skinny jeans and black silk kippahs wandered around clinking beer bottles and sharing cigarettes. It was a scene Boaz had never tapped into, the stray kids, the ex-penguins. They came from religious homes, Ultra-Orthodox families, the real black and white type, but they had strayed from that path. Everyone was looking for a good time, to rebel, to break loose. They stared at Shoni as he walked past them in his panda mask, the cassette player in his hand. At least, as a panda, he was also dressed in black and white.

I saw Chair Girl at the other end of the room, dancing with a girl. They were swaying to techno music from somebody's cell phone and touching each other's hips, leaning in and whispering and laughing. Chair Girl looked different; she was wearing the same shirt, but it was unbuttoned, revealing a bra strap. Her skirt was shorter, above the knee. Her nose was pierced with a silver hoop. She probably only wore the conservative outfit at home. She saw us now, and pulling her friend along, they came up to Shoni, ignoring me completely.

"You again, Mr. Panda."

Shoni nodded, acknowledging the fact of their meeting a second time as if it were preordained.

"How do you do?" her friend asked, stretching out her hand. Shoni shook it. They were obviously drunk.

"Isn't he cute?" Chair Girl said. "We need to go find you some bamboo, don't we?"

She held out her hand, which he took, and led him away as if to look for a nearby bamboo forest tucked away behind a synagogue.

Her friend shrugged and kept dancing. Boaz introduced us. "I'm Moriah," she said.

"How about your friend?" I asked.

"I thought you already knew each other. She was feeling pretty comfortable with your panda."

"I don't know her. Not really."

"Well, go ask her then."

I left Boaz with Moriah—he was already whispering something in her ear—and went over to the corner where Chair Girl was talking to Shoni, who had taken a dreidel out of his pocket and was explaining a complex gambling game involving the spinning top and the letters *gimel, nun, shin,* and *hei.* I stood next to them, but they ignored me.

I put my hand on Chair Girl's shoulder to get her attention. "What's your name?"

"Her name is Batsheva," Shoni said.

"I always thought Alte Sachen drivers were old Arab men," Batsheva said.

"And I thought Haredi penguins all wore long skirts and modest clothes," I said.

She laughed. "You can take all the penguins to the junkyard, for all I care."

She was on her way to becoming a *datlashit,* formerly religious, and there was something new and fresh and exciting about her. She hated traditions, wanted to move to Tel Aviv, work as a barista in a café in Masarik Square all day, go out dancing at night at the Pasáž Club, swim naked in the sea at dawn.

After telling me about her impossible future, she asked if I liked collecting junk. I told her I didn't know whether I liked it or not, it was just what I did. There were things about being a junk collector that I liked. The stuff you could find, the secrets people's objects revealed to you. It wasn't just garbage. These were objects that had stopped working, old technology, outdated devices. It was like working in a time machine. We were excavators and archaeologists, not scavengers and dumpster divers.

Shoni whispered in my ear that he was tired and wanted to go home. I told him that we couldn't go home now. He bowed his head and hung his arms low and moaned. I ignored him. He was always sabotaging my plans with girls, but not tonight.

Boaz, Shoni, and I left the abandoned house together with the girls, walking down Aliyah Bet Street, passing the tower of the Ottoman Saraya fort, and taking the path down to the Old City, through its shuttered shops and galleries, cafés, syna- gogues, and restaurants, where years ago artists used to sit, sip white wine, and eat plates of grilled fish with slices of lemon, pale blue smoke curling from their cigarettes, drifting past the balconies and street windows, and disappearing into the night sky. Now the winding alleyways were desolate and uninhab- ited, a maze of empty streets in a silent ghost town.

Batsheva and I walked ahead, and she told me about her family, her eleven brothers and sisters, her strict home. She felt like something was missing—she found no meaning in her par- ents' way of life, it was like living in a home with no furniture. All they wanted for her was to be a good wife, to find her a *shidduch,* an arranged marriage with a learned Torah scholar, to prepare all his meals, to set silver candleholders and warm challah on a waxy tablecloth, to bathe and purify in ritual mikveh waters, and to produce as many children as there are stars in the sky. I looked back at Moriah and Boaz walking with their arms wrapped around each other, stumbling around and laughing.

Shoni pretended he could fly, zooming around the narrow

street and bumping into the limestone walls. He had stolen a long piece of tattered curtain from the abandoned house, and he was using it as a superhero cape.

We went to the junkyard on the hill in the Cana'an neighborhood, passing by the Ethiopian Immigration Center, where, under the light of the moon, we saw the Falash Mura women, known by the light blue cross tattooed on their foreheads, walking around in robes of white, carrying baskets heaped with crushed red peppers. In the junkyard, I saw pipes piled one on top of another, the skeletons of cars, paint peeled, wheels gone, skin stripped away. A stray cat jumped out from under a sheet of corroded metal, puffed up its tail, and hissed at us. Shoni hissed back, even though I'm pretty sure pandas don't hiss. The cat slunk away, watching us from behind a rubbish heap of splintered wood.

"We need mood lighting, man." Boaz flicked on his silver Zippo, but its flame hardly lit up anything.

I remembered the first time Aba took us to this junkyard. It was a playground of rusted dinosaurs, carcasses of cars spilling metallic guts, rusted spinal cords, dust-coated engine hearts. Everything ended up here, at one point or another. Shoni and I had waited by the shell of a crushed car, when suddenly Aba rose out of a pile of burnt tires, in an armor of tinfoil and aluminum sheets, corroded silver pots dangling from his arms, the word EMET scrawled onto his forehead with charcoal. He was the Golem, chasing us down, bellowing in a deep voice like an earthquake.

Aba had told us the story many times. The *tzadik* Judah Loew ben Bezalel, a sixteenth-century rabbi of Prague, crafted a statue made of clay from the dirt of the banks of the Moldau

River. To breathe life into the Golem, the rabbi inserted a scrap of parchment with the word EMET, truth, written on it, and stuck it on its forehead. The Golem was the rabbi's helper during the day, sweeping and cooking, and at night the rabbi put it to sleep. Until one day, on the Sabbath, the rabbi forgot to make the Golem sleep, and it went on a rampage through the Old City, wrecking everything in its path. To destroy it, the Rabbi erased the first letter of the word EMET, leaving only MET, death. I imagined Aba on Purim, on his back in the street like an overturned dung beetle, legs flailing in the air, clutching his heart that had stopped beating at the age of forty-three, on his forehead the word MET.

If Aba returned anywhere as a spirit, I thought, surely it would be here, to haunt this assortment of abandoned things. An hour had passed since we left the party, and now clouds covered the moon, providing us with darkness. Boaz and Moriah found an abandoned sofa. They stretched out on it, on top of each other. I heard giggling and shushing, then silence, only heavy breathing. I saw the brightness of Shoni's eyes under his mask, glinting like a cat in the moonlight. I felt a hand groping me, feeling my chest and neck, until it settled on my face. Batsheva's nose grazed mine. I felt her warm breath, smelling slightly of arrack. Her lips reached for mine, and her tongue was warm, slippery. I hoped Shoni couldn't see, but I didn't care. I pulled her close to me, and we held each other. I ran my fingers through her hair, kissed her.

A harsh, mechanical sound cut the silence in the air. *We take it all, Alte Sachen, Alte Sachen! Beds, cabinets, desks, chairs, fridges, gas stoves, sewing machines, sofas, carpets, Alte Sachen, Alte Sachen!*

I turned on my phone's flashlight, my eyes slowly adjusting, and saw Shoni sitting inside a bathtub, his makeshift cape wrapped around him, the cassette player on his lap, with one arm dangling over the rim of the tub. He looked like a tiny prince in a garbage kingdom, ruling over scraps—the only thing missing was a crown of twisted metal. Batsheva giggled. I felt humiliated. I was so angry I started shaking. It wasn't fair. Not only did he ruin my chances with this girl, who probably already thought we were freaks, but he had to keep playing Aba's voice, over and over again, never giving me a break, he couldn't let me forget about him, not even for a second, all I wanted was one moment without thinking about Aba.

I made my way to Shoni, snatched the cassette player out of his hands, and threw it against a rusted car skeleton, smashing it in two. The voice became distorted and garbled, then cut off abruptly, and it felt as if Aba had died for a second time.

Shoni got out of the bathtub and started crying, the tears dripping from the bottom of his plastic mask. He balled up his tiny hands into fists and hit me repeatedly, and then he went to the broken pieces of the cassette player and tried to reassemble them, his chest heaving. "Where is he?" he said. "I need to hear him! Where did he go?"

Batsheva tried to comfort him, putting her arms around his body, but he pushed her away. He was crouched over the broken device, making small noises like an animal.

"What the hell does it matter?" I said.

"He's in here," he kept repeating. "He's in here. He's in here."

After that night, Shoni got worse. He kept pretending Aba was right next to him, and he would talk to him, keeping

up a constant stream of narration that was even more un-
nerving than his silences had been. He talked late into the
night, often repeating the Alte Sachen refrain over and over
again, like an incantation. Sleeping in the bed above him, I
couldn't block him out. I would get angry and shout at him
to stop talking. He wouldn't stop, he kept going all night. I
wasn't sleeping. I woke up with dark circles under my eyes,
cursing him under my breath, until one night, when he began
chanting, I couldn't stand it any longer, and I punched him
hard in the chest. His breath left him in one whoosh, and he
gasped, choking.

He didn't make a sound after that. I told him I was sorry. I
kept repeating it, *Sorry, sorry, I didn't mean to hurt you, Shoni,
but you wouldn't shut up, you just kept talking and talking
and I couldn't sleep, I'm sorry.* He refused to talk, he only
looked at me with his eyes glinting from underneath the panda
mask. Sometimes he tiptoed to Ima's room to sleep in her bed,
but more often than not it was empty. She was always out until
late at night at her friend's place in Rosh Pina. Once I bumped
into her in the bathroom, her lipstick smudged, and neither of
us said a word. Unnerved by Shoni's silence, I read aloud to
him, stories by Mendele Mocher Sforim, tales of Jewish ped-
dlers traveling around in a wagon, never crossing beyond the
Pale.

Batsheva and I never saw each other again. Sometimes I
would take the truck through Ha'Ari Street and call out *Alte
Sachen, Alte Sachen,* but she would never open the door. I
thought I saw a curtain move once, but it could have been one
of her eleven brothers and sisters. We didn't have Aba's recording anymore, and it was tough going without it. I had to yell

out *Alte Sachen* every day for hours and hours, until my voice was hoarse and cracked.

Shoni never said a word. He was about as useful as a ghost. I kept talking to him, even though he didn't reply or acknowledge my presence in any way. I talked about Aba and the stories he used to tell us, about life after death. I told him Aba was never in the cassette player, I had just made it up.

On Purim, the happiest day of the year for most, a day when it was a mitzvah to celebrate and be merry and to drink to oblivion, the streets were filled with children in costumes, gift baskets dangling from their arms, twisting *raa'shan* noisemakers, singing and dancing. "My Little Clown" blared out in an endless loop from Rafi's Hardware Store. Shoni and I sat on the bridge overlooking the Midrahov, sharing a box of Oznei Haman cookies and watching the parade of costumed children go by. For once Shoni did not look out of place in his panda mask. There were fairies and witches, zombies and mermaids, Batman and the Joker, Yoda with a plastic green lightsaber walking hand in hand with a Gal Gadot Wonder Woman.

A few children pulled along a toy red wagon, filled with random objects: a two-legged barstool, a one-eyed teddy bear, and an old transistor radio. They were dressed up as Alte Sachen drivers. Shoni and I watched them go by, carrying their things in a little cart, with their parents following closely filming them on their phones. It was strange watching them, like looking at ourselves through a cracked mirror. The children were yelling out a mangled, broken version of the *Alte Sachen* call: *We want your junk! Alte Sachen, Alte Sachen. Give us your trash! Alte Sachen, Alte Sachen.*

Shoni laughed. "They got it wrong."

I felt as if I could finally exhale again. Those were the first words he'd spoken to me in weeks. I looked at my little brother beside me, laughing, and knew he was going to be okay. I watched the costumed children disappear down the street with their toy red wagon, listening to their voices getting fainter and fainter, swallowed up by the bright chaos of Purim celebrations, until I couldn't hear the *Alte Sachen* call anymore.

The Man Who Sold Air
in the Holy Land

Simcha was the man who sold air from the Holy Land, not to be confused with those unimaginative con artists who sold oil from the Oily Land or water from the Dead Sea. One summer he tried his luck selling oil; he picked enough olives from public gardens and private lawns to make a few decanters' worth. As for selling water, he filled up carafes from the tap in the kitchen sink and added plenty of salt to make it authentic, as if it were siphoned directly from the Dead Sea. These projects all proved too much work, too risky, and too costly. Air was everywhere, he didn't need anybody's permission to bottle it, and most important, it was free.

Like the Mediterranean cabernet sauvignon of the Judean Valley, Simcha's product came in boutique bottled packaging designed for the sophisticated customer with the discerning palate. He made little sticker labels for each bottle with his daughter Lali's help. On each label, she drew a bearded old man blowing a gust of wind. Apparently, he was a Greek god of some kind she studied in school, but Simcha thought he looked more like the Miser, the owner of the falafel place down the street, who enjoyed quoting biblical verse from Kohelet and sold half a measly pita for a small fortune. Together, Simcha and Lali polished the empty glass bottles with a rag, placed them side by side in the blue trolley, and went out in search of tourists willing to buy air.

With his keen eye and sixth sense—a tingling sensation in the presence of the very wealthy—Simcha zeroed in on them from all the way across Dizengoff Street, window-shopping. Two middle-aged American tourists, Jewish of course, and proudly patriotic with their I ♥ ISRAEL shirts, probably with plans to marry their daughter off to an El Al pilot. Simcha got closer, innocently pulling his trolley along. He could tell they were rich by the shine of their teeth. The husband's wallet practically bulged out of his back pocket, plump as a peach. The man was flushed, sweat pooled under his arms and made his turkey neck shine. The young wife, petite and dressed impeccably in white linen, was starstruck by a golden necklace in the window, playing with the diamond ring on her finger. Her hair, like the necklace, was golden. Although Simcha knew that her hair was not really spun of solid gold, it did give her a certain advantage. If in dire need, she could cut off her own hair and sell it to the highest bidder.

Simcha pulled his trolley along in the tourists' direction, empty bottles clanking and clinking as he went, while Lali came over from the other end of the street, wearing her adorable dress spotted with starfish and sea snails, holding Moshe Dayan, the one-eyed cat, in her arms. Simcha reached the tourists, who were peering at the display in the front store window of Zehava's Jewelry and Judaica: silver goblets and mezuzahs, pearl necklaces, blueberry-size diamond earrings sitting snugly in a green velvet case. Lali stopped in front of Simcha, admiring the bottles of air arranged in the trolley, while Moshe Dayan, curled up in her arms, groomed his fur, licking his forepaw with his quick, scratchy tongue.

"Mister sir," Lali said, in the English they had practiced, "what do you have there?"

"Oh, this? I'm only selling air."

"Air? Why would anyone buy air?"

"This isn't just any air. It's very special. I'll tell you a secret."

Lali leaned in, and her father whispered gibberish in her ear. The tourists stopped and were staring now, dumbstruck by the interaction.

"I want ten of them!" Lali said.

"Ten? You couldn't afford even one, my dear."

"I can sell my cat, Moshe Dayan. Please."

"This cat? He only has one eye. How much could he possibly be worth?"

The tourists looked mortified. The golden-haired wife clicked her tongue in disapproval, as if it were unkind to remind the cat that he only had one eye. *Visually challenged feline" is the correct term,* Simcha imagined her saying at an annual dinner for the charitable foundation she set up in support of downtrodden and dim-sighted kittens. The rich couple stopped to stare, and now came the final blow. Lali went over to the tourists, the visually challenged feline in her arms, stared at her shoes, and gave her speech.

"Hello, ladies and gentlemen," she said. "I offer you my

cat, Moshe Dayan, to purchase. He may only have one eye, but he doesn't break things often. He is named after the famous Israeli war hero who lost his eye in the struggle for our nation's freedom."

"We can't buy your cat, honey," the American lady said. "It wouldn't be right."

Lali hid her face in the cat's fur.

"What's in them anyway?" the American man said.

"Oh, in these?" Simcha said. "Nothing. Only air."

"Then why does she want them so bad?" the husband said. "How much are you charging?"

"Fifty shekels per bottle, for the usual customer. For the girl, I will give a very special discount, fifty percent off! Now only twenty-five shekels per bottle."

The wife looked at her husband, raising one eyebrow like a golden bow.

The husband seemed annoyed, drumming his fingers on his thighs. *It's nothing,* she mouthed. The husband looked at his wife, and Simcha imagined him trying to calculate the cost of refusing to buy the bottles of air. Would they fight for the rest of their vacation? Would she give him the silent treatment and act as if he didn't exist? Would she leave him for a younger Israeli man, who ran ultramarathons and worked in tech, a man who bought bottles of air on a whim, just *because,* without thinking twice, because money meant nothing to him? The husband sighed, nodded wearily, accepting his fate with modest bravery.

"How many bottles would you like, honey?" the wife asked.

Lali stayed with Simcha in his shabby apartment on Bugrashov Street on Fridays, and that was only because her mother wanted to get drunk in a dimly lit bar downtown in Florentin, where it was too dark for the lonely middle-aged men to see her wrinkles. Simcha's ex-wife got custody for six days, while he only got one. She worked at a beauty parlor on Ben Yehuda Street, which wasn't exactly Wall Street, but the judge wouldn't listen. Apparently, Simcha wasn't as financially stable. *It's all castles in the air how you make a living*, said the judge, waving an arthritic hand, as he casually proclaimed his sentence of doom. On Fridays, after selling bottles of air to American tourists, Simcha took Lali to Katsanelson's ice cream factory, and they picked out the misshapen Popsicles, the mistakes in production, which were free, and then they went to HaAtsmaut Park and played with other people's dogs. They had their tradition of going out to eat falafel at the Miser's after a big sale of air, and then visiting the Dolphinarium.

The Miser's Falafel was a tiny place, so small it could fit only the Miser himself. He hired no other employees, since he was too cheap to pay them their wages. Simcha and Lali joined a long line of customers who were waiting for their falafel. The Miser took his time, frying the chickpea balls in his bubbling, sizzling grill, where the oil, possibly as old and bitter as the Miser himself, was never replaced.

"Hey, king of the falafel," Simcha said, "I want two pitas with falafel, hummus, tahini, pickles, salad, and cabbage. Don't leave out the spicy mango *amba* sauce!"

"Did you get a haircut?" Lali asked the Miser.

"There is nothing new under the sun," said the Miser, quoting his favorite passage from Kohelet. His hair did look different, lopsided, shorter on one side, as if he had gone to the barber's and changed his mind halfway through. There was no way, Simcha thought, that the Miser would ever pay full price for a haircut.

"Can I have one extra falafel?" Lali asked, as she always did. "I'm hungry."

"All the rivers flow into the sea, and yet the sea is not full."

"Come on, Miser," said Simcha. "Give my daughter one extra falafel."

"What profit has man in all his toil under the sun?" said the Miser. "It will cost you. I have my reputation to consider."

The Miser had known Lali ever since she was "this big"—he always mimed her size by lowering his hand to the ground—but even so he refused to give her an extra falafel. It was a matter of principle, and Simcha respected him for his steadfast miserly ways but cursed him for the very same reason.

As usual, Simcha and Lali split the money from the sale of bottled air. He kept half and handed her the other half, which she tucked into a tin box with a peeling castle floating in the clouds on the cover. Her mother didn't know about the arrangement.

"If your mother asks," Simcha said, "tell her I gave you some pocket money."

"Okay," she said, licking her fingers.

"Your bat mitzvah is coming up," he said, as he did every time they met.

"No, it's not. Not for another"—she counted using the fingers on both hands—"seven years."

"That doesn't mean we can't start celebrating. Where do you wanna go today?"

They went to the Dolphinarium, as was their tradition.

Years ago the Dolphinarium used to be an aquatic zoo, where people paid to watch dolphins perform tricks, flips, and other acrobatic feats. At the center of the arena was a circular pool, where the dolphin trainers stood on artificial islands, wearing white shirts and serious expressions, and tossed handfuls of mackerel and sardines for the dolphins to catch in the air. The crowds would come and applaud the talented dolphins, but pretty soon it became unfashionable, because the animal rights groups protested every day by the entrance, parents stopped bringing their kids, who started seeing the cruel side to the enterprise, and the Dolphinarium was shut down and transformed into a nightclub. The club—which kept the enormous pool at the center, as well as the arena-like structure, and played electronic dance music until dawn—was destroyed in a suicide bombing years ago, during the Second Intifada, before Lali was even born, but everyone still called the wreckage the Dolphinarium.

Simcha and Lali would go watch invisible dolphins do their tricks, which was the best and cheapest entertainment around. There was a secret way into the Dolphinarium: if you followed the wave-breaker boulders toward Yaffo and slipped through a hole in the fence, you could climb into the remains of the arena. The pool, long dry by now, was painted with all kinds of sea creatures, lionfish, zebrafish, catfish. Every combination of a fish and another animal was represented. Even combinations of inanimate objects and fish were there, like swordfish and hammerhead sharks. The bottom was cracked and dusty, scattered with plaster debris, and the seats of the arena that surrounded the pool on all sides were long gone, too. Simcha and Lali sat in their reserved seats at the very center of the empty pool, where their voices carried and echoed in the empty space.

"Look at that one!" Lali said, clapping her hands. "It's so fast!"

"What a fantastic swimmer, top notch."

"Nice flip!" Lali said.

"Would you stop feeding the dolphins, sir?" Simcha said. "That peanut snack is not healthy at all!"

"Don't stick your head in its mouth!" Lali said.

"I wish I had a tail like that," Simcha said.

The sun sank lower and lower in the sky, painting the cream-colored clouds shades of rose water, just like *malabi,* Lali's favorite dessert. The attraction of an empty arena, so full of hidden promise in the daytime, slowly faded as it grew darker. Lali got sleepy, her head rested on Simcha's shoulder, and the dolphins around them were invisible once more. Pretty soon she would be too old for this, and he would have to take her to see real dolphins in real aquariums. The arena was completely deserted, except for a seagull that perched on a rusted metal beam. It flapped its wings and left, too. Simcha scooped Lali up and hung her off his shoulder, like a sack of potatoes, and they made their way home.

After he returned Lali to her mother, Simcha sat in the living room staring at the pile of unpaid bills on the table. Letter upon letter upon letter, all with red warnings, towered to an impossible height. The electricity and water were going to be shut off soon. He couldn't have Lali sleep in here when it happened—it would be too terrible. No hot water for a shower, no television. She would be miserable. She would tell her mother, and then he would never see her again. The judge would grant her mother full custody.

He could just picture the courtroom. *And what exactly is your occupation, sir?* the lawyer would ask him. *Are you a salesman?*

I am a sommelier of air, he would reply grandly, *specializing in oxygen from the Holy Land.*

Everyone in the room would laugh, and Lali would be taken away. He'd never see her again. She would forget who he was, pass by him on the street without a second glance, as if he were completely invisible, like one of the dolphins in the Dolphinarium.

He sat on the stoop of his house, on the first floor of his apartment building, with the trolley of empty bottles. When he got bored, he called out to potential customers, trying to sell his air. *Selling the freshest air, straight from the Holy Land, step right up and get your air, you won't regret it! It's flying off the shelves right now. Who doesn't need air? Don't miss this opportunity to get two for the price of one! Air, everyone, air!* Someone walked by and shouted, *We're breathing it for free, you donkey!* It wasn't any use. Without his daughter, he was nothing. He couldn't sell air even to the most gullible American tourist.

That Friday he arranged to meet Lali at the reception room of the Hilton, wearing his flamingo-pink suit. Lali dressed up in her Audrey Hepburn costume from *Breakfast at Tiffany's,* another favorite of theirs. When she entered the hotel, wearing a faux fur shawl, satin dress, and plastic tiara, he bowed and kissed her hand, calling her "my lady." The hotel served a buffet lunch of pancakes doused in golden syrup, mountains of raspberries and blackberries, plums in ice, honey dripping off the comb, clusters of granola, overnight oats and century-old wine, rhubarb and apricot crumbles with scoops of vanilla ice cream, and a meter-tall, edible white chocolate centerpiece in the shape of the Wailing Wall, complete with tiny marzipan figurines of praying Haredim. They heaped their plates and ate it all, speaking in their assumed roles. *Pass the marmalade, darling. Delightful crumpets! Have you tasted this scrumptious Scandinavian smoked salmon, my lady?*

Simcha waved the waiter over. He was a tall man with hair parted to the side, dressed in a dark suit jacket, a blue and white flag pinned to his lapel. Simcha always found it hilarious and grotesque when Israelis dressed up. There should be a law against it. Unless they were professional actors or perpetrating an elaborate scheme that required a disguise, it was ridiculous and downright offensive for Israelis to wear anything but flip-flops and swimming shorts. They weren't fooling anybody. The waiter looked like some kind of *tsabar* version of the mythological British butler.

"Jeeves, old chap, we'd like one *malabi*, two spoons," Simcha said. "We want all the toppings, and don't skimp out on the rose water!"

The milk pudding *malabi* came in a little glass cup, topped with rose water and sickly sweet syrup, heaped with pistachios and crumbled peanuts. Simcha and Lali clinked spoons, like honorable adversaries, and battled for dominance over the dessert. It was gone in thirty seconds. Lali licked her lips, bright red from the rose water.

When the time came to pay, Simcha told the waiter to put it on his room tab and drew a number in the air, three-oh-one.

"I'm afraid we don't do that, sir," he said.

"I seem to have misplaced my wallet. If you would be so kind to put it on my room tab, I will make sure to take care of it."

"That's not possible, sir. We take cash or card."

"Come on," Simcha said. "Just this once. Do it for the girl."

"Sorry, sir. That's not our policy."

"Damn it! Just do it." Simcha slammed his hand down on the table. He wiped the sweat from his brow.

"Daddy, here," Lali said. She placed a tin box on the table, with the peeling castle in the clouds on the cover. Inside was her share of the profit from selling air to the American tourists last week.

Simcha got up from his chair and grabbed the waiter by his collar. "Are you going to let me, a grown man, take money from my own daughter?" He let his hands hang there. Then he patted the waiter's chest, once, twice. "I'm sorry, so sorry." He sniffed. They paid using the money in Lali's tin box and left the hotel.

The next week and the one after that, Lali's mother refused to bring her over, perhaps because she heard some version of what had happened at the hotel. She probably thought he was using their daughter to make money. He could hear her self-righteous voice in his head. *Simcha, you should be ashamed of yourself. This is the last time you treat our daughter like a walking ATM card.* But it was just a game, a bit of playacting that Lali loved, and it never really hurt anybody.

Simcha spent his time sleeping on the couch and hatching plans that he never acted upon. One plan was to steal Lali in the middle of the night, to hitchhike to the airport and board a flight to Zanzibar as stowaways in the cargo section. He could picture them flying through the air in the plane's belly, with all the dogs barking in their cages nearby. They would open a few oversize suitcases and eventually find a delicious meal that someone had managed to sneak past security. They would eat someone's homemade roast and potatoes and give the scraps to the dogs, who were whining and howling like crazy. They would live on a remote island, eating coconuts and training monkeys to fish for them. They would grill the fish and use their bones to pick their teeth, leaving the scaly skin for the monkeys, forming a perfectly self-sufficient society.

The next week, when Lali still hadn't come, he headed to the Dolphinarium on his own. The arena was gone. The construction crew's trucks had come by and demolished whatever remained, completely erasing it, as if it had never existed at all. All that was left were a few blocks of stone and plaster, fragments of the painted pool. He picked up one of the pieces from the pool, on which a small green fish was chasing after a scrap of kelp, and put it in his pocket. He felt like that fish, lost in the big sea, always chasing after scraps, getting tossed here and there by the waves, pushed to the side by the great white sharks, watching his small kelp daughter drift away from him. It was almost like the plot of that movie *Finding Nemo*, except Simcha wasn't as overprotective as Nemo's dad, Marlin. He imagined taking that one piece of painted rock he'd found and multiplying it, using it to build a castle in the air, hovering right over Sheinkin Street, in the heart of Tel Aviv. The castle would be made up of hundreds of thousands of painted tiles, with all the sea creatures in the world, and in the middle of the living room would be a huge aquarium with stingrays and dolphins. Lali would have her very own room and a waterbed, and he would teach her to love sushi.

When Simcha returned home, there was a bold-lettered eviction notice on his door. He hadn't paid rent in months. Inside his apartment, his closet was overturned, and clothes hung out of drawers. His bottles of air were gone. He stumbled back outside, to Bugrashov, and saw that his furniture and belongings were tossed all over the street. His trolley was being hauled off by two teenagers—one of them sat inside it, while the other pulled. A man with crumbs in his beard was trying on one of Simcha's jean jackets. He saw his bottles of air shattered in the dumpster behind the terrible kosher Chinese fusion restaurant that served kung pao latkes, Peking kugel, and General Tso's knishes. Once he ordered their famous fortune cookie hamantaschen, and the note inside read, *Don't worry about money. The best things in life are free.*

Simcha sat on the steps of his former home, as people wandered by and took what they wished. In his pocket, he still had the piece of painted rock. A kid in baggy jeans and an oversize T-shirt rolled by slowly on his skateboard, looking oh-so-cool eating a slice of pizza and flicking his long blond hair back to get his bangs out of his eyes. Simcha asked him if he ever considered donating his hair to charity, and the kid gave him the finger. In the afternoon, Lali came by on her way back from school and sat next to him on the steps. Ever since the Second Intifada bus bombings years ago, he made sure Lali always walked home, never took public transportation. It was the one thing Simcha and his ex-wife agreed upon.

Lali took off her ocean-themed schoolbag, which had pictures of seahorses on it, and sighed, sounding older and wiser than her years. The air was hot, thick with humidity. Across the street, along Ben-Zion Boulevard, gnarled ficus trees swayed in the breeze. Simcha closed his eyes for a moment, enjoying the wind, until a green garbage truck crawled by, with its scent of rotten eggs and sewage, followed by a taxi whose driver was honking and cursing loudly. Sometimes Simcha wondered what it would have been like to live somewhere polite and boring, where no one ever raised their voice, and the phrases *thank you, you're so kind,* and *please, after you,* and *sorry, it's my fault,* so rarely heard in the Hebrew language, were used on a regular basis by calm, generous drivers.

"Why is all your stuff on the street?" Lali asked.

"I'm having a yard sale."

"Cool! Can I buy anything?"

"Sure. What would you like?"

"How about this shoebox?" She held up a washed-out piece of cardboard from the street, which wasn't even his.

"That's too precious." He winked at her. "I'm not sure I want to part with it, actually."

Lali brought him back to her house on Ahad Ha'am Street. Her mother was still at the beauty parlor. Simcha searched for his face in the photographs hanging on the walls and resting on cabinets and bedsides, but he wasn't in any of them. Moshe Dayan was sleeping in an armchair in front of the television, his one good eye closed. He'd lost his other eye in a surprise attack masterminded by a vicious, merciless tabby named Fifi, on the holy day of Yom Kippur. The fishing channel was on. The floors were clean, the lights worked in every room, the shower didn't have any hair in it, and the water from the tap was so hot it scalded his hand.

"Mom won't be home for another hour," she said. "When Moshe Dayan is alone, I always put this channel on. The fish calm him down."

Simcha and Lali sat in her room on the soft blue carpet. Stickers of sea creatures were plastered all over her closet, and her bedframe was shaped like a wave. They listened to her sea sounds playlist, which she put on every night before going to bed. The whooshing of the waves calmed Simcha. He placed the painted rock in the palm of her hand.

"Have you seen any dolphins around?" he said.

"A few."

"Your bat mitzvah is coming up."

Lali did not answer him this time. She was playing with the painted rock, making it swim across the carpet. "Where are you going to sleep, Daddy?"

"What do you mean? Anywhere. The Hilton, the Dolphinarium, a castle in the air. I have beds everywhere."

"No, really." She looked hard at him, her forehead creased with worry. She was waiting for him to answer, and he really didn't want to disappoint her. That was the worst feeling in the world.

For the first time, Simcha wondered if, when they sold bottles of air to tourists, she had been the one humoring him, rather than the other way around. He told her that there were plenty of things that he could do to make money to buy a new house, where they could be together. They could both join the circus and perform as a duo, jump through hoops of fire and glide through the air, held by invisible ropes. They could build a farm and raise chickens, paint their eggs golden, and sell them for a fortune. They could collect strangely shaped rocks and sell them as rubble from the moon. They could break open clams and take their pearls. They could train parrots to talk like the dead at funerals, for those loved ones who had missed the final conversation. They would say things like *You were always my favorite son,* or *I kept a secret portion of the estate for you,* or even *I forgive you.* He kept talking and talking, even though he knew that she'd stopped listening anyway— soon she would stop believing him, just as he had stopped believing himself.

Checkpoint

I still search for Adam's face among the soldiers whenever I come to the checkpoint. Every soldier's uniform reminds me of doing his laundry, when he used to come back from the base on weekends. The dark green spinning and spinning in the machine, the surge of water, the frothing soap, then the sensation of drowning. I can't do laundry now without thinking of Adam. For days after his funeral, I washed his old uniform. I sat and watched it spinning in the machine. When the wash was over, I'd put it in again. I dried his uniform in high heat, again and again, imagined it shrinking until it looked like baby clothes, until it got so small it was all gone. I'm afraid that Adam, spinning around and around in my head, will disappear completely one day.

It's dawn; first light glows orange, simmering beneath the heavy clouds. Leading up to the checkpoint are partial roadblocks, earth mounds, and rubble piles. Construction workers, clothes still dirty from yesterday's shift, are waiting in line to be searched and checked, crammed into a single tight enclosure. A few women in hijabs shuffle their feet and hold their children's hands tightly. Many of them arrived hours ago, in the middle of the night, due to the long delays that keep them waiting at the crossing point.

The sun is white hot now, and the line is endlessly long and unbearably slow today, filled with men smoking their cigarettes down to the filter, drinking strong coffee, standing under a corrugated tin roof that provides some shade. The gate is shut. Adam was killed four years ago, and still I go to the checkpoint every week. Nothing has changed—things have only gotten worse. An endless cycle of violence. The Nation State Law, settler price-tag retaliations, the demolition of homes and the burning of Palestinian olive groves in the West Bank, every two years or so another war in Gaza.

I've been volunteering at the checkpoint for almost two decades. My job is to document whatever happens. I write reports and take pictures and record videos. I'm here every Sunday for my shift, from five to eight in the morning, making sure the Palestinians aren't mistreated with casual cruelty and that the soldiers and border police are doing their job properly. I know the checkpoint inside and out, all its secrets, down to the very last detail—just as I know Adam's room. All the things he kept hidden in his desk drawer. A pale seashell from Caesarea beach, a deck of old Yu-Gi-Oh! cards, a pack of Marlboro Reds with three cigarettes left, a packet of extra-safe condoms, and one of his milk teeth, wrapped in crumpled tissue paper.

I always have my bulky old video camera with me, a relic of the '90s. When I film the men in their tight-fitting jeans and knockoff Nikes, they whistle and hold up two fingers, a V for victory. Children hide behind their mothers, peeking at my camera. Through my lens, I can see the elderly staring blankly back at me, their wrinkled features etched with countless daily sorrows and humiliations. All the other women volunteers, most of them grandmothers, use their iPhones to document the checkpoint, but I kept my old video camera, since all our memories, our footage of Adam growing up, is there, backed up in three different USBs, but still I wake up in the middle of the night thinking that we have lost it all.

I remember Shaul using the very same camera to film the newborn baby Adam lying on the bed, the quilt from Kathmandu spread out and his tiny body between us, telling him his first bedtime story. We filmed Adam's first bath. We washed him in the sink because he was so small. He was born premature, pink and wrinkled, weighing about as much as a small bag of rice. When he was three years old, he pretended to open up a restaurant. He sat us down in the living room with napkins on our laps and folded paper menus. He recited the specials of the day: pasta Bolognese, mashed potatoes and schnitzel, chocolate cake and vanilla ice cream. *I'll take the pasta Bolognese,* I said, and Shaul ordered mashed potatoes and schnitzel. *We're all out,* Adam said. No matter what we ordered, Adam would somberly shake his head and announce that the kitchen had run out of it. No pasta, no potatoes, no ice cream. I wanted to do the same thing when he turned eighteen, when the army came knocking on our door, I wanted to say, *I'm sorry, we have no boys left for you.*

The soldiers do their job with utmost boredom. The earth is dry and cracked, sparsely covered with withered plants. A herd of sheep grazes in the yellow grass next to the highway, and the sun is high in the sky, even though it's still early morning. The concrete wall is spray-painted with slogans: DON'T FORGET THE STRUGGLE, TO EXIST IS TO RESIST, and my favorite, MAKE HUMMUS NOT WALLS. The men and women are funneled through a narrow passageway, where they shove and jostle for space, pass the spinning steel turnstiles, go through the metal detectors, and finally they reach the station where jaded soldiers sit behind bulletproof glass and check IDs, matching a picture to a face.

Everyone is waiting for the soldiers to decide to open the gate. Meanwhile some Palestinians purchase coffee and cigarettes from the wandering vendors and hawkers. Tired children are crying, bleary-eyed workers are late for their shifts. A man in a gray hoodie is shouting and waving his hands. He is told to lie down on the ground. A soldier yells out commands in broken Arabic, stumbling over the words like a schoolchild reciting a poem he can't quite remember. The man puts his head to the ground, as if listening for a heartbeat. His hands are cuffed behind his back, and he is led away to the *jora,* the detention area.

"Why are you taking him?" I turn on my camera.

The soldier who leads the farmer away raises a hand to cover his face. "Stop filming! Will you get out of here already?"

"*Yalla, yalla, yalla,* keep it moving," another soldier says, speaking into a megaphone. "This isn't an Airbnb."

He waves to the rest of the people, who stare after the receding figure of the worker. In line, the Palestinians are mostly grim and silent now, knowing that if they argue they might not be able to pass at all. They have families to feed, jobs to go to.

Today it is this worker—tomorrow it will be another. *Yom assal, yom basal.* A honey day, an onion day. One of the children in line, a small boy with a mischievous grin, sticks his tongue out at me. I wonder how long it will take for him to harden, become bitter and angry, how many more humiliating days spent waiting at the checkpoint, being strip-searched or interrogated, until he begins resisting with a group of other boys from his village, throwing rocks at passing settler vehicles, and confronting soldiers with riot gear and tear gas canisters and rubber bullets, until he's hauled off to prison for throwing one stone too many.

Last week a settler kid stuck his tongue out at me, too. I seem to attract this kind of attention from children. I was waiting at an intersection on the way home after my shift at the checkpoint, when I saw a family of settlers in their four-by-four with a FIGHT TERROR, SUPPORT ISRAEL bumper sticker, the husband with a woven kippah, the wife with a *mitpachat* headscarf, their three children peeking through the windows, blond *pe'ot* curls dangling from their cheeks, holding gleaming lollipops and melting Popsicles. One of the kids narrowed his eyes and stuck his tongue, painted purple with Popsicle, out at me. How long until he becomes resentful and inflamed, driving down the highway, his car pelted by stones thrown by Palestinian boys from the side of the road, his father getting out of the vehicle with his M16 and firing an entire magazine into the air for deterrence, how long until the child picks up a gun himself and, vowing revenge, takes the law into his own hands?

One young settler, slightly overweight and tall, with *pe'ot* locks and a scraggly beard, comes from a neighboring village in the Occupied Territories to harass the Palestinians. When-

ever he opens his mouth to scream at them, I catch sight of his
buckteeth. He's red-faced and enraged, throwing his hands up
in the air. But despite his loud theatrics and intimidations, he's
got the quiet, dejected look of someone who used to be the
shyest boy in school. He appears to be one of the extremist
hilltop youth, No'ar HaGava'ot, living in one of the illegal
outposts in the West Bank.

The settler has been eyeing me. I'm conspicuous with my
video camera. He steps toward me. "Go work in the kitchen,
Arab lover *zona*!"

I've read somewhere that when you're confronted with people you don't particularly like, give them a costume—it will
help ease the nerves. I picture the settler in a Tudor monarch's
clothes, like those worn in the ridiculous portraits of King
Henry VIII, a round wide hat on his head, pinned with ostrich
feathers, a puffy collared shirt, a coat lined with white ermine.
Somehow this makes me feel slightly better.

"*Arabushim*, this is our land!" yells the Tudor settler. "It's
been our land for two thousand years!"

"If you don't keep quiet, you will be removed," says one of
the soldiers.

"You love moving us with force, don't you?" says the Tudor
settler. "You would move us all and give up the whole land of
Israel to the Arabs!"

"I'm not giving up any land to the Arabs," says the same
soldier, "but if you don't shut up I'll remove you from here
with force."

"We gave the Arabs so much, and still they want more. All
they want is to kill us, for Esav hated Yaakov. It's not politics!
It's the truth from the Torah."

The soldiers stare. Some of them laugh, but none intervene anymore. Formally, they have given a warning, their job is done, now let the settler talk. The Palestinians, the soldiers, the settler, and me, the middle-aged activist working for the women-only human rights group, mourning her son, the soldier. It would be a wonderful theater production in three acts. Something by Hanoch Levin, staged at the Habima Theater, called *Requiem for a Checkpoint*. It would be violent, obscene, and grimy. All the best Israeli actors from Tel Aviv would play the Palestinians. And we, the audience, would rise from our seats and clap and say how powerful it was, how political yet nuanced, how very *real*. And who would they get to play my Adam? A complex character: a soldier, the son of a left-wing activist, killed in action.

There's a commotion: the soldiers are busy with an old man who has metal in his heart and refuses to go through the detector. The old man keeps pointing at his chest and shaking his head. A young girl's schoolbag is being searched: a fine-toothed comb, a science textbook, and a pencil case decorated with Hello Kitty stickers all spill to the ground. With her ponytail held up by a green scrunchie, the frightened girl clutches her father's hand tightly, knuckles white. The father's face is gaunt, deeply lined with worry, and there are sweat stains under his arms, darkening his short-sleeved FLY EMIRATES shirt.

The soldier doing the security checks eyes him with suspicion. "*Tawaquf,* stop!" Quickly and efficiently, he pats the father down. "Show me your ID."

He searches him, then he motions for the little girl to go through the metal detector. The soldier's eyes travel to my camera, then back to the girl.

"Why isn't she at school? *Madrassah, madrassah,*" the soldier says.

"*Madrassah,*" repeats the father, nodding his head eagerly.

"She's going to school," I say.

"I didn't ask you. Stop talking."

I don't say anything further because I don't want the soldier to punish them if I do. I look at the ground. *Let them pass, please, she needs to go to school.*

"*Yalla,* get out of here," the soldier says. He waves them through, and the girl's father nods at me wearily.

"You can't be here," he says, addressing me now, and I notice his *yehida* insignia, the shoulder tag with the sword and olive branch of the District Coordination and Liaison Officer. "This is a military zone."

"I'm not talking to you or to your men. I can be here."

"This area is under my jurisdiction, and I will tell you where you can or cannot be. Anyway, you're wasting your time here."

"As long as these checkpoints exist, I need to be here," I say.

"No. As long as these checkpoints exist, *we* need to be here," he says, gesturing to the other soldiers. "You can be at home making couscous for your kids right now."

I flinch at the word *kids.* Plural.

"You got kids?" the soldier asks.

"Yes."

"They serve?"

"My daughter, Yael, is only twelve years old. My son, Adam, was in Golani."

"And this is what you do? You must hate each other," says the soldier.

"I don't hate you. You're doing your job, I'm doing mine. I'm here to make sure you treat these people fairly. Legally."

"I bet your son hates you. I would, if you were my mother." The soldier returns to monitoring the metal detector, ignoring me now.

I feel so tired suddenly, even though it's not yet eight o'clock, I arrived almost three hours ago. I woke up so early to be here, when it was still dark outside. On the way I was so exhausted, I hardly thought of Adam. Not until I reached the checkpoint. I don't want to wait. I want to leave now, to just get back in my station wagon, the one Shaul and I don't really need anymore, and turn on the AC and drive out of here. My friend Nechama, that seventy-six-year-old firecracker, will come to replace me soon, but I don't have the patience to wait.

The parking lot is far, and the air is so oppressively humid, like a sauna but without any of the fun. Winters at the checkpoint can be tough, too, with the rain and wind and bitter cold seeping into your bones, but there are also moments of strange beauty. I remember, six years ago, there was a heavy snowstorm. Adam was still alive then, the day it snowed at the checkpoint, and the heavy flurry of flakes settled on the concrete wall and the barbed wire, and I watched a bizarre and lighthearted snowball fight between a Palestinian family, a mother and her sons, and two Israeli soldiers.

I watch the long line of people yawning, coughing, spitting, and smoking. It feels as if it has finally caught up to me, all those years of fighting for equal rights for the Palestinians, protesting the evictions in the Sheikh Jarrah neighborhood in East Jerusalem, attending meetings with members of Combatants for Peace, organizing the joint Israeli-Palestinian Memorial Day Ceremony, all for nothing. Most people who are my age are already starting to prepare for their retirement, looking at brochures to go on yacht cruises in the Bahamas, learning to play the mandolin, building model airplanes, or at the very least sitting at home and doing the *Haaretz* crossword, but here I am, arguing with eighteen-year-old soldiers.

I make my way to the parking lot, down the long stretch of empty highway, surrounded on all sides by dry grass and pale, craggy boulders, and it really is all very dramatic, this Promised Land, this so-called Judea and Samaria, with its rolling green hills and ancient olive groves, the chirping of hummingbirds, the gurgle of natural spring waters. There are many things wrong with this country, but its landscape doesn't lack any natural beauty, if we can only keep it that way. Adam was always telling me to appreciate the stark Israeli landscape. I used to love going on hiking trips to the Galilee or the Negev, and Adam and Yaeli would toast marshmallows on our open campfire, and the smoke kept away all the mosquitoes, and I slept so peacefully in my husband's arms, hearing my children breathing right next to me.

After a few minutes of walking rather absentmindedly in the direction of my car, I notice that someone is behind me, the settler from the checkpoint, and that he is singing, in a strangely beautiful and mournful voice, "Hatikvah," our national anthem, which always makes me cringe with its two-thousand-year-old longing for a Jewish homeland. I ignore him, walking purposefully. *Nefesh Yehudi homia.* I'm no longer young, but I do my best to walk quickly, and my hips ache, my back hurts, my shoulders are tense. *Ulefati mizrach kadimah.* The soles of my feet are sore from standing around. *Ein*

Le Zion Zofia. My head hurts from being out in the sun, and his booming, thunderous voice, which has the qualities of a *hazzan* cantor, isn't helping with my migraine. *Our hope is not yet lost, the hope that is two thousand years old, to be a free nation in our land, the land of Zion, Jerusalem.*

The settler's words are drawn out, melting into each other like the stream of *El Malei Rachamim,* the prayer Shaul insisted we recite during Adam's funeral. I thought that Yehuda Amichai's ironic version of the prayer for the dead would be more appropriate. *If God was not full of mercy, mercy would have been in the world, not just in Him.* With each repetition of the chorus, the settler gets closer and closer, the more my throat closes up, and the more constricted I feel, as if I am being buried alive. *I, who plucked flowers in the hills, and looked down into all the valleys. I, who brought corpses down from the hills, can tell you that the world is empty of mercy.* I imagine the settler standing over me, reciting a funeral prayer, shoveling dirt until I can't see, can't hear, but still my thoughts keep spinning, spinning in the void. Keep walking, he'll back off at some point, just keep walking.

The settler gets closer and closer, and now I can hear his footsteps behind me, but I keep walking, staring straight ahead. Walk quickly, faster now, faster, but don't run. Running signals that you're scared, that this is actually real and happening. He would never hurt me. He wouldn't dare. The highway is desolate. He could grab me, pull me by my hair, toss me under the shade of an olive tree or leave me out in the blazing sun and do whatever he wanted. I walk faster. He's caught up. He flanks me, pressing in.

I look back. I'm too far from the checkpoint, but I can already see the parking lot in front of me. The settler starts walking alongside me, his *pe'ot* locks bouncing with each step he takes, and now his steps match mine, we are synchronized, and for some reason, this bothers me more than anything, because I don't want anything in common with this man, not to share the same air, not to eat the same food or drink the same water, not to speak the same language, and not even to walk in the same rhythm as him. That's when I start running.

"Hey, where are you running off to? Gaza is the other way!"

He runs after me. He is overweight but surprisingly quick. He reaches me, pulling me to him by my wrist. I struggle free and push him away.

"Because of you, the brothers of Israel, the sons of Abraham, are being murdered!"

I aim my kick between his legs, but he grabs my foot, seizing my shoe. Momentarily I'm caught off balance, and then he lets go and clutches my arm instead, holding me in place. He is a mountain, a thick big block of a man. I slap him, hard. The sharp crack resounds, startling a pair of small birds to fly away, and everything is silent for a moment. He steps in front of me, blocking my way, and I bump into his chest, which smells surprisingly sweet, like laundry detergent.

"Get out of my way!" I cry.

He presses his fingers into my shoulder. His face is contorted, his hot breath makes me want to vomit. He laughs, flashing his buckteeth. Spittle flies in my face.

"What did you say to me, *shikse*? I am in your way? No. I think you're in my way."

I bite his arm, and he yelps in pain. I seize the opportunity to take out my car keys, the metal sticking out like a knuckle duster, and try to get away, but his grip is back and stronger than before—his fleshy hands are on my neck. My vision is blurred. Black spots dance in front of me. I raise my hand, clutching the key, and aim for his face, but he hits me above the eye, knocking me down. The impact takes the breath out of me, scratches my cheek. The burning tarmac of the road sticks to the palms of my hand. I can feel blood trickling down my forehead, and I start shaking uncontrollably.

I'm on the ground. I can hear a noise, far away, but getting closer and closer. The roar of an engine. I can make out a military jeep in the distance, a desert-colored Sufa off-road vehicle, speeding this way in a flurry of dust, and for a moment, I think it's not going to stop, and for a split second, I hope it doesn't. Do the soldiers really hate me that much, that they would leave me here? Would they just drive by? Run me over? Would I really care if they did?

The jeep stops with a screech of wheels on dirt, and a soldier jumps out, leaving the engine still running. "*Yalla!* Get out of here!" he says.

From my position on the ground, with the soldier standing over me, his AK-47 hanging off a strap at his side, I notice that between the rubber bands tucking in the pant legs of his uniform and his dusty black combat boots, there is a hint of color, a red sock, which is technically breaking the rules. Only black and gray socks are allowed. This hint of color makes me like him a bit.

The settler, who is standing to my left, frames the other side. He is wearing Shoresh sandals, the straps forming an X below his ankle. He doesn't back down—fearlessly he spits on the ground, very close to me.

They face each other, my body between them, the prize at the end of the fight.

"Go, get out of here!" the soldier says. "Start running!"

The settler doesn't move. Is he carrying a weapon? Most of the settlers are armed nowadays, but because they're Jewish no one thinks of them as terrorists. I can hear the soldier cursing under his breath, and the settler takes a step toward him, and the soldier raises his weapon and shoots a few rounds into the air as a warning. The bullet casings drop all around me, but I can't hear them hit the ground because my ears are ringing, a high-pitched frequency, like the one Adam used to complain about after he went out dancing, standing too close to the speakers in the Block, a techno and house club on Salameh, by the old train station in downtown Tel Aviv.

The settler starts loping away, clumsily, and trips once or twice. I lie there for a moment more, feeling the warm road vibrating against my skin with the rhythm of the jeep's engine, and thinking why it is that I wish the soldier hadn't come. A dull buzzing in my head, but the ringing has stopped. Leave me alone. Let me bleed out, right here on this highway, be found the following morning: *Nurit Abramovich, mother of Adam (1996–2014) and Yael, wife of Shaul. Political activist.* And what else? What have I done that would be worth mentioning? I have sent off my son to be killed in a war I don't believe in, fighting for a government I hate. And I made him feel bad about going to war, as if he even had a choice.

"Hey! Hey, wait a second," the soldier says, as I get up and start heading in the direction of the parking lot. He's speaking, but I can barely hear him even though he is right beside me. It's the same soldier I argued with at the checkpoint, the

District Coordination and Liaison Officer. His face is concerned, like he's helping a grandmother cross the road. Really, that's what I must seem to him, a grandmother. The truth is I'll have to wait awhile until I have grandchildren—Yaeli hasn't even had her first boyfriend yet.

I'm wobbly on my feet. My head is throbbing. I dab my eye with the sleeve of my shirt.

"You're bleeding," the soldier says.

"What?"

"You can hardly stand, you shouldn't be operating a vehicle—"

"I don't have to stand to drive."

We finally reach the parking area. It's not difficult to find the station wagon, since there are only three cars in the entire lot.

"Do you have anyone you can call? Your husband?"

"I don't want to scare him. Besides, this is our only car. No, I'll be fine."

"Wait a second."

He walks a few steps away, making a call. Getting permission, I assume. I want to call Shaul, to tell him everything, to cry into the phone, but I can't.

Ever since Adam died, he's hardly said a word. He's never been the talkative type, but now he's almost completely silent, retreating so far into himself, I'm not sure he knows how to talk anymore, how to move those tired muscles. It's as if his wife and daughter have ceased to exist, and there is only Adam, Adam, Adam.

When Adam was sent to Gaza, Shaul replaced our door. He got the idea from David Grossman's novel *To the End of the*

Land, where a mother is haunted by visions of army officers knocking on her door and bringing her news of the death of her son. If they come to tell me he is dead, I don't want to see their feet in the door, the mother says, and taped a piece of cardboard to block out their boots. Our door, like the fictional mother's, was made of glass. Shaul replaced our glass door with a heavy, dark door, but it still wasn't enough to keep them out—the soldiers can come through any door and tell you that your son is dead.

The soldier will drive me home and take a bus back. It takes less than an hour to get from the checkpoint to my home in Tel Aviv, on Dubnov Street. We leave the military jeep and take my station wagon. I get in the passenger seat. Looking around in the back seat, he finds a sandy towel. He hands it to me, and I touch it to my forehead.

When Adam was very young, he would frequently get high fevers. I remember pressing a cold cloth to his burning forehead. He was shivering. Only a small boy, thin arms, freckled face. I stroked his damp reddish hair.

Ima, Ima, I'm scared.

What are you scared of? It's just a fever.

Ima, am I going to die?

Die? Don't be silly. What nonsense.

"Press on it," the soldier says.

"That's the surest way to get it infected. You know how dirty the sea is?"

I take the towel anyway, so I can cover my face, so he won't be able to see the tears in my eyes. For the longest time, I have been numb. The pain feels good. I am grateful to feel something, anything. The sand sticks to the blood on my face.

"I could have taken care of myself, you know."

"It didn't look like it from where I was standing."

"Well, you were standing far away."

"You're lucky I was taking the jeep for a supply run."

"Yes. Very lucky," I say with a sigh. Even luckier if I was dead on the highway.

He turns on the radio, flicking through channels as if we were two friends going on a road trip, until he settles on Galgalatz, the military broadcast station. They're playing oldies. "You like this kind of stuff, right?"

He is making fun of me, *mistalbet.* "Why? Because I'm old?" But I do like this kind of stuff, he's right.

He shrugs.

Patches of earth, low bushes, dry grass to our sides. Adam would always laugh at my taste in music. *Ima, why do we always have to put on Leonard Cohen? All his songs sound exactly the same. So whiny.* The soldier's left hand is on the steering wheel. His right hand is on his thigh. Thick blue veins. Hairy fingers. The fingernails are chewed off, and gun grease darkens his knuckles. Adam used to bite his nails so fiercely, we had to spread bitter polish on them. I want to pat the soldier's hand, to tell him thank you, but I don't.

I imagine the soldier's body relaxing, just for a second. Just the way my Adam would lounge on the couch when he came back for the weekend. The army had made him silent, more like his father. For brief moments, he would return to his old self. *Ima, make me schnitzel and p'titim. I'm so hungry.* He was like a little boy again. Demanding, childish, pretending to be powerless. Then he would snap to attention. Show no weakness. That's what they teach them.

"Have you got a name?"

"Nurit," I say. "You?"

"I'm Tamir."

"You know, Tamir, I can't imagine how hard it is to do this shitty job if you don't believe you're doing something important, useful."

"It's shitty, all right."

Tamir has long, dark, almost feminine eyelashes. A hint of stubble on his cheeks. He keeps one hand on the wheel, and with the other he undoes the buttons of his uniform, revealing a white shirt and a silver *diskit* dog tag that glints in the sun. He wipes the sweat from his forehead and turns on the AC.

"Where are you from?" I ask.

"Kiryat Ata."

They always send these kids, from places like Kiryat Ata, Ashdod, Netanya, to guard the checkpoints, kids who barely graduated high school, one wrong step away from Ofek Prison, angry kids.

"You said your son was in the Golani Brigade, right?"

"Yes. He fought in Operation Cast Lead."

No reaction. Well, who didn't fight in Gaza? Everyone knows someone who did, especially at his age. Everyone knows someone who knows someone who died. Around the country, those who make it out alive organize half-marathon runs in memory of the dead classmate, the dead friend, the dead son. I think of the military funeral they organized for Adam. The honor guard firing their rifles, the coffin draped in the flag. Sometimes I imagine Adam's funeral as a dance choreographed by Ohad Naharin or Pina Bausch. Darkness onstage, drums beating, then a bright spotlight. *Batsheva* dancers dressed in white burial shrouds stand in a semicircle. They shiver and convulse, shaking uncontrollably, as if their bodies are being torn apart. The drum beats faster as they thump their chests and stomp their feet and let out a wail, raising their hands to the heavens in a cry that will go unanswered.

"I mean, I never thought he was a fighter when he was growing up. I thought he would go do intelligence work at 8200, but he had a different plan. He joined a fitness group to prepare. He was never the strongest boy, but he was stubborn. He would get this tremble in his lower lip as a boy. I don't know why I'm telling you this."

Tamir's jawline is hard. I can't imagine his lips trembling. The back of his neck is burnt and peeling from the sun. The AC is working full blast now, and the hairs on his arms are all erect. Over his shoulder, I can see the stone homes of the Palestinian village At-Tira, the mosque tower sticking up like a long pale finger, sheep grazing in fields of tall grass, thorns and brambles growing in patches on the ocher-colored dirt, under a vast, pale blue sky, clouds moving quickly across the horizon.

"I know what you think of me, of what I do. My son also hated my volunteer work at the checkpoint. The night before he left for the operation, I wanted to be sure he knew I loved him even though I didn't support the government or the war he was fighting in."

When I think of Adam's last night at home, I have this claustrophobic feeling, as if everything is closing in on me, and I want to scream, but I can't. I'm like the mouse in Kafka's "A Little Fable." Alas, said the mouse, the world is getting smaller every day. The long walls have grown narrow. I'm running, forever running, toward the trap. You only need to change your direction, said the cat, and ate it up. But as I'm talking, I feel as if a barrier is being lifted, ever so slightly. There is a small opening, and by talking and talking, maybe I can squeeze through.

"But somehow, instead of telling him I loved him, we had this big argument the night before he left. We were standing in the kitchen—I was making a cup of tea. He told me he was ashamed to tell his friends what I did at the checkpoint. He told me it was hard being my son, that he hated me sometimes. I didn't look at him, but I knew he was crying. I poured the hot water into a mug and let the teabag soak. Then I went to the living room without saying another word to him, without even looking in his direction. Why didn't I at least look at him?"

Tamir stares straight ahead, betraying nothing. The countryside zooms pasts us, in row after row of electricity pylons, and shades of yellow and brown, and the red-roofed homes of the settlement of Beit Horon, where last year a twenty-three-year-old Israeli woman was stabbed in her home by two Palestinians in a deadly terror attack.

"It was just a few days later," I continue, "he was killed. Friendly fire."

I can feel Tamir tense beside me. He turns to look at me, his lips part for a moment, but no sound comes out, then he turns his eyes back to the road, pressing down on the gas pedal and overtaking a green Egged bus.

"I'm sorry," he mumbles.

"And you know the last thing I said to him?"

Tamir shakes his head.

"I was still angry at him from the night before. It was a Sunday, early in the morning, and Adam needed to go to the pickup spot. He said he didn't mind taking the bus, but my husband, Shaul, suggested we drive him. I refused, rather childishly, insisting that I needed the car to get to the checkpoint in time for my shift, that it was difficult to reach by public transportation, that he was a big boy now and could take the bus by himself, couldn't he? Adam looked so hurt. And he took the bus to go to war."

Tamir sighs. He starts tapping his hand nervously against the dashboard. *Tap. Tap. Tap.* I want to keep talking. I have thought about this so much that the story comes out automatically, mechanically.

"Three officers came to our house. I heard the doorbell. Shaul and I stared at each other. It rang again. When I opened the door, I just looked at their feet. I knew from their boots that they were coming to tell me that my son was dead. We sat in the living room. The officers were confirming Adam's information with us, but I wasn't listening—physically I think I was unable to hear them. My ears shut off. I refused to listen to what these people had to say. I stared at the painting hanging in our living room, a Gershuni with these thick brushstrokes, a cross in the earth. And then I heard one of them say: 'Sergeant Adam Abramovich.' Shaul corrected him. This was the only time that Shaul spoke when the officers were in the house, so I remember it well. He said: 'No, he's a corporal. He hasn't been promoted to sergeant.' I had no idea what rank our son was. And the officer replied: 'When a soldier falls in the line of duty, he gets promoted automatically. He's a sergeant now.' He said *falls,* not dies. As if Adam had slipped and grazed his knee."

We pass the city of Modi'in-Maccabim-Re'ut, built on the

ruins of Palestinian villages, with its sloping wadis and identical white homes. In half an hour I'll be home. The blood on my face has dried. I touch the wound to feel the stinging again. "Sometimes I wish Adam had never been born." I watch Tamir's face for a reaction. Nothing. My face hurts. My whole body hurts. "What if I had a son who wore overalls and smoked feisels with hash? An artist who didn't go to the army. Someone who grew a beard and squatted in an abandoned building off Allenby Street, and constantly talked about that one time the bouncer let him into the Berghain in Berlin and ate *masabacha* in Abu Hassan every day and tried to speak in Arabic to all the staff. A son who would say things like *The occupation corrupts us*."

Tamir's laugh sounds like a low growl.

"You know the type. Well, Adam wasn't like that. When he was little, he liked building Playmobil cities, with tiny plastic people, always smiling, Swedish cottages and bridges, construction workers and pirates, and a remote-controlled train going in circles. His favorite figurine was a French Revolutionary soldier, with a red jacket and a large black Napoleon hat. He was so serious with those toys. Adam and Shaul would play for hours in his room, making up stories and battles and sieges, two coconspirators planning an elaborate military strategy. A few months after Adam was killed, I caught Shaul playing with his toys. I don't think he saw me watching him. He'd taken the toys down from the attic, where they had been stored for years in a dusty Tupperware box, and he was holding the French Revolutionary soldier, Adam's favorite, and then he cleaned it with his shirt sleeve and put it in his pocket."

Creedence Clearwater Revival on the radio, "Have You

Ever Seen the Rain?" This land hasn't seen rain for a long time. There will never be enough rain. I want to feel clean, to think simply. Everything here sticks to you, dirtying you. Suddenly I feel very old. I want to be home, in my bed, not on this empty highway with this soldier who reminds me so much of Adam.

"You know," I say, "when David Grossman gave a speech calling for a cease-fire in Lebanon? Writers and intellectuals were gathering, protesting in Rabin Square. Grossman demanded an end to the bloodshed. His son, Uri, was among the soldiers fighting. Three days later Uri was killed in action. The following morning a cease-fire agreement was reached. I remember watching on TV, Grossman standing over Uri's grave in Mount Herzl. I listened to the eulogy, thinking I can't imagine what he feels like, what it would feel like to lose your son.

"Eight years later I knew exactly what he was feeling. I remember he had said, *Every thought begins with no. No more coming home to you, no more talking to you, no more laughing with you. This is a war we have already lost. As a family.* You know, most days I don't feel like getting out of bed. I just lie there. But I have a daughter, too. My Yaeli. When Grossman told his daughter that her brother was killed, she sobbed at first. Then she said, *But we will live, right? We will live and trek like before, and I want to learn how to play the guitar.* Grossman hugged his daughter and told her, *We will live.* When my daughter, Yaeli, asked me the same question, I couldn't answer her."

We turn off of Highway 1 to Ayalon Freeway, at the La-Guardia Interchange, and suddenly we've reached Tel Aviv, the monstrosity of its three Azrieli towers, and to my left the Sarona market, all fancy shops and swanky restaurants, and right in the middle of the city sits the Kirya military base with its barbed wire and tall fences, and we turn from Kaplan onto Ibn Gabirol, then down the quiet, tree-lined boulevard, and finally we get to Dubnov Street, to my home overlooking the public garden, where all the children are running around and crying in the colorful playground, and the pretty young mothers, rolled-up yoga mats tucked under their arms, chat to one another, and all is well, and for a moment, when I go up the three flights of stairs and unlock my front door, and walk down the cool, carpeted hallway leading to the living room, past the Gershuni painting and the spacious windows and tall bookcases and pale white orchids and bright healthy succulents, fleshy green leaves spiraling forever inward, I forget that Adam won't be there.

The Sephardi Survivor

I was always jealous of my Ashkenazi classmates for having grandparents who were Shoah survivors. My brother, Zohar, and I were Sephardi; our parents came from Egypt and Libya, their parents came from Syria and Morocco, and somewhere way back our ancestors were expelled from Spain. We wished we had a Shoah story in the family to be proud of, but we didn't, so we were always on the lookout for survivors to adopt. This year, on the week before Shoah Memorial Day, we brought Yehuda home. We found him wandering around Moshe's Superzol, between the gefilte fish and kugel aisles, muttering with a glazed look on his ancient face. Most important, he didn't have one of those caretakers following him around everywhere like a devoted bodyguard. He was shuffling along in his house slippers at an agonizingly slow rate, as if he were a nearly extinct reptile, the last of his kind.

"What are you standing around for?" he said. "Help me carry these."

He struggled with the shopping bags he carried in his veiny, liver-spotted hands. On his left forearm was a Band-Aid with turtles on it. Each of us grabbed a bag, stuffed with a variety of raw earthy roots, celery stalks, parsnips, and radishes—the kind of tasteless vegetables I imagined a blind, burrowing mole-rat would enjoy.

"They ran out of beef tripe," the old man said.

"It's a win-win situation," Zohar said to me, ignoring him. "He could use the company, and we need a survivor to bring to class on Memorial Day."

"But he doesn't look anything like us," I said.

I stared at the old man, with his eyes the color of gray porridge, his pale wrinkled skin, and tufts of white hair sticking out on the sides like Ben-Gurion. He would make a strange-looking grandfather, like a clownfish among sea urchins. It was true that with our dark poppyseed eyes, our curly black hair, and our angular faces we didn't look anything like him.

Zohar shrugged. "Doesn't matter."

We decided to take him home with us and convince him to pretend he was our grandfather for Shoah Memorial Day at school. The walk from the Superzol to our house wasn't too bad—it was only down Golomb Street, past four different auto repair garages, then Tzvika's furniture store, Lior's pet store, where we bought our pet turtle last year, and a building materials store called HaBonim, off of Ayalon Highway, then up the three flights of stairs to our apartment, 4 Daled. It seemed to take forever with the old man huffing and puffing behind us. His legs shook, the two bony knees bumping into each other, and he leaned on the banister for support. He was about as fit as nine-hundred-year-old Methuselah. When he finally made it up, he was triumphant, the first-ever mountaineer to scale Everest's peak. He was sweating so much that his Band-Aid slipped off, revealing a series of numbers tattooed on his left arm. Bingo.

The old man didn't seem to notice or particularly mind that he wasn't in his own home. We led him through the kitchen, where he admired our mother's spice rack, a four-tier chicken-wire mount with rows of brightly colored powders arranged in a spectrum of tints, from the different shades of green, cardamom pods to cilantro, to the oranges and reds of turmeric and paprika, and finally at the very end, the dark, fallen autumn leaves of ground sumac.

We slipped past Dad, fast asleep as usual on his sofa-chair in the living room. We didn't have to worry about Mom, who wouldn't be back from work yet for another hour. We led the old man to our shared room and gave him my bed. My brother and I decided to take turns sleeping on the floor. The old man tapped the cage in the corner of the room, where our turtle was munching on a piece of lettuce.

Zohar picked up the turtle, whose scaly feet were clawing the air.

"What's its name?" the old man asked.

"Ghetto Lodz," Zohar said. "Because he's a fighter."

"My name is Yehuda," the old man said. "Because I'm Jewish."

"Were you in Ghetto Lodz?" I asked.

"Ghetto Lodge?" Yehuda said. "I don't stay in hotels very often."

Zohar and I exchanged glances.

"First thing," Yehuda said, "I need you to write a letter to my son."

There was a computer in Dad's office. Yehuda didn't even know how to turn it on, so we opened an email account for him. We used the numbers tattooed on his forearm as the password.

"That way you'll never forget it," Zohar said.

Yehuda's son grew up in Tel Aviv, but for the past fifteen years lived in the wealthy Charlottenburg neighborhood of Berlin, close to the Zoological Garden. He worked as a doctor in a clinic on Kantstrasse, made shopping trips to Kurfürstendamm, and in the evenings took his wife to the Deutsche Oper. Yehuda knew all this from the handful of times his son visited Israel, but soon he stopped coming for holidays and summers, always with the excuse of work or school or money. They hadn't spoken in four years. His two granddaughters were avid fans of Bavarian pretzels and sauerkraut but barely knew any Hebrew. Yehuda was terrified of his son's wife, she was a real Alp-climbing, milk-chugging Frau with platinum-blond pigtails, named after the legendary shield-maiden Brunhilda. In the email to Yehuda's son, we asked him to come visit and to bring his wife, too, who might be interested in touring the sites, like Yad Vashem Memorial Center for the Shoah, which can be a heartwarming experience for the entire family.

Yehuda read over the email several times, his crooked finger pressed to the screen, following the words as if he were reading a newspaper. He seemed pleased with the phrasing, and after he made sure there were no spelling mistakes, we sent it. He sat eagerly on the bed and waited for a reply. He kept asking us if his son had written back yet. We told him it didn't work like that. He turned the radio on to Kol HaMusica, the classical music station. Before I fell asleep, I could still see him waiting for his son's reply, tapping his fingers on his knee.

I woke up to the sound of clanging pans. That night we discovered Yehuda had wandered into the kitchen and cooked Sephardi food, using our mother's spices, rolling up his sleeves to stuff vine leaves with pine nuts and turmeric rice, and fry okra and zucchini in garlic. He paced around, talking to himself as he stirred the various bubbling pots and sizzling pans, adopting a Sephardi accent, emphasizing the guttural *chet* and *ayin*. He was no longer the Ashkenazi survivor we had found wandering the Superzol, shuffling between aisles, resigned to the tasteless life of a root vegetable, but someone else entirely, a spice-crazed Sephardi survivor.

In the morning, Yehuda sat at the kitchen table, acting as if nothing had happened, admiring the assortment of dishes. I could see the yellowish stains of turmeric on his hands and smell the burnt garlic on his clothes, but despite all this insurmountable evidence piled against him, he denied the accusation again and again.

"Your mother," he said, "she can really cook, huh?"

We didn't have the heart to tell him that he was actually a Sephardi in the body of a Shoah survivor Ashkenazi, so we piled his plate high and watched him eat. Afterward he licked his lips, withdrew an embroidered handkerchief from his breast pocket, and dabbed his chin. We explained to our parents that we had to take care of a survivor for a week for a school project. We promised we would keep him in our room, and he wouldn't be disruptive in any way. Mom and Dad left for work, and we had to leave for school, so we left Yehuda on his own for a while, retreating out the door guiltily, as if we were leaving a puppy alone for the first time. We left a key on the table and told him he could go out to the yard if he wanted to but not to stray too far. The yard wasn't in good shape—the only *freier* who ever took care of it had moved, and no one else volunteered for that sucker's job.

After school we found Yehuda sitting in the yard, dejected. The ground was covered in dead leaves and rotten branches. He picked up a branch, and an ant crawled up his sleeve.

"Are you going to clean this up or what?" Yehuda said.

"Okay," Zohar said, "but do you promise to pretend to be our grandfather on Shoah Memorial Day?"

Yehuda shrugged. "What about this garden?"

"You rehearse your Shoah story while we clean up," I said.

We made a deal. We would tend to the garden, and plant new flowers and vegetables, while he worked with us on his Shoah story. He was still waiting on a reply from his son. We convinced him that the future email from his son could be read only on our computer, since that was where we sent our message from. Yehuda decided to stay in case his son wrote back. We felt a little guilty tricking him about the email, but we figured that without us, he wouldn't even have known how to write to his son in the first place.

Yehuda's story of survival wasn't as exciting as some of the other Shoah tales around. I mean, it wasn't bad, but it wasn't the best, either. He was born in Warsaw, where his Polish mother, a seamstress by profession, having always wanted a little girl, taught him to sew. He was talented and could make fashionable dresses with a patient, steady hand and an eye for detail. The war broke out when he was eight years old. The Luftwaffe bombers circled the sky while he was working on a knitted cap for his younger sister, the panzer division tanks crossed the border while he was putting the finishing touches on a pair of Polska mittens, and the Wehrmacht troops laid siege to the city as he clutched his sewing needles, paralyzed with fear. When the infantry divisions cut off all supply routes and there was great hunger, Yehuda peeked from his window overlooking Nowy Swiat Street and watched a starving, hollow-cheeked woman in a fur-lined overcoat pick a piece of meat off the skeletal remains of a dead horse sprawled on the cobblestones, and by then his hands no longer obeyed him.

He was separated from his parents and younger sister, whom he never saw again, and for three years he lived in the Warsaw Ghetto with his uncle, a barber, until they were both sent to Majdanek. The Nazi officers heard about his talent for making clothing, and he was given a job with the camp's seamstress. As part of his job, he would occasionally leave Majdanck, escorted by a German soldier, to examine and purchase cloths and textiles. He kept leftover garments and scraps of fabric in his pockets, hiding them under his prisoner's uniform, to combat the cold. One day he had the idea of weaving a dress for himself, as a disguise, to escape. Little by little, day by day, he made the dress. It was a black and white geometric-patterned dress in the haute couture style of Coco Chanel. Ironically it was some of his finest work, despite the odds stacked against him. Luckily, he was sometimes mistaken for a girl anyway, due to his delicate features, high cheekbones, and elfin chin. He'd acquired a wig from his uncle, the camp barber. Secretly, his uncle kept the hair he shaved off the men and women in the camp and glued it together to create a wig. On his next trip to town, while the soldier guarding him was chatting to a beautiful customer in the back of the shop by the changing rooms, Yehuda managed to slip on the dress and wig undetected and escape, blending into the crowd of the textile district.

It was a pretty good story, I thought, but Zohar wanted Yehuda to make it more exciting. Zohar was a year older than I was, so I usually deferred to him. We asked Yehuda if, when he was telling the class, he could change his version a bit, add some more action.

"Maybe you grew up in the woods," Zohar said. "You were raised by wolves in the Black Forest."

"Wolves," Yehuda repeated.

"Okay," I said, "maybe not wolves. What other animals do you have in the Black Forest?"

"Nazis," he replied.

"This year we're going to have the best Shoah survivor story," Zohar said.

We kept our part of the deal and worked on the garden. We didn't have shears, a wheelbarrow, or a hoe, so we spent most of the day tearing weeds out with our hands, and then we went out to a gardening store to buy mulch. The next day we pulled dead leaves and branches off the tree. I whacked the wizened bougainvillea bush growing along the wall with a broom, and hundreds of pale moths flitted away. We uprooted thistles and cleared out thorns. Sweat ran down my back and made my arms slick. My pants were covered in mud. My shirt was stained, dead flowers stuck to the soles of my shoes. I had to take a break. I put my head under the tap and drank the lukewarm water, then washed my face and hands. I took off my shoes and rubbed my feet. After the break, we walked to the highway, where, by the side of the road, a boy sold prickly pear and potted plants. We returned with a handful of bags. We planted passion fruit vines, cucumbers, and cherry tomatoes.

Yehuda was Ashkenazi by day, Sephardi by night. After midnight, he cooked elaborate and mouthwatering feasts and baked *ma'amoul* cookies filled with dates and walnuts, powdered with sugar on top, which were so tasty even our mother approved of them. At dawn, he transformed back into his old self, and by the time we woke up, he was a confused old man again, wiping crumbs off his chin with his handkerchief.

We made him recite his newly improved Shoah story to us, which was a mishmash of all the World War II films we had ever seen, with a few embellishments. We made Yehuda into a world-famous pianist, a tortured but brilliant artist who managed to stay alive in the death camps by playing Beethoven's *Moonlight* Sonata to the Nazi officers. Yehuda loved this part of the story, since he was a big fan of classical music. He also managed to escape to the Black Forest, where, and this was our favorite addition, he lived with wolves and picked up their mannerisms and behavior, proving himself as the alpha by biting the lead wolf's ear off. He led the wolves in several successful ambushes against Nazi patrols. He became a household name in Baden-Württemberg, a feared man-beast, known only as the Wolf Jew.

At first, the story was too complex, and Yehuda kept forgetting important details, like the fact that when he was leader of the wolf pack, he wore the skin of his enemies like scarves around his neck, or that he hid a pistol inside the grand piano, which he would later use on the mesmerized officers listening to the *Moonlight* Sonata. We didn't give up, even when Yehuda fumbled the story completely, making up a version about a wolf that played the piano. *Practice, practice, practice. That's the only way you get to Carnegie Hall,* Yehuda liked saying. We drilled it over and over again, relentlessly. It was a grueling routine, with very few breaks in between, based on Itzhak Perlman's nine-hour practice sessions, fiddling away at his Stradivarius. We practiced until Yehuda could recite his Shoah story without a hitch, until it was perfect.

On the morning of Shoah Memorial Day, Yehuda was gone. He'd been staying with us for a week now, and we'd planned to take him to school with us and stand together during the siren, like all our classmates did with their grandparents, but we couldn't find him anywhere. Maybe he had walked out the door and got lost or had managed to hatch another escape plan involving a handmade dress and a wig. I imagined the frail man sitting alone on a park bench wearing a dress stitched together from my old Pokémon T-shirts. Pikachu, Bulbasaur, and my favorite psychic trio, Abra, Kadabra, and spoon-bending Alakazam, who always reminded me of Uri Geller. On Yehuda's head, I imagined a bird's nest wig made out of the hairs my mother left in the shower drain. Why would he want to escape? He didn't seem miserable. He knew how important bringing a survivor to Shoah Memorial Day was to us. How could he be so selfish? Besides, he was still waiting to hear back from his son.

Eventually, we found him in the Superzol. It was nearly ten in the morning, almost time for the memorial siren. We should have been in school two hours ago, and we were going to be punished for being late, but the only thing that mattered was bringing Yehuda back. We would have to smuggle him out during the siren. The best time to steal a survivor was during the siren, when the entire country stood mute, with their eyes closed, for an entire minute and a half. Zohar kept watch. When the siren started, its tone steady and uninterrupted, I took Yehuda's hand and pulled him toward the exit. We made it outside with a few seconds to spare, stood stock-still, and closed our eyes until the siren petered out.

When the competitions were held at school, the grandfathers and grandmothers were paraded around like slow-moving trophy dogs. *Look at that one,* Zohar said, pointing at Klara Kuggelmas's grandmother, a tiny elderly lady with rouged lips and a purple cane. He nudged Yehuda in the ribs. *Not bad-looking, eh?* Yehezkel Yankeluvich brought in two survivors, double trouble, twin sisters with matching silver braids, who had been experimented on by Dr. Mengele. Dana Davidson brought in her grandfather's second cousin, a bean-pole who had testified at Eichmann's trial. The best survivors of all were so shrunken, they were almost pocket-size. They were carried around from event to event, pulled out at the last minute, and used as excuses for not completing homework on time. *I'm sorry, I couldn't study because I was listening to my grandfather's Shoah story* was a common reason for failing a math test.

Our sworn enemy was Matan Mordechai Mendelbaum, who always had the best Shoah story. His grandfather was not only a survivor, he was also a respected historian, a world specialist in the field whose books on the Shoah had won awards and prizes. The Mendelbaum home was filled with shelves of his books, translated into dozens of different languages, all with swastikas on the cover. I imagined all the Mendelbaums sitting together at the breakfast table, picking at crusts of baguette and expensive smoked salmon, quoting their favorite parts of *Schindler's List* to each other, and I was so jealous I wanted to wring Matan Mordechai Mendelbaum's neck. Thankfully, the Elvis of the Holocaust, as Mendelbaum frequently referred to his grandfather, didn't live in Israel. My brother and I would have surely lost if he were coming to class to tell his story.

When Zohar and I brought Yehuda in, shuffling forward nonchalantly down the corridor, the other kids called him the "Sephardi Survivor" behind his back. Little did they know of his nightly transformations. We looked like a strange trio walking together to class, holding hands, each of us more nervous than the others. The school was filled with survivors, all wearing their best clothes for the big day, their hair slicked back on a bright scalp or covered with a flat cap. They brought Tupperware boxes of foul-smelling soups, swimming with *kneidalach*. Our nemesis, Matan Mordechai Mendelbaum, was wearing his starch-white bar mitzvah shirt, lugging a suitcase filled with his grandfather's books, and looking smug. He stared at us walking past, one eyebrow raised. When we passed him, a noticeable chill crept over me, and I shivered, as if he had brought an eastern European gale of freezing wind with him to the hallways of Janusz Korczak Middle School.

"You're late, boys." Anat, our teacher, stood in front of us, blocking our path, hands on her hips. "You missed the siren."

"But we have a survivor this year," Zohar said.

"I can see that," she said, looking Yehuda up and down. "So, how are you related to the boys?"

"He's our grandfather!" I said, too quickly.

"I'm their friend," Yehuda said.

"What he means," Zohar said, "is that we're so close it's like he's also our friend. But he's actually our grandpa. You know, by blood."

"Listen, boys, there's nothing to be ashamed of if you don't have any relatives that are Shoah survivors. Not all of us can be as lucky as Mendelbaum."

It was time to share stories. Each survivor came up to the front of the class. Some of the miniature ones preferred to sit in a small chair fit for a child, while others stood up to their full, unimpressive height or leaned against the chalkboard. Sitting next to me, Yehuda was looking nervous, even paler and more Ashkenazi than usual. Zohar was massaging his shoulders, preparing the lightest featherweight boxer in the world for his big fight. *Float like a butterfly, sting like a bee,* Zohar whispered when Yehuda's turn came. He stood in front of the class, introduced himself as Yehuda Finkielkraut, born in Warsaw in 1931, the son of a seamstress. Then he put his hands in his pockets and took them out again, scratched the back of his almost-bald head, tugged at his collar. He was sweating now, rubbing his hands along his pants, leaving marks. He hummed a tune, drumming his fingers.

"So, are you a survivor or not?" Matan Mordechai Mendelbaum said. He was sitting at the very front row, hands neatly folded in his lap, with his grandfather's books, there were so many of them, piled on the table in front of him. "What's your story?"

Yehuda nodded vigorously. "Yes, yes, I am. My story, well, let me tell you my story."

He stopped speaking and gazed off at a speck on the wall. But no one was paying any attention, everyone was talking and laughing. In the back of the room, one of the survivors was showing off a magic trick he had learned in the ghetto, producing a five-shekel coin out of thin air, then making it disappear again, to thunderous applause and cries of *Do it again, please, one more time!* Anat gave me a look, as if I had personally failed her, and shook her head, disappointed. I couldn't believe Yehuda was blowing it like this, after all the rehearsals and pep talks, our endless support and unwavering encouragement. This year we were finally going to have the best Shoah story, but he was ruining it. Yehuda looked at me, pleading. I couldn't save him, no one could.

"This is a tragedy," Mendelbaum sighed. "Like sheep to the slaughter."

"Tell them about the forest," Zohar said, "the wolves."

Yehuda let out a small sound, like a balloon deflating, and without another word or even a glance in our direction, he walked out of the classroom. Anat summoned the next survivor promptly, Klara Kuggelmas's grandmother, a heavily made-up woman with a purple cane, but I didn't listen to a word of her story. I couldn't stand the gleeful look on Matan Mordechai Mendelbaum's face. He let his hand rest on the tower of his grandfather's prize-winning books and smiled at me in a way I knew meant he had won. I kicked the wall, desperate and humiliated, then hung my head and carved X's on my desk, pretending it was Matan Mordechai Mendelbaum's face.

When school ended, we took the long route home, cursing Yehuda the entire way. He'd double-crossed us, stuck a knife in our backs—Us! His own people—just like the traitorous *Judenrat*. I didn't know where Yehuda was, and I didn't care. He wasn't going to get a second chance, no way, he blew it with us. We took care of him, and this was how he repaid us? Even if he came crawling back and promised to deliver a three-hour PowerPoint lecture on the Warsaw Ghetto uprising in front of the Mendelbaums, I'd still say no. Never again.

"He's probably wandering around the Superzol again," Zohar said, "searching for the ingredients to make *cholent* and muttering to himself."

We went to the garden, which, though the dirt looked neater than before, had not grown at all. We stomped on the ground and kicked around some dirt, transforming it back to its usual miserable state. Yehuda finally returned an hour later. He stood in the decimated garden and shouted at us, waving his arms around like a reed blowing in the wind. I wondered if he was in a trance. He took off his flat cap and threw it onto the ground, stomping on it, too, as if it weren't already flat. His eyes were coated in a thin, translucent film that resembled the foam of skin in a cup of warm milk. He picked up a stick and swung it. *Hooligans, barbarians, maniacs, delinquents.* He swung again. Zohar managed to wrestle the stick away, and Yehuda sat on the earth, exhausted and defeated. His head was bent down, the bright pink of his bald spot showing, shoulders shaking slightly. He wiped his eyes with his embroidered handkerchief. We led him back into the house, feeling sorry for him suddenly, embracing him like a long-lost relative.

Over the next few days, he didn't act like a survivor at all. He played instead the part of a rebellious teenager, hanging around the neighborhood with a cigarette dangling out of his mouth and the sour smell of arrack on his breath, whistling lewdly as perfumed girls in miniskirts sauntered by, snapping gum. He challenged the other men in the neighborhood to arm-wrestling contests. He didn't care about gardening or cooking anymore, he only ordered takeout from the greasiest food joints. He ate falafel every day, the tahini dribbling down his shirt and staining his lips white. When he started listening to Mizrahi pop music, I told Zohar that it was over. Yehuda was a lost cause. No Shoah survivor listened to Omer Adam. *I'm your beauty, you're my beast, welcome to the Middle East.*

Yehuda still lived with us, sleeping in our room and waiting for an email from his son, but we had given up on the idea that he could be our survivor grandfather. We wondered if we should start training our turtle, Ghetto Lodz, to be Yehuda's replacement next year on Shoah Memorial Day. Turtles lived for hundreds and hundreds of years. We could tell everyone that Ghetto Lodz had not only survived the Shoah, he had also fought in the First World War. We would use our colorful markers to draw a yellow star on his shell, teach him to hold his wrinkled head high in front of the class, and train him to bite Mendelbaum's fingers off.

On Saturdays, Yehuda sat on a discarded leather sofa and played backgammon with Chaim, our neighbor who had two chins and a silver Star of David necklace. I had never met an Ashkenazi who was good at backgammon before, it was a rare sighting, like witnessing the silvery guardian of the skies, Lugia, the most legendary Pokémon of them all. Yehuda was the oldest backgammon wunderkind ever, rolling sixes the entire time. He looked so overjoyed when he won, and he rubbed it in Chaim's face, who most certainly wanted to punch Yehuda in the face. I was afraid he would get his teeth knocked out—but at least he wasn't acting like a victim anymore.

"This is the life," he told us, reclining on the sofa. "I feel like I'm seventeen again."

It was like that movie *The Curious Case of Benjamin Button,* I thought, when Brad Pitt ages in reverse, becoming younger as the years go by, but starring Yehuda Finkielkraut. It would be a box-office disaster. Yehuda had also gotten a bunch of tattoos: a snarling dragon on his chest, a Chinese symbol he claimed meant "passion" on his ankle, and a naked lady riding a Harley-Davidson that obscured almost entirely the numbers on his forearm.

"How're you going to remember your email password now?" Zohar asked in a small voice.

Yehuda let out a laugh. He took a cigarette out of his front pocket, where he used to keep his embroidered handkerchief, lit it, and exhaled. "It's never too late to change your story."

We played along. I jumped on the sofa next to him. "What's your story, Yehuda?"

We let Yehuda tell us a different version of the events, since it seemed to please him. He ran his fingers through his cloud-like, almost nonexistent hair, and sat up a little straighter. He told us that he had been born in Marrakesh, to a wealthy family of textile merchants. He could make the lightest cotton pants. In the summer, they were weightless, like wearing cotton candy. The King of Morocco himself ordered a handful of pants in burgundy, saffron, and turquoise. He was so pleased by the pants that he appointed Yehuda to be his personal tailor, and from then on Yehuda lived with his wife and son in a spacious house with a lush garden on the palace grounds. It was a beautiful home, Yehuda said, his voice crackling like a caramel wrapper. *My wife and I would stroll each morning in the garden under the dappled shade of citrus trees, the air fragrant with blooming pale purple licorice and white jasmine flowers, as my son chased the wandering palace peacocks, who were always wearing golden collars.*

The Sand Collector

I fell in love with Salim almost twenty-five years ago, when the last Israeli soldiers were withdrawing from Sinai. It was 1982, I was fourteen, and I remember watching on television as the Egyptians raised their flag with the eagle of Saladin atop the fence that marked the new border, lit torches in Cairo, Sharm al-Sheikh, and Rafah, sang and danced until midnight. I grew up in the desert, so I knew what it was really like, how uncaring and cruel. The wind seized the tiny golden grains, swirled and tossed them away without a second thought. And I knew the wind not only picked up sand but sometimes carried off entire makeshift homes and flung them into the air, spinning them around and around, letting them fall where they may, like a roll of the dice.

The Bedouin tribes, once free to roam the chalkstone hills, shepherding their black goats through the desert, were now stranded on either side of the new Israeli-Egyptian border. Salim lived exposed to the elements, behind a blue tarp hung over a box of rusted scrap metal and plywood in one of the largest unrecognized Bedouin villages in the State of Israel. His village was made up of tents and tin shacks, only a few hundred meters from a poisonous waste dump. The men in the village worked in the hazardous waste disposal facility. The facility caught fire many times, and the flames spread like quicksilver, engulfing the village in a toxic cloud. Some of the villagers developed breathing problems, children's teeth began falling out, women lost the babies in their wombs, and Salim's father died of cancer at forty-seven.

I lived only four kilometers away, in Be'er Sheva, on the northern edge of the Negev Desert, a city that is now home to programmers and coders from the Silicon Wadi high-tech industry, scientists working in the nuclear reactor southeast of Dimona, and chess masters from the Soviet Union. When I was growing up, it was only a midsize city surrounded by sand. I was a lonely girl, described by some of my teachers at school as quiet and unapproachable. I liked to think of myself as self-sufficient. In the Negev, the air was too dry for epiphytes, those plants that grow on other plants. Like a true desert dweller, I never wanted to rely on someone else. I hardly spoke at all until I met Salim. Instead of confiding in my mother or a classmate, I went out into the desert, to the sand dunes, and talked and talked into the void, venting frustrations, whispering my biggest secrets to an empty landscape. I think it was Salim's broken Hebrew, his thick accent, that made me want to speak to him. Once I started talking, I couldn't stop. I wanted to drink and drink from Salim, like a never-ending pool of clear water, but when he was finally mine, he dissipated between my fingers like a fata morgana, the distant mirage of an oasis, a ray of light bent through layers of air.

By the time Salim was sixteen, he was already a smuggler. Unlike his older siblings—all five of them, brothers, who worked at the toxic waste facility—he went to school. He didn't go down the block like I did—he traveled to the next village in the early morning darkness, then walked back for hours, arriving home exhausted, bone-weary, unable to keep his eyes open long enough to do his homework. He promised himself he would never work in the waste disposal facility like his father and brothers, but he dropped out of school and became a smuggler, because he had seen how they lived, with their perfumed homes and ornate rugs, with their blazing firepits and goat meat sizzling on skewers. He became a smuggler because he needed the money. Knowing Hebrew wasn't enough to get a job; nor was a high school diploma, unless he wanted to do what his father did. He knew the risks of smuggling. He could get caught by the Israelis, by the Egyptians, even by his own people.

Smuggling is a different business now, I read on the news, since Egyptian troops increased their numbers. Soldiers patrol the border, walkie-talkies crackling. Dimly lit underground tunnels snake their way between Gaza and Egypt. Tracks, carts, and pulley systems transport the goods: canned pickles and olives, fuel and gasoline, weapons and medical supplies, jars of tomato sauce. In some larger tunnels, they smuggle cars without license plates: a mud-splattered Volkswagen, a beat-up Subaru. Once they even sneaked across animals that made their way to the Gaza zoo: a rare white tiger, and a baby elephant with his huge, wrinkled mother, her ivory tusks shining under the glow of bare lightbulbs.

At night, I liked listening to the various sounds of the desert, separating them like instruments in an orchestra; the slithering of blue-headed lizards, the rattle of death-stalker scorpions lifting their sting, the *clump clump clump* of ibexes' hooves and the clash of their horns, hard as fossilized stone. I joined the orchestra with my own sounds, telling the desert about the new bush of dark hair that sprouted between my legs. My embarrassing breasts that had somehow gotten bigger since last summer, forcing me to buy expensive new bras. I complained about Mom sitting rapt in front of the television every night, ignoring me completely, watching Haim Yavin present the news on *Mabat*. I admitted to the desert that, surrounded by people, I always felt especially lonely.

Almost every day after school, those long afternoons in the early spring, I rode my banana-colored bicycle down Highway 40 in search of desert flowers. They were out in abundance, carpets of red anemones, pink cyclamen in full bloom, pale luminescent clusters of Solomon's seal. I remember the first time I saw Salim, a slender figure with a shirt tied around his head to protect himself from the sun. He had a small black pouch strapped across his waist. The sand was littered with pieces of sheet metal, plastic bags, and empty cigarette packs. He grabbed a thin piece of sheet metal and used it like a skateboard, sliding down the dunes, blending into the sand with his dusty tracksuit. I was close enough to him that I saw his different-colored eyes: the left was green, and the right was blue. There was a scar on his cheek, pale as a *sahlab* orchid. Later, he would tell me that he got the scar from climbing over a border fence and tossing over a package. When the Egyptian troops opened fire, he panicked and cut himself on the barbed wire, dropped into the darkness, and fled, his face bleeding onto the sand.

I grabbed another piece of sheet metal and slid down the dune, wordlessly. Salim followed, skidding across the sand. We played this sandboarding game, without really acknowledging each other's presence except for a few stolen glances. I liked how he could be quiet, like me. He didn't draw attention to himself but instead waited, endlessly patient, like a lizard basking in the sun. I noticed his skinned knees, a pale pink in contrast to his skin. He took off the shirt tied around his head and shook his messy hair peppered with sand. From his pocket, he withdrew a disk of colored glass and held it up to his eye like a telescope, then passed it to me. I saw the world tinted, a dark ivy sky. I liked to imagine he saw half of the world green with his green eye, the other half blue with his blue eye. In the distance, a pickup truck stopped by the side of the road, and someone stepped out in a Spider-Man shirt, called out, *Salim! Salim!*

"I am Salim," he told me in heavily accented Hebrew. "That is my friend, Spider-Man."

I stared at the ground, afraid to say anything, but then, surprising myself, I mumbled, "With great power comes great responsibility."

"Exactly." He smiled, revealing a crooked front tooth. "Same time tomorrow?"

When I returned to the same spot on the sand dunes next to Highway 40, there he was, waiting for me. We walked around slopes of chalkstone, and he picked the stems of the fibrous sparrow-wort bush to knead into a rope. He had brought me the tiny skull of a kitten, pale against the palm of his hand. It probably belonged to a sand cat. The ear canals were very wide, a sign of the creature's enhanced hearing capacities. I wondered if this was a sign that, finally, I had met someone other than the desert whose ears were big enough to listen to me.

"Does this make me Catwoman?" I asked.

From his pouch, he took out an empty glass jar and a long silver spoon. He scooped up sand and put it into the jar. He did this again and again, until the jar was half full. Then he took out a black felt-tip marker and wrote on the jar in Arabic.

"And I am the Sand Man."

Only when I was no longer a child did I read the story of the Sand Man, who sprinkled sand in the eyes of children to get them to fall sleep. He had a silken coat that constantly changed colors, green to blue, just like Salim's eyes. He had two umbrellas, one under each arm. The first umbrella, which he spread over good children, made them dream the most beautiful stories. He spread the second over naughty children, who slept a heavy, dreamless sleep. Of course, by then, I also knew the evil version of the Sand Man, the one you didn't hear about in the fairy tale. He was the thief in the night who sneaked up on children who couldn't fall asleep and stole their eyes. Sometimes Salim was the evil Sand Man, with my stolen eyes in his pocket, and other times he was the good Sand Man, spreading his umbrella over me, and I stared up at the pictures and dreamed of beautiful things, of lapis lazuli and opals, rubies and emeralds.

"I must leave now," Salim said.

We set up a time to meet again on the dunes by the highway, and he disappeared, leaving me with the skull of the sand cat in the palm of my hand. When we saw each other again, he didn't mention his sudden disappearance. We walked together in silence until we passed a yellow sign, BEWARE OF CAMELS NEAR THE ROAD, and Salim began talking about camels. He told me about the *ardha*, the camel-racing show held at an abandoned desert airstrip. The al-Hejin racing camels were lean, slim, and agile, like him. *But many of us don't raise camel herds anymore*, he said. *We can transport our possessions in the back of a pickup truck. Besides, when you ride a camel, there's no air-conditioning.* He laughed, winking at me. He told me about the Tulu wrestling camels from Turkey, pitted against one another in competitions, who used their long necks as leverage to push down their opponents. For a moment, I imagined his neck struggling against mine, his hot breath in my ear. I wanted to leap onto him, to wrestle him down, but instead I sat on my hands, afraid of what I might do if they were free.

After that we started meeting on the sand dunes every day after school, by the mauve horsetail knotweed waving in the wind, the fleshy leaves and pink flowers of the violet cabbage shrub growing out of the stone. Salim brought me tiny gifts every time we met, spiced olives and sweet *madjhoul* dates, Egyptian postage stamps, invisible ink, a hand-carved wooden camel. I had no idea where he got it all from. Once he brought an assortment of music boxes, each one a different size, each one playing a different tune. I turned the lever, and the music sprang out of the tiny box, echoing across the emptiness of the desert. As we listened to the music, our foreheads almost touching, Salim reached into the pouch around his waist and retrieved a jar and a spoon. He scooped up sand with the spoon and put it in the jar, then took out a marker and wrote something on the side of the jar in elegant calligraphy I couldn't read.

I invited Salim over to my house, thinking he would never come. To my surprise, he accepted. I wondered if he'd been to Be'er Sheva before, or to any big city, for that matter. I realized how little I really knew about him or about his culture. The only Bedouins I had ever met were the vendors in the market on Thursdays, selling copper kettles, jewelry, and woven crafts. Most of my neighbors were suspicious of them, fearful even. But he probably felt the same about us, distrustful of our urban lifestyle. Maybe it was strange for him to see immovable ocher- and dune-colored buildings dominating the cityscape, wind-ravaged and sand-battered hulking bone behemoths, vast graveyards of concrete. These structures seemed to me to be fixed and secure, anchored to Be'er Sheva, so different from the temporary, makeshift tent-homes of his village, which could be swept away and dismantled in an instant. I lived in Neighborhood Bet, home to the Hapoel Be'er Sheva football club, which wasn't the best team but also wasn't the absolute worst. I didn't care about football, although I thought he might, so I told him about the stadium. He didn't care about it, either.

Mom wasn't home, so there was no need to explain why I had anyone over, let alone a boy like Salim. We sat in my room, underneath the open window, the white plastic shades were partly open, letting in slats of sunlight, a warm breeze. I grew up hearing about the hospitality of the Bedouins, and I felt inadequate. I wanted to offer him something, to reciprocate his generous gifts, but what did I have that was special? We had cottage cheese and milk in the fridge, cereal and bread in the cupboard. There was a mint plant in the kitchen. Some of its leaves were brown and withered, but a few were salvageable, bright green.

"Would you like tea?" I asked.

He nodded. "I like it with a lot of sugar."

I tore off a handful of healthy mint leaves, dropped them into two glass cups, then spooned a generous amount of sugar. The kettle boiled, and I stood by the steam for a moment, letting it heat my face, taking a deep breath to calm my nerves. My hand shook when I poured, and I spilled a little. Salim slurped the hot tea and nodded like a grown-up. At least I didn't ruin the tea. We stood in the kitchen, listening to the hum of the refrigerator. I started noticing everything Salim might not own and felt strangely guilty at the sight of the landline phone and the toaster. Salim wasn't interested in any of the electrical appliances—he was staring at a photograph of my third birthday party that we celebrated in Mitzpe Ramon. My cheeks were puffed up like a hamster's, I was inhaling as much air as I could, hovering over a sponge cake with three mismatched candles.

"We can make a cake," I said.

Standing on top of a stepstool, I collected the necessary ingredients. What a stupid idea. I couldn't even remember Mom's recipe. I should have paid more careful attention when she made it. A big plastic bowl, flour, sugar, a carton of eggs. I poured the flour into the bowl and cracked the eggs into it. The yolk was bright orange, radiant. I tossed aside the cracked shells. Whisking it all together, I slid a finger into the batter, a dripping gooey mixture, and slipped it into my mouth without thinking. Salim was watching me—I licked my finger clean. The batter was too sweet, probably just the way Salim liked it, if his taste in cakes was anything like his taste in tea.

"Now your turn," I said, handing him the bowl, as if this were how cake was made.

Salim slid his finger along the rim of the bowl. His face transformed once he tasted the sweetness. He smiled very widely, laughing like a child. I was pleased with myself. We ended up sitting on the cold tile floor, eating the raw batter with our fingers.

"What is your earliest memory?" he asked.

"My mother was in the kitchen. She was talking to a friend. I knew it was about me. She said she was worried because I didn't talk. I felt terrible. It made me want to talk even less."

"You do talk."

"I guess," I said. "What's your earliest memory?"

"A scorpion sting."

He told me that when he was just a baby, his father went out to hunt for a scorpion. His father came back with the dangling yellow creature and crushed it under his sandal. He burned it and mixed it with oil, creating a poisonous paste, which he smeared on Salim's tender skin. Ever since then, he had hardly even felt a scorpion bite. He brushed it off, like sand.

Salim disappeared for days. At the time, I didn't know yet that he was meeting his friend Spider-Man to drink coffee under the carob tree and discuss their next smuggling operation along the new Egyptian-Israeli border in Sinai. Spider-

Man was a spotter with only three fingers on his left hand. As a spotter, his role was to be on the lookout for patrols. He knew the land better than anyone. He wanted to be a tracker for the IDF's Minority Unit. A number of Bedouins volunteered each year, although I never understood why they would want to serve. Spider-Man taught Salim to walk backward. Many smugglers, knowing their pursuers will follow the direction of their footprints, learned how to walk backward. The real way to distinguish the direction a person is headed is by noticing how sunken the footprint was, where the most weight had been placed.

On one of their first smuggling missions together, Salim's friend brought along his precious Spider-Man comic book. While they waited for their contact in Sinai, they took turns looking at the comic, wondering why the superhero took photographs of himself in his Spider-Man costume and sold them to the newspapers. They loved the pictures of Spider-Man swinging from his web, dangling from the Brooklyn Bridge or the Empire State Building. They both agreed that Spider-Man would make an excellent smuggler, and if they had his abilities, they would be filthy rich. Spider-Man got his nickname that day because he was so engrossed in his comic book that he hardly noticed when their contact finally appeared, and Salim made fun of him ever since.

One day we had a running race. We sprinted down the sand, which sloped like the hips of a fat woman, running until we could hardly breathe. We lay on our backs, exhausted, and I rolled up my bell-bottom jeans, exposing my pulsing calf muscle. Salim stroked my leg, gently wiping away the sweat. It was the first time we had really touched. I watched his chest heave up and down, up and down, until it slowed, relaxed, regained its natural rhythm. I stared up at the darkening sky that had just begun to show a few stars.

"Don't you have stars in Be'er Sheva?" he asked.

The wind got stronger, cold gusts made the hair on my arms stand up. Sand got in my eyes, and I curled up, shivering, next to Salim. He placed his arms around me, held me. I felt the rapid pace of my own heart. I took his hand, interlaced my fingers in his. I was grateful for the dark. I didn't want him to see how scared I was. Before I could think about it, I kissed him on the lips.

"Wait," he said. He reached into his pouch and took out a jar.

"I want to remember this moment," he said.

"This moment is still happening, idiot."

The next time we met, we drank tea together again, but this time black tea whose leaves Salim brewed in a kettle over an open flame, adding wild sage, cardamom pods, cinnamon bark, and plenty of sugar. Salim told me he wanted to work in the tourist industry. His dream was to go to a resort in Sharm al-Sheikh to scuba dive with rich Europeans in the Red Sea, pointing out congregations of pilot fish weaving their way through the lionly manes of seaweed beds, and loggerhead turtles floating motionless, heads bobbing, eyes half shut.

Salim invited me to his home, to his tent with the sheet metal roof, the one that could be blown away by a gust of wind. The following week, in the midafternoon, I left school and rode my bicycle four kilometers south to Salim's village. We met at the entrance to the toxic waste facility, looking out at the incinerator for hazardous and organic detritus, the gas turbine units, the shadow of giant steel frames and crisscrossing piping. All around us, sewage piled up, bubbling and gushing like a living thing, producing a sharp stench that made it difficult to breathe. I did everything I could to stop myself from coughing because I didn't want him to think it affected me. I tried to smile weakly at him, but I could only manage a grimace. The air was thick and yellow, the venomous cloud I'd heard about hanging over the village, and the earth itself looked gray and dead—it had been poisoned, spoiled. The tin-roofed shacks jutted out from the earth, while the factory chimneys in the distance expelled tunnels of dark smoke into the sky.

Sensing my anxiety, Salim tried to put me at ease by telling me he used to play on the trash heaps with his brothers. They would chase each other down the derelict piles. He used to build little toys out of the refuse: cardboard planes with rotating plastic propellers, wooden boats with working rudders, fire engine trucks painted red. When Salim was very young, he walked around the trash heap with his father, hand in hand, after his shift at the facility, asking him questions: *Are there seven wells in Be'er Sheva? Why is an orange in your hand bigger than the sun in the sky? How many cherry hearts can you swallow before a tree grows in your belly?* His father always knew the right answer, or else he made it up.

"My father taught me all the old Bedouin names of places in the desert," Salim said. "Before the Zionists came and changed all the names."

I didn't like the way he said "Zionists." It felt like he was saying a bad word. I had no idea what he was talking about, but I wasn't going to admit it.

"We didn't change any names," I said, trying to sound confident.

"Yes, you did. My family has been here for a long time. I'm from the Al-Azazmeh tribe. We had our own names for our places, and you changed them all."

"That's not true," I said. "How did we change the names?"

"The Committee for the Designation of Place-Names in the Negev."

"You just made that up."

"Yeruham, close to your home, was actually called Rahma."

"Why do you care so much about the names, anyway?"

"Because my father taught them to me. He died of cancer when I was eight. He got it from working at that waste facility. There were many others just like him. And no one cared."

I wanted to apologize to him, but I didn't know how, and besides I was still angry at the way he said "Zionists." Why did it matter if we changed some of the names of places in the Negev? He could call them whatever he wanted—in the end, it was just sand. Walking through the village, everyone greeted Salim as we passed by. Everywhere I looked, there were children scampering around, their colorful clothes faded. A group of young girls, their hair in braids, followed us around, giggling. One of the girls was holding a shy-looking chicken in her arms, patting its head, while several other clucking chickens followed in her wake, pecking the earth. A young boy strutted by proudly on a horse, circling and taunting us, until Salim shouted at him, and he galloped away. Several boys sprinted past us, chasing after a football, raising a cloud of dust in their wake. Two men wearing long galabias and white headcovers were communicating using sign language, their fingers tapping and pointing, making circles and waves. An elderly woman in a dark robe, her tattooed face as wrinkled as a prune, hung clothes on the line and stared at me, unblinking.

We passed a truck parked next to a solar panel, a water tank, and a flat *tabun* oven for frying bread. An enormous pile of rubble and debris rose up in the distance. Salim explained that the soldiers came with bulldozers and a demolition crew last week, razing stone homes and animal sheds, supposedly built illegally on state-owned land. "We are only allowed to live in tents," he said. "We don't have permission to build permanent houses, since according to your government, we don't own the land. You act as if the Naqab Desert is empty, as if Bedouins don't exist." I hated how he kept saying "you" and "your government," as if I were the one personally tearing down his home.

When we reached his tent, he took my hand and squeezed it. I was both grateful and sickly anxious, fluttering wildly between loving and hating him.

Inside, there was a single bed and a shabbily made wooden shelf with three levels. Arranged on each level was a row of identical glass jars filled with sand. Each of the jars was labeled in that same beautiful calligraphy.

I picked up a jar at random. "What does this say?"

"That one says 'Broken Leg.'"

I picked up another. "And this one?"

"'Best Shawarma.'"

"It doesn't look like shawarma."

"I collect memories," Salim said. "Whenever I have an experience I want to remember, I fill a jar with sand from the spot where it happened." He looked at me, his blue and green eyes glinting.

"But they all look the same."

"Exactly. The sand jars are all the same, but each memory is different."

It was a kind of collection, he told me. The jars were identical, but each evoked a very specific, intimate memory for him because of its label. The most recent jars were all about experiences he and I shared, like the first time we kissed. When he picked up the jar, it reminded him of my stumbling tongue, flicking in and out of his mouth, and my chafed, dry lips. Another jar reminded him of my calf muscle pulsing, after we ran our race down the dunes.

"So, all your sand is from here?" I asked.

"My backyard is the desert. All my memories are from here. Why would I go anywhere else to collect them?"

Salim offered me tea in a copper pot and dates, toffee candy, and almonds on a decorated silver platter. He kept refilling my glass with sweet tea, again and again, until I put my hand over the empty cup, covering the rim, and shook my head. I really had to pee, but there was no toilet. I heard the sound of an engine running outside.

"Spider-Man is outside," Salim said. "I must speak with him."

While he was gone, I stayed inside, sitting on his foldout cot, staring at the blue tarp and swinging my feet. I got up to look at the sand jars again. I tried to remember what little Arabic I learned in school. There was a jar with JAMILA, meaning "beautiful," and BINT, the word for "girl." I wondered if it was about me. Did he think I was beautiful? But it could have been about some other girl, more beautiful than I am, with hair like honey and golden bracelets around her thin wrists. A girl who liked gifts.

I started pacing around the room. Maybe Salim had a gift for every girl he met and liked, and then he took them here, to his home, where he showed them his glass jars full of memories for each of them, and made up a story about collecting sand and his dead father. I was hurt and angry at myself, embarrassed by my own paranoid thoughts. I sat down on the bed and swung my foot—it bumped against a wooden crate.

I leaned over and saw a metal latch attached to the crate. I opened it. At first I thought that inside would be more sand. Did he also collect it cemented in slabs, wrapped in cloth? But it wasn't sand he was collecting in the crate. Whatever it was, it had a distinctive musk—it smelled like a combination of moss and spider flowers.

Just then, Salim came back inside. His face darkening, he closed the crate and pushed it back under the bed. "Don't touch that."

He'd never spoken to me like that before. All I wanted was to leave, to get away from him, from his tiny tent in this desolate village by the waste dump. I wanted to be in my own bed, safe under the blankets, listening to the sounds of the desert.

We didn't meet so often afterward, once or twice a week at most. I started noticing little things after that: hushed late-night conversations, mysterious disappearances, crates in Spider-Man's truck, bundles of cash under Salim's mattress. Once I was looking for signs, they were hard to miss. All his gifts and little presents—stolen goods. I became quieter and quieter around Salim, fading into the background, like a dust-coated shrub in the sand. Out on the dunes, he wanted to kiss me again, but I didn't let him. It hurt him, to be pushed away.

One afternoon I realized I'd once more lost my ability to speak, which used to be so easy with him. Salim didn't look me in the eye. He didn't even acknowledge that there was a problem between us, an ever-widening chasm. Instead of talking about it, he gave me a silver necklace with a crescent moon, studded with diamonds.

"Can I put it on your neck?"

I took the necklace from him and flung it into the sand. "I don't want your gifts," I said. "You're a liar."

"I'm not a liar."

"Then tell me what those things really were in the crate under your bed."

Salim's jaw clenched, and he answered me in a low voice. "You really want to know? Fine, here's the truth. It's three hundred and twenty-five grams of hashish."

When Salim started telling me about his life as a smuggler, the sky was blue with a few feathery clouds, and he talked and talked, sometimes struggling to find the right words in Hebrew, and the sky slowly became tinged with pink and peach, and when he couldn't find the right word in Hebrew, he cursed in Arabic under his breath, and then he sighed and picked up the story where he left off, speaking until the sun was a tiny red speck. He told me he knew the risks. The leaders of his tribe discouraged smuggling and punished those who were caught attempting it. They had their own forms of punishment, where innocence was proven in the *bisha'a* fire test. The accused was brought before the judge. The *mubashe* heated up a silver rod for the fire test. Once the rod was scalding hot, he placed it on the accused's tongue. The tongue of a liar would burn. The anxiety of lying dried out the tongue, causing the burning metal to scorch the flesh. The truth was to be revealed through pain.

The sky darkened, and dusk settled over the desert when Salim told me he could never see me again. "What do you think they will do to me if I'm not only caught but they discover I'm in love with a Jewish girl?" And then, in the same breath, he said he could taste me on his tongue still, and he thought of my smooth skin, the smell of my shampoo. He told me he thought of collecting all the sand in the desert, all the gifts in the world, and giving them to me, so I would forgive him.

But it wasn't the smuggling I needed to forgive—it was the fact that we could never be together. I felt it the first time I walked through his village: I didn't belong in his world, I was an outsider, and he didn't belong in mine. I imagined my mother's crazed reaction if she ever discovered I was in love with a Bedouin boy, and shuddered. I wanted to tell him something dramatic, like *You'd better grab a handful of sand and put it in a jar right now, because this is the last time you're ever going to see me.* In the end, I didn't say anything. I just got up and walked away, didn't look back at him.

I never saw Salim again. In the weeks that followed, I kept riding my bicycle searching for desert flowers, but he was never there. Maybe he had gone to smuggle hashish across the border, or perhaps he was watching me from afar. He knew how to evade detection, to blend into the sand. But a month later, when I returned to the spot where we used to meet by the dunes next to Highway 40, I discovered a single glass jar, filled with sand, that he left for me to find. This was his parting gift to me, I imagined. We wouldn't share memories anymore. He wrote the label this time in Hebrew, his writing shaky, but the words clear: CATWOMAN. It was his way of telling me he would remember me. I still keep the jar of sand in my room on my bedside table, by the pale skull of a sand cat, and sometimes imagine what could have been.

Scheherazade and
Radio Station 97.2 FM

During Operation Peace for Galilee, when Ziv was thirty-two and serving in the paratroopers reserve unit, he was sent to take over a radio station in West Beirut. Ziv and his fellow unit members, Nadav and Mazal, were among the many reinforcements called for combat duty via special immediate order. Their objective was to stop the subversive transmissions from 97.2 FM, an English-language radio station in Lebanon. Most of the transmissions coming out of the station were stories for children, fairy tales that their commanders believed contained coded messages for the Palestinian Liberation Organization. They had expected to discover a large-scale operation with high-tech broadcasting machinery, state-of-the-art technology, and countless technicians, researchers, and reporters, but to their surprise, the radio station was operated by a single woman, who called herself Scheherazade.

The station was close to the Museum Alley Demarcation Line, a dangerous crossing point between East and West Beirut. As they passed the National Museum on Damascus Road, the four columns of its ocher facade riddled with bullet holes, Ziv saw militiamen, automatic weapons strapped across their chests, carrying what looked like priceless artifacts to an un-marked van—ancient painted pottery, alabaster burial urns, and a heavy stone bust of Anubis, the Egyptian god of death, mummification, and the afterlife, with a golden jackal's head. For a moment, Ziv was tempted to go inside the museum, but they weren't here to see an exhibition, there was a war going on, and they needed to get to their destination.

The station was on the top floor of a run-down three-story building, encircled with barbed wire. A massive signal antenna towered on the roof, like a lone steel Lebanese cedar tree in a forest of satellite dishes.

They found Scheherazade alone in the dimly lit broadcast-ing room of radio station 97.2 FM. She was sitting at a long desk outfitted with a turntable and a reel-to-reel tape recorder, preparing for her broadcast, when Ziv and his men burst into the room. For a moment, her eyes were wide and terrified, but she recovered quickly. She was wearing a formal evening gown of black velvet, as if she were on her way to an elegant ball, a turquoise clutch bag hanging from her shoulder. Her long dark hair was lush and thick as night, her face pale as wax, jaw clenched tight.

She crossed her arms over her chest. Her wrists were slim, Ziv noticed, her long fingers like the ivory keys of a grand piano. The way she hugged herself, as if in protection, was the only indication she was nervous. Otherwise, she seemed ut-terly unaffected by their hostile takeover. She snapped open her clutch bag, and for a moment Ziv imagined her retrieving a sleek pistol and calmly shooting him between the eyes, but with a flick of her slender wrist she took out only a pack of Camel Lights and a gleaming silver Zippo.

"If you're going to kill me," she said in lightly accented English, "you may as well do it now." Her voice did not waver. It was resolute, resigned to a lifetime of instability and violence. She inhaled deeply, the cigarette burning amber, then let the smoke out slowly.

"We're taking you prisoner," Ziv replied in English. "No one's going to die."

She sat up very straight, looked at each of them in turn, then stamped out her cigarette against the table. She gathered her hair in a bundle and tied it up with a golden brooch shaped like a honeycomb. It was a habit of hers to tie her hair before every broadcast, she later told them. With her hair out of the way, Ziv found himself admiring her delicate collarbones, and the single beauty mark on her long neck.

"May I broadcast my show now?" she asked. "I was just about to begin."

"Not tonight," Ziv said. "We're taking you off the air. We're shutting the station down." He grabbed the turntable, yanked the cord from its socket, and smashed it against the wall. Then he destroyed the recorder, too, pulling the seemingly endless reel, letting it spiral on the floor.

"That's right," Mazal said. "Veni, vidi, vici."

"Very well," Scheherazade said with a sigh, drumming on the table with her long fingers. Then she smiled shyly and asked, "But can I tell you a story off the air?"

"Yalla, let her tell a story," Mazal said. "It's been years since I've heard a good bedtime story."

Once upon a time there were three little piglets, Scheherazade said, her sonorous voice soft and low, as if she'd smoked two packs of those same Camel Lights every day for the past ten years. The first pig was lazy and built a house out of straw. The second pig was not particularly industrious either—he built his house out of sticks. The third pig was a hard worker and built his house with bricks, putting in the effort even to add a chimney and a fireplace. A wolf passed by, saw the straw house, and smelled the succulent pig, licking his lips, thinking he would make a fine mouthwatering meal. He knocked on the door. Little Pig! Little Pig! Let me in! But the little pig saw the wolf's big paws and cried, No!

"I know this story," Mazal said. "The wolf huffs and puffs, and then the house comes down."

"And the first pig," Ziv said, "runs away to hide with the second pig."

"And the second pig," Nadav said, "runs away to hide with the third pig."

"And the pigs end up eating the wolf," Scheherazade said. "But this isn't how this story will end."

Ziv had a bad feeling about staying in the radio station. It wasn't going to be a fairy tale with a happy ending or an easy moral. "We should move on," he said, speaking in Hebrew so Scheherazade wouldn't understand. "We can look for a different place to lie low. There are plenty of abandoned bombed-out buildings in this city. We can find somewhere else to spend the war."

"Like a Club Med?" Mazal said.

"Anywhere but here," Ziv said. "Come on, we've still got a few hours before it gets dark."

"And become cannon fodder for RPG kids?" Nadav said.

On the first day of the war, they had met the so-called RPG kids, named for their weapon of choice—the rocket-propelled grenade. It was June 6, 1982; their unit of ten had just entered Lebanon in an armored vehicle, along with the entire platoon. Tank after tank thundered forward, water carrier trucks and gasoline trucks, an endless procession of steel-gray Centurions and beige Merkavot in a hazy fog of bluish exhaust smoke. They went through southern Lebanese villages, with stone houses and lemon trees, and Ziv felt strangely excited, as if he were going on an adventure, watching the blur of banana groves, sunflower fields, and cypress trees swaying in the breeze, admiring the bright Technicolor sky and the distant sea, radiant and ablaze with light.

When their platoon of armored vehicles passed Rashidieh, a Palestinian refugee camp about five kilometers south of Tyre, they came upon a school building. The playground was a mess of broken earth. A large black raven was pecking at the overflowing trash bins in the yard. Suddenly, bullets whizzed past Ziv's ears, shrieking like deranged mechanical hornets. All around him, men were crawling on the ground. Ziv crouched behind a thorn bush, lungs choked with dust. Nadav and Mazal took cover behind a mound of dirt. Amid the foliage of silver birch trees surrounding the school building, Ziv saw a child wearing a dirty red-and-white-striped T-shirt, aiming an RPG. The kid couldn't have been more than twelve years old. Ziv froze, his finger on the trigger—he couldn't bring himself to shoot. When some of the soldiers opened fire in the kid's direction, the boy threw the RPG on the ground and ran away. He was too small to carry the heavy weapon. At that moment,

Ziv decided that the best thing for him to do was to try to avoid the war at all costs.

They fought another battle at the Ain al-Hilweh refugee camp, in the suburbs of Sidon, and lost more men. Air raids took down entire buildings, leaving behind only wreckage: twisted metal beams, broken white window shutters, crumbling walls. When they got to El Mansourieh, many of the homes were abandoned, the streets were deathly still. Cherry trees with pink petal blossoms grew on the hills, their stone fruit a rich, dark red. There was a tall, pale-brick building, a tower with a cross. Several young men with rifles strapped across their chests, members of the Christian Phalangist army, sauntered out of the church in a careless and arrogant kind of way. A woman in a torn floral dress was stumbling around in a daze, wailing. The Phalangists whistled at her, then laughed mercilessly. Ziv knew Israel's fight wasn't with the Phalangists— they were allies. At that point, he had no idea who they were fighting. Everyone was a potential enemy.

For weeks, their forces had West Beirut under siege. Frequently, the entire electrical grid would switch off, leaving the city under a blanket of night, darkness so thick it was biblical, a plague from the Book of Exodus. Once in a while, the sky would light up with a white flare, illuminating for a moment everyone's dirt-stained faces, the skyline of Beirut, fighter jets streaking through the air, followed by heavy bombardment. Bursts of fire, walls of flame licking the air, heat so terrible Ziv felt it gnawing at his skin, infiltrating to the marrow of his bones. The earth shook, and the sky was filled with thick, acrid smoke. Entire buildings collapsed in heaps of rubble.

When they invaded the city, it was complete chaos and anarchy. By then, their unit of ten had shrunk to three. Their armored vehicle rolled into a maze of small streets, smelling of cordite from artillery fire and the decaying stench of bodies rotting in the sun. There were snipers at every window, and checkpoints at every corner, each manned by a different militia. Stunned, dead-eyed civilians fled, clutching suitcases over their heads. Scrawny dogs scrambled over fallen rubbish bins, sniffing through the remains of a halal butcher's shop, snarling and biting each other over entire rotisserie chickens, grilled legs of lamb, tenderloin filets, and rib eye steaks. Children dug through the rubble of a candy shop, pulling swirly lollipops and colorful pastel candy-chain bracelets from a heap of broken glass, while an old man was tenderly wiping the dust off of his gray Peugeot, whistling the tune of Edith Piaf's song about having no regrets.

That first day inside West Beirut, they had no clear objectives or directions from their commanding officers. Amid the devastation of flattened buildings, blackened by fire, Ziv saw a pretty young woman in a leopard-print dress watering her flower garden. Nadav was playing with a plastic toy ring hanging from a chain around his neck. He had found it in a blown-up video arcade and amusement park. He wandered inside, lured by a pinball machine, its glass cabinet lit up with brilliant lights. He saw the best modern coin-operated arcade games: Donkey Kong, Space Invaders, Battlezone, and Pac-Man, frozen in time, stuck in the maze forever, surrounded on all sides by colorful ghosts. Nadav found the toy ring in a yellow claw crane machine, its glass front smashed, all the plush toy frogs and giraffes spilling out. "When I get back home," Nadav said, "I'm going to propose."

Ziv didn't have much to look forward to back home. He didn't have a girlfriend waiting for him. His father was dead and had left him nothing but a worn copper field compass, the North faded almost entirely. His mother was in a care facility, her brain foggy with early-onset Alzheimer's. Ziv worked in a kibbutz in the northern Golan Heights, picking pears and nectarines. It was steady work but difficult, leaving him blistered, sunburned, and worn out. On weekends, he went camping alone, pitching a tent on the banks of the Sea of Galilee. He liked the early mornings, the lake shrouded in mist. He would fish in the murky waters, snag several red-bellied tilapias, and fry them on his grill until their bodies were charred, the pale flesh moist and ready to eat. If he died in Beirut, no one would notice.

Finally, the opportunity to avoid the war presented itself when they received an order over the communication device to take over a radio station in West Beirut. Noting the waypoint coordinates, they plotted the shortest route there. They didn't want anyone to think they were cowards, so they would go on their mission and then hide away in the station until the war was over. *See no evil, hear no evil, speak no evil.*

But after meeting Scheherazade, Ziv changed his mind. They could go to an abandoned factory or mall, someplace their guys would never think to bomb. He was unnerved by Scheherazade's calm stoicism, but he was also feeling protective of her. He thought of her slim wrists and delicate collarbones. She was so alone in the station, broadcasting her stories, while mortar shells fell from the sky, and Beirut went up in flames.

"We should leave her and keep going," Ziv said.

Mazal insisted they stay. "Nobody will come looking for us here. It's the perfect cover. We did our job and stopped her from broadcasting. Now all we have to do is hang around until the war is over."

"It could take years," Ziv said.

"Let's give it a week," Mazal said.

"That doesn't sound like a bad idea," Nadav said.

Mazal got what he wanted—they stayed in the radio station waiting for the war to end. He was the luckiest guy Ziv had ever met. That was how he got his nickname Mazal, meaning "luck." He could tell Mazal was lucky from the first moment they met in reserve duty. Mazal had come in late to roll call, cocky and hungover, in a faded leather jacket, with three days of stubble and beautiful curly hair tumbling to his shoulders. The commander recognized Mazal from a silent meditation retreat in Dharamshala that they had both gone to in their early twenties, and he let him get away with it. Mazal had hated that retreat. For two entire weeks, on a remote, snowy mountain peak in the Himalayas, he'd sat on a wooden mat in a tiny room and didn't say a word. It was absolute torture for him, the most difficult period in his life, even more terrible than war. Eventually, he couldn't take it anymore. He went to the head monk, a British yogi in orange robes who always looked clinically depressed, and told him he was leaving. The yogi held a finger to his lips. *No talking,* he mimed. Mazal smiled respectfully, told him where he could shove that finger, and left with a bounce in his step.

Ziv notified Scheherazade that he and his men would remain in the radio station for the foreseeable future. He made it clear to her that she wouldn't be able to leave the premises without his permission. At gunpoint, she gave them a short tour of the facilities, acting like a gracious host, forced to put on a smile and escort a pack of wild children trailing mud through her elegant foyer and ransacking her home. The only sign of her discomfort was a vein throbbing on her forehead, a slight tremor of her hands. She showed them the broadcasting room, toilets and shower, the well-stocked kitchen and supply closet. "Down the hall," she said, "there's the elevator. I warn you: its descent is quite slow, and it plays terrible Muzak." It was a vintage metal-frame birdcage elevator with an interior of polished sandalwood and plush blue carpeting. Apparently, it took its sweet time descending to the basement, which Scheherazade affectionately called the Underworld.

They followed her into the common area, with its tattered green sofas and orange shag carpet. Some of the windows were shattered, and the walls were damaged from stray bullets fired from outside. There were shelves crammed with hundreds, maybe even thousands, of LP albums. Ziv spotted *Sgt. Pepper's Lonely Hearts Club Band,* his favorite. Years ago the Beatles were supposed to come perform in Israel, but they were denied entry to the country, because Golda Meir feared their music would corrupt the youth. *Sgt. Pepper's* had been released fifteen years ago, when Ziv was in high school—he had just moved with his family to the Golan Heights after it was seized from Syria in the aftermath of the Six-Day War. He didn't make any friends at his new school but spent all his time drinking liquor stolen from his father's cabinet, smoking cheap Noblesse, and listening to *Sgt. Pepper's.* Those were his last months of freedom, before he was drafted for mandatory service.

That night Scheherazade tied her hair up and told them

another story. Briefly, the shelling outside stopped, as if in suspense of her story. Ziv felt like a kid again, sitting in front of a *kumsitz* campfire with his friends, listening to a scary *chisbat*. Nadav was perched eagerly on the edge of the sofa, nervously playing with his red beret. Even Mazal, who normally never stopped talking, was silent in anticipation. One of the overhead lights flickered and died, leaving only the illumination of a single lightbulb hanging from the ceiling. Scheherazade's face was cast in shadow. She looked at each of them in turn as she spoke. Spellbound by her beautiful voice, Ziv felt the hairs on his arms stand on end and his heart beat faster. For a moment, he was so captivated by her tender lips that he forgot that she was their prisoner.

Scheherazade told a story about an old fisherman who cast his net into the sea. One day he pulled up a dead donkey. The next time he cast his net, he scooped up a pitcher full of dirt. On the third attempt, he found shards of pottery. Finally, on his fourth try, praying to Allah as he cast his net, he hauled a jar, emblazoned with a six-pointed star, the seal of Solomon. When he pried open the lid, a jinni appeared, who promised to grant the fisherman a choice: he could pick the way he would die.

"How do you want to die?" Mazal asked, interrupting the story.

"I'd like to die on the toilet," Nadav said.

"I want to die having sex," Ziv said. He turned to Mazal, the lucky one. "You?"

"In my sleep," Mazal said. "Think about it, man. If you die in your sleep, you don't feel a thing."

"No," Nadav said, "it's much better to die on the toilet. You're already sitting down, it's peaceful."

Mazal and Nadav started arguing passionately about the best way to die, going back and forth with great speed like the racquet players on Tel Aviv's Frishman Beach. Mazal flicked away Nadav's limp emotional points like a professional *matkot* player, hitting back with his expertly worded rubber ball of tightly controlled logic. With each serve, Mazal knocked down another one of Nadav's verbal defenses, until a tense silence settled over the room.

"Well, that was fun," Ziv said. "I'm going to bed."

"I'll take the sofa tonight," Mazal said.

"Sweet dreams," Nadav said. "May all your wishes come true."

They set up a guard rotation to watch Scheherazade, who had left the room and made herself comfortable on a foldout cot. When it was Ziv's turn to watch her, he made a pot of black coffee to keep himself awake. She was sitting on her cot, wrapped tightly in a cocoon of bedsheets. At any moment, he expected her to shed her chrysalis and transform into a black and orange butterfly, wings like the stained-glass windows of the church in Nazareth he visited once as a kid on a school trip. They sat in silence for some time, and every once in a while Ziv heard fighter jets fly by, one after another, recognizing them by the sound their engines made. The whooshing Phantom, the screeching Ayit Skyhawk, the sonic boom thunderclap of the Mirage. He heard a mortar shell explode, tanks climbing over heaps of rubble, and rapid gunfire in the distance like the drilling of an insistent woodpecker.

"Can't sleep?" Ziv asked, adjusting the strap of his Galil rifle.

"No." She shook her head. "Just like my sister. She can never fall asleep, either."

He sipped his coffee. "Tell me about her."

Her sister was the spelling bee champion of Lebanon. She spent every day memorizing long, complicated English words. Her parents hired the best private English tutor in Beirut, who liked carrying an engraved whiskey flask and a worn copy of *A Midsummer Night's Dream* in the breast pocket of his green velvet waistcoat, a gentleman known as Shakespeare al-Lubnani. Her younger sister was the gifted one, a prodigy. The reason she could never fall sleep was her brain wouldn't rest. Words drifted by every moment, letters arranging themselves in her mind in endless combinations. She recited them again and again, walking down the long and winding corridors of the alphabet. Many geniuses, Scheherazade said, were somnambulists. *Somnambulism* meant "sleepwalking," she told Ziv. It was one of the spelling bee words that had crowned her sister a champion of Lebanon. Another one was *chiaroscuro*, an artistic style with strong contrasts of light and shadow. Her favorite, *vivisepulture*, meant "being buried alive."

"How about you quiz me?" Ziv asked.

"Okay," she said. "Spell *kaleidoscope*."

"K-A-L-"

"Yes?"

"Is it I-E or E-I?"

"That's why you're not the Lebanese spelling bee champion."

"I'm not a champion of anything."

"Maybe you're lucky. My sister is blessed with an incredible memory, that's true, but it's also a curse."

Scheherazade told him how her sister could remember exactly what she had for breakfast last month on a given day. She knew the color of the bus driver's cap, who drove her to the bookshop at the city center on a Tuesday afternoon ten years ago. She remembered how many age rings looped around the severed tree trunk in their backyard. She could tell you the number of turquoise tiles lining the kitchen wall of her childhood home. She could recite the lyrics to all of Fairuz's songs, memorize the order of a deck of cards in under a minute, and tell you the details of their father's autopsy, including the type of bullet used to kill him and the diameter of the hole in his chest.

"How did he die?"

"It's very easy to die in Beirut, don't you think? He died six years ago now, a year after the civil war started. Shot by a sniper when he was on his way to the pharmacy to buy my sister lemon-flavored cough drops."

The coffee was cold in his cup, but Ziv sipped it anyway, just for something to do. "You live in the radio station?" he asked.

"Yes, this is my home. And you are the big bad wolf, coming to blow it all down."

Ziv grew up on stories of the big bad wolf from Lebanon, sending rockets to their villages in the north. They kept rebuilding and rebuilding, and now their homes were no longer made of straw, they were made of brick. They were defending themselves, pushing the PLO operatives back past the forty-kilometer line from the border, making sure they wouldn't keep suffering attacks like the Coastal Road Massacre. At least that was what he was always told. Scheherazade must have grown up on different stories. He kept thinking of her father with a hole in his chest, and her sister reciting the information from the autopsy report, the width and depth of the bullet wound, over and over again, in a room full of turquoise tiles.

When Scheherazade fell asleep, wrapped up in her cocoon, Ziv went to check on Nadav and Mazal, both curled up on the two sofas in the common room. Nadav slept with his M16 in his hands, probably dreaming of his girlfriend. Mazal was sound asleep, his stolen Kalashnikov rifle, looted from the corpse of a Palestinian fighter, peeking from under the sofa cushion. Ziv could hear him snoring lightly, his breath coming in waves.

Suddenly, gunfire erupted from outside, shattering the shelves. Ziv ducked for cover, as the stacks of LPs came raining down. Nadav rolled to the floor, clutching his M16, but his eyes were not on the window. He was staring at Mazal, who was lying very still, a bullet in his forehead. Blood ran down the side of his face, staining the sofa, dripping to the floor, pooling on the shag carpet.

Ziv remained crouched, his heart pounding, waiting until he was sure it was safe again before going to Mazal's side. *At least you died in your sleep,* he thought, cradling his friend's still warm head on his lap.

They needed to find someplace to store the body. They didn't want to risk leaving the radio station, so they decided the best option was the basement. Ziv took Mazal's Kalashnikov and slung it over his shoulder. He grabbed Mazal under his arms, the uniform soaked with blood, and Nadav took hold of his legs, and on the count of three they lifted him from the sofa, dragging the heavy body down the hallway. They put him in the birdcage elevator and propped him up awkwardly in the corner, legs sprawled. They took the slowest elevator in the Middle East down to the Underworld, avoiding each other's eyes, while some hidden electronic speaker emitted unnervingly soothing Muzak.

When they finally reached the basement, a kind of storage room, they laid Mazal's body among cardboard boxes filled with old radio scripts, worn books of poetry by Khalil Gibran, and a crumpled newspaper with a photo of militia commander Bachir Gemayel on the front cover. Nadav touched his right hand to his lips, then to Mazal's forehead. Ziv took out his father's worn compass, stroked the copper frame, then put it in Mazal's rigid hand. Mazal might as well have the compass—it didn't work anyway. The stubble of Mazal's beard was light blond and reddish. His curls tumbled down, excessively luscious for a man, let alone a dead man. His lips were parted as if, even in death, he wanted the last word.

"Do you want to say anything?" Ziv said.

"If Mazal was alive," Nadav said, "he wouldn't be able to stop eulogizing himself."

Ziv was waiting for Mazal's death to affect him in some way, but mostly he felt numb. He stared at the peeling plaster wall, etched with drawings of fuzzy black and yellow bumblebees. It was like discovering the old painted cave walls in France, with the buffalo, deer, and bears. The drawings on the radio station wall, however, were not ancient—they must have been done by Scheherazade in honor of her sister, the spelling bee champion of Lebanon.

After their improvised funeral ceremony for Mazal, they

sat on the bloodstained sofa in the common area, exhausted and shaken. Slowly the sun rose, bathing the room in a golden glow. Ziv closed his eyes, feeling the warmth on his face. He could hear Nadav quietly sobbing, so he kept his eyes shut, knowing that if he opened them, he might cry, too.

A few hours later, Scheherazade walked into the room, her hair slightly disheveled from sleep. She didn't seem surprised to see the blood on the sofa, or two soldiers instead of three. She stifled a yawn and wordlessly went to the kitchen to make coffee. She seemed completely at ease, while they were steadily losing control. Ziv began to wonder if they were in fact her prisoners and not the other way around.

He didn't want to admit it, and certainly not to Nadav, but he was afraid Nadav would actually die on the toilet seat. So now, whenever Nadav went to the bathroom, Ziv followed him. At first, he tried to do so discreetly. He would pretend to make himself something to eat in the kitchen, but after a while, he didn't care anymore. Nadav had many things to look forward to when he returned home from the war, he just couldn't die on the toilet seat.

When Ziv showered, he caught Scheherazade watching him. He was rubbing a bar of coarse soap on his body, thinking about dying during sex. He imagined Scheherazade coming to him in the night, slipping out of her dark velvet dress, tiptoeing naked to his foldout cot, crawling under the blankets to keep him company. That wouldn't be a bad way to go. For the time being, however, he would abstain. Once he left Lebanon, he would be free to have all the sex he wanted and to tell the tale afterward. Scheherazade kept watching him shower, and he had nowhere to hide his arousal, so he shut off the water, even though his body was still covered in soap, wrapped himself in a pink towel printed with flowers, and grabbed his Galil. Scheherazade giggled when she saw him—how stupid he must have looked, walking around with a pink towel around his waist, rifle slung across his back.

If she wanted to look, let her look. Ziv would make it easier for her. He grabbed a sledgehammer from the supply closet and broke down the bathroom door, imagining he was Sylvester Stallone in *Rocky III*. He splintered the thin wood and kicked it apart until all that was left was a gaping hole. He broke down the walls, and they came tumbling down in a heap, just like the houses of the three little pigs, and all that was left was a pile of rubble. He ripped the teal-colored shower curtain from its rod. The toilet seat was now in plain sight, between the broadcasting room and the kitchen, and the view to the shower was unobstructed. At least now Ziv would be able to watch over Nadav, so he wouldn't die on the toilet. He was panting heavily, and his forehead was damp with sweat. He really needed to shower again.

"Look at you, man," Nadav said. "Whoever started the rumor that reservists are lazy was totally wrong. This station is starting to look just like the war outside."

The night after Mazal died, Scheherazade tied her hair up. She wanted to tell another story.

But Ziv interrupted her. There was no way he was going to let her tell another story that would endanger him or Nadav. "You're lucky you're still alive," he said.

"Doesn't it make sense, though, that I tell another tale? That way, the new story will override the old one. I can tell a story with a happy ending if you like."

"Which story?"

"One about an archaeological expedition that crossed the Sahara to search for the City of Brass. Along the way, they met marionettes that danced by themselves, without strings."

"That doesn't sound like it has a happy ending. Tell me about yourself instead."

"That's not a story with a happy ending, either, but okay, if you want, I'll tell it.

"I was a lonely girl," Scheherezade told him. "I didn't have many friends at the Grand Lycée or in my neighborhood of Achrafieh. There was one place I loved: the National Museum. It was my refuge, my hiding spot. I wandered the marbled floors of the main gallery, visiting the exhibits as if they were my friends. The precious sarcophagus of Ahiram, engraved with winged sphinxes, was my favorite. I conversed with the mummified queens of Tyre and the statue of Aphrodite, confessing how much I hated my classmates, those rich and spoiled, superficial girls. My real friends were made of stone and marble, bones wrapped in gauze and faded robes of cotton. To me, this collection of ancient and dead things was more present and alive than anything."

Ziv didn't want to tell her about the militiamen he'd seen looting the museum on his way to the radio station. He was wondering if the sarcophagus of Ahiram, Scheherazade's favorite exhibit, was safe—when an explosion shook the building. Dust and debris, shattered glass all around. Ziv instinctively protected Scheherazade, covering her body with his own. Lying on top of her, he felt her soft silk dress against his cheek, smelled rose water in her hair. He felt her rapid heartbeat against his chest. He got up, shakily, and ran out of the room, but it was too late; he found Nadav slumped on the toilet seat, pants hugging his knees, head lolled to the side. Shrapnel had pierced his neck, and now poor Nadav, too, had gotten his wish.

Ziv lifted up Nadav's pants to cover his skinny thighs and the dark hair around his genitals. He felt like a father dressing his son, teaching him to use the toilet for the first time. For a moment, struggling with the button, Ziv thought: *Why does this matter? He's dead, he won't be needing pants anymore.* He took Nadav's M16, then he knelt beside the body, trying to remove the toy ring hanging on a chain from his neck, but it got caught in the buttons of his uniform. He tugged at it, forcefully, and the chain snapped. The ugly plastic ring was bloodstained. Ziv cleaned it with his sleeve. At least it wouldn't be bloody when he gave it to Nadav's girlfriend.

For her birthday last year, Nadav had taken her to the guesthouse of a kibbutz in the Galilee for the weekend. They had shared an enormous breakfast of omelets, yellow HaEmek cheese, warm pitas, and a finely chopped salad. They spent their evening on an outdoor swing, under a Syrian juniper, drinking cheap white wine, looking out at the fertile plains and rolling hills, when a hoopoe bird settled on a branch above them, spread its wings, and shook its crown feathers in a mating dance. Then, lying in the thick grass, naked in the cool night air, they made love in the dark.

Ziv managed to drag Nadav's body from the bathroom all the way to the elevator. He rode down to the Underworld, laughing hideously at the terrible Muzak, and at the thought that he had no one else in the entire world to share this bizarre nightmare with except for Scheherazade. He dumped Nadav's body next to Mazal's bloated corpse, gagging and coughing at the terrible stench in the storage room.

If all the ways they imagined dying came true, would he never have sex again?

"This is your fault," Ziv said, when he reemerged and saw Scheherazade smoking a cigarette in the hallway. He pushed her against the wall, trapping her between his arms. He was breathing heavily, shaking.

"I'm so sorry about your friends," she said, her face as indecipherable as a marble death mask. "Let me cook dinner for us."

"How do I know you won't poison me?"

"You're being ridiculous. I'll taste all the food before you eat it," she said wearily, and stubbed out the cigarette on the wall.

She whisked a bag of bulgur wheat, lentils, and three small onions from the supply cupboard. She boiled the bulgur and cooked the lentils, the steam rising from the pots, onions sizzling and caramelizing in the pan, the flames lighting up her face with an orange glow in the dark kitchen. She made *mujadara*, the poor man's food in Lebanon. She served them each a portion, heaping it into two bowls. Ziv watched her eat, spooning the bulgur gently, chewing without taking her eyes off of him for even a moment. She ate an entire bowl before he even touched his. It had been so long since he last had a warm meal, and it was so delicious, he could barely stop himself—he ate quickly, gratefully.

That night Ziv placed his Galil, Mazal's Kalashnikov, and Nadav's M16 under the sofa cushion. He watched Scheherazade sleep in her foldout cot, listening to the rising and falling of her breath. In the morning, he woke up to the sound of running water. She was showering, her back turned to him, water cascading off the delicate wings of her shoulder blades, trickling down her vertebrae. Her silk-spun midnight hair fell past the curve of her hips, down to her pear-shaped buttocks. He shut his eyes, pretending to be asleep and waiting for the sound of the rushing water to cease, but it kept going and going. He felt a droplet on his face. When he opened his eyes, she stood over him, gloriously naked with the dark mound of her pubis, the triangle hills of her breasts.

"I'll chop your head off," Ziv said.

Scheherazade slunk away, hips swaying, and switched off the water. She squeezed the water out of her sopping wet hair and gathered it up with her golden honeycomb brooch, but she didn't put her clothes back on. She started walking around the radio station naked. Over the next few days, they developed a comfortable routine that revolved around mealtimes. He'd had girlfriends before, but he'd never gotten married, and he assumed this was what married life was like, a kind of uneasy truce between enemy nations, a fragile cease-fire that required a constant redrawing of the battle lines. He felt trapped but happy in his prison. He lost track of time. The dazzlingly long and uneventful days blended into each other, repetitive and monotonous, sitting on a bloodstained sofa, next to a naked woman, imagining the war outside.

One night, unable to sleep, Ziv noticed Scheherazade wasn't in her foldout cot. The common room was empty, and no one sat on the toilet seat or stood under the shower. For a moment, he wondered if she had escaped the station, but finally he found her sitting in the broadcast room, on the floor, her hair tied up with her honeycomb brooch. He wondered what she was thinking and if she missed her sister. He sat down next to her, crossing his legs. Neither of them said anything, and Ziv found himself once more thinking of the nearby National Museum, imagining its treasures, mosaics of lions and tigers, gilded figurines, and golden sarcophagi.

"Would you like to see the view from the rooftop?" Scheherazade said.

"Let's take the stairs," Ziv said. "The elevator is out of order."

They stood on the roof, amid dozens of dusty dish antennae, sprouting up like mushrooms after the rain. The station's enormous steel Lebanese cedar tree stood tall and proud, a sentinel with forked branches of signal antennae overlooking the smoldering night sky, bursts of orange and yellow, rain of fire and white ash, choked with plumes of dark smoke. Ziv felt the heat on his face, his nostrils tingled with the acrid smell of burnt rubber. Watching the bombs falling on Beirut, the flames getting higher and higher, he understood that he would never go back home. He would die here, in the radio station, while having sex with Scheherazade.

Ziv felt surprisingly calm and free of fear, as if he were re-enacting a scene from a play he knew by heart. His hands were steady as he laid down his Galil assault rifle. He put Mazal's Kalashnikov and Nadav's M16 on the ground. He took off his heavy Ephod Combat Vest, which held twelve magazines, three hand grenades, a first-aid kit, and binoculars. Then he slipped off his uncomfortable red paratrooper boots and dark socks and massaged his tired, dirty feet. He unbuttoned his uniform and pants, pulled off his T-shirt and underwear, and cast aside his silver dog tag. He left everything behind, until he was completely naked. He reached out to Scheherazade, caressed her hair, and stroked her delicate collarbones, then he pulled her toward him, holding her in his arms.

"Can I tell you a story this time?" Ziv whispered in her ear.

"Very well," she said, half a smile on her lips, poised as ever. A cool breeze blew by, and she shivered, her slim arms covered in goose bumps. A strand of dark hair escaped her honeycomb brooch. She tucked it behind her ear. "Tell me a story off the air."

"Near where I grew up in the Golan Heights," Ziv said, "there are hundreds of thousands of active land mines. The only inhabitants in these dangerous no-go zones are a rare breed of cunning wolves, so small they don't weigh enough to trigger the explosives. They've made the dangerous landscape their home. They stalk the ranchers' cattle and drag their prey back to their lair, where the hunters cannot go. When I was a teenager, I was unhappy and liked to get drunk by myself and wander away from home in the dark. One night I walked too far, it was pitch-black, and without noticing, I stumbled onto a field of land mines. Any false step, and I would be blown away, reduced to nothing but dust. I waited and waited, paralyzed with fear, unable to sit down or even move my feet. Suddenly, I saw a pair of glimmering green eyes. A wolf appeared out of the darkness, and somehow I knew that I needed to follow it. I walked slowly, a few paces behind the wolf. I stepped where it stepped, followed its exact movements, trusting it completely with my life, and it led me out of the field of land mines and back to my home."

High Heels

O n the corner of Mazeh Street, by the old water tower, a crooked sign hangs on the front door of Sandelmann's Shoes: OPEN AIR-CONDITIONING. Sroch knows this is a lie. The air-conditioning stopped working a long time ago. His father's shop is crowded with shelves of sneakers, sandals, mountaineering boots, plastic waders, and ballet slippers. But however hard Sroch and his parents work, it doesn't seem to matter. Competition is steep. Mass-produced footwear outlets and new boutique shoe shops, selling fleur-de-lis-patterned slip-ons and curved moccasins that resemble birds' beaks, are taking away Sandelmann's customers.

Sroch helps the customers try on different pairs. Most of the boys like leather boots, while the girls prefer sandals. The regulars are usually elderly and unable to pay for new shoes. Sometimes his father, Shmulik, who keeps track of expenses but is terrible with managing the shop's finances, refuses to take their money. His mother stays in the back of the shop, sitting on a small stool by a table with tools scattered around: scissors, pliers, measuring tape, a rotary cutter, needle and thread. She does small repairs: stitching, polishing, replacing worn laces. Almost no one gets their shoes repaired anymore, they just buy new ones. Sandelmann's is one of the last shoe repair shops in the country.

There is one pair of high heels, kept on a shelf above the cash register, that they will never sell. They belonged to a Polish-Jewish prima ballerina named Franceska Mann, the dancer who killed a Nazi officer with the tip of her heel. Her story begins and ends with a pair of heels. They are called stilettos, his father tells him, the Italian word for a long sharp knife, since the eight-inch blade of the heel resembles a dagger. They were made in a shoe factory in Chelmek, in the south of Poland. The black shoe, a size thirty-seven and a half, was supposedly made up of two hundred and eighty different parts. They were shipped to Sztylet, a high-end shop in Warsaw, where they were purchased by the dancer and her mother.

It was never entirely clear to Sroch how Franceska's high heels came to be in his father's possession. Shmulik told a convoluted story about receiving the shoes as a gift from a long-lost relative and collector of historical footwear, Mr. Zalman Lauterpacht, who purchased them in a secret auction for stolen Jewish possessions. All kinds of miscellaneous knick-knacks were sold at this underground auction of Jewish paraphernalia, although their authenticity could not always be absolutely verified. Besides Franceska Mann's high heels, Lauterpacht spoke of a long-lost letter from Walter Benjamin to his wife, Dora, two Olympic silver medals by the Austrian-Jewish swimmer and fencer Dr. Otto Herschmann, and the

1757 Guadagnini violin of Alma Rose, niece of Gustav Mahler, who directed the Women's Orchestra of Auschwitz. Rose led a group of young, female Jewish musicians who performed for their captors in order to stay alive, playing German marching songs to boost morale and, a particular favorite of the camp commandant, Franz Hössler, Schumann's *Träumerei,* the dreamlike reverie that makes up movement seven of opus 15, *Kinderszenen,* "Scenes from Childhood."

In his fantasy, Sroch likes to imagine the dancer visiting Sztylet with her mother to buy a present for herself. She is radiant after coming in fourth place in the international dance competition in Brussels. She removes her faded pointe shoes, unravels the layers of lambswool and chamois leather padding, revealing her bare feet, damaged by years of dancing. Her soles are calloused and blistered, her flesh purple and bruised, one nail is black, her toes stiff and injured from standing on point. She flexes her muscles, in control of every single separate segment of her ankle and foot, each toe as obedient as another. She slips on the high heels, a perfect fit. She is still unaccustomed, however, to walking in them. Attempting to cross the room to her mother, she nearly twists her ankle.

"Do I have to teach the prima ballerina how to walk?" her mother asks.

Shmulik has a favorite saying: "The shoemaker's son always walks barefoot." Every day he warns Sroch: "Don't neglect your family. Don't forget those closest to you." Shmulik knows that his son sneaks out at night. From a relatively young age, Sroch has been rooftopping in Tel Aviv, discovering new parts of the city with limited access to the public, creeping into construction sites and building zones. His favorite activity is climbing cranes. He does it alone, preferring the solitude and concentration it allows him. There are so many cranes on the skyline that the advertisements for construction work have invented a new nickname for Israel: Crane Nation. Sometimes the cranes are so high, they reach over the tops of skyscrapers, hanging like the curved arm of an orangutan. Sitting on a thin metal beam at the top, he feels like he's visiting a kingdom of air. Shmulik just doesn't understand why his only son would waste his time breaking into construction sites to climb to the top of a crane. "It's dangerous," Shmulik says, "and foolish. Besides, look what it's doing to your sneakers, they're always scuffed."

Shmulik is a distinguished professor of shoes, and he knows everything about high heels. He's researched them to the point of exhaustion, and even his wife doesn't want to hear about them any longer. At the dinner table, while they eat roasted peppers stuffed to the brim with ground beef and pine nuts, he tells her that it was ancient Egyptian butchers who were the first to wear high heels, in order to avoid stepping on the carcasses of slaughtered animals. For their thirty-year wedding anniversary, Shmulik and Shoshana ride horses in the Golan Heights, and he tells her the Persian cavalry wore heeled boots to keep their feet in the stirrups. When they watch a movie about a big shot academic at Harvard, he tells his wife that in Massachusetts in the sixteenth century, women who tempted men into marriage using the seductive sexual allure of high heels, known as the horns of the devil, were considered witches. During Operation Cast Lead, sitting in the dusty bomb shelter with the Jacobsons, he tells her that Louis XIV wore high heels embellished with scenes from the battle of Saint-Denis, the siege of Maastricht, and other skirmishes of the Franco-Dutch War. During Sroch's bar mitzvah celebrations in the Kotel, Shoshana complains that they've been standing around too long next to the Holy of Holies, the Western Wall, and that the soles of her feet hurt tremendously, so Shmulik tells her about the ungodly Turkish invention, thirty-inch high heels, that required the wearer to use a long cane or a dedicated servant to keep from tripping. His wife, barefoot, considers asking him for a divorce.

At three in the morning, Sroch puts on his skull-knit black cap and double-checks the four AA batteries in his headlamp. Like most people in Tel Aviv, he wears only black, but not because he's a hipster. It's the uniform of an urban climber: jet-black cargo pants, dark shirt, scuffed sneakers. He makes sure even his socks are dark. He needs to be invisible. Urban climbing is risky business. If anyone sees him, they'll call the police, and he could be fined for trespassing. He could also slip and break his neck. There are many construction sites around the city, all closed off for the night.

He decides to go to one near Meir Park. He's scouted the site beforehand, noting entry and exit points, as well as the time when the crane operator arrives. Everywhere there are warning signs about trespassing, but after years of staring at OPEN AIR-CONDITIONING, he doesn't believe them. It's easy to break in. He scales a fence, climbs the scaffolding around a building, jumps down to the construction site. He makes his way to the base of the crane, tiptoeing through rubble and debris, tools, helmets, and uniforms strewn around everywhere, passing two massive tractors, those majestic mechanical dinosaurs.

The eighty-meter-tall crane sways in the wind. Sroch climbs the base, a concrete slab, all the way up the steel-trussed sections of the mast, heading to the operator's cab. The metal is cold and slick against the palm of his hand. He looks only in front of him, the glow from his headlamp illuminating each rung in the ladder, as he steadily makes his way up. He goes fast. At any moment, he could be seen. Once he reaches the operator's cab, he makes his way along the jib. At the very top, he switches off his headlamp and savors the darkness. He's walking on a metal beam the width of his shoe, eighty meters off the ground. It's just as easy as walking on the pavement. He strides forward, like a gymnast on a tightrope, aware of his movements, using his ankle as a pivot point, positioning his center of mass directly over the base of support. He's weightless, he could just drift away on the wind. It's so very quiet at the top.

Creaking metal, footsteps, low voices. Two people approach, silent as shadows. There's nowhere to hide, only one way up and one way down. Sroch switches on his headlamp. He can make out a man and a woman, both in black hoodies. They're neither police nor part of the construction crew. They're night climbers like him. The woman waves a gloved hand, like the Queen of England, and for a moment, Sroch imagines the frail British monarch balancing on the balls of her feet on a crane, eighty meters in the air, her crown slipping from her head and tumbling down into the darkness. God save the queen.

The man walks without hesitation, his movements efficient and razor sharp, as if this were his natural habitat and he was born eighty meters above the ground.

"I see we have guest," the man says with a thick Russian accent.

"I can go," Sroch says.

"*Nyet,* stay."

The man grasps the yellow metal beam above Sroch's head and lowers himself to a sitting position next to him on the steel bar. The woman, catlike, follows elegantly and sits next to the man. Three sets of feet now dangle eighty meters off the ground.

"You don't have photographic device?" the man asks.

He doesn't have a camera.

"You are political?" the man asks.

Sroch shakes his head.

"We're not political either," the woman says. "Why do you climb?"

Sroch shrugs. He doesn't know really. He just started doing it one day and couldn't stop.

"I like how quiet it is," Sroch says, then regrets it immediately, thinking they might get the wrong idea. The truth is, he doesn't mind company.

"What's your name?" asks the woman.

"Everyone calls me Sroch," he says.

The woman bursts out laughing. "Like shoelace?"

Sroch is a nickname that stuck because he's long and slim and works in a shoe store. They introduce themselves. The man is Monkey, the woman is Gecko. Most night climbers have nicknames or use fake identities, to avoid detection by the authorities. The less evidence that can be tied back to them—a name, a face—the better.

"Why are you called Monkey?" Sroch asks.

Monkey tells him he made aliyah together with his parents, from the former Soviet Union, when he was fourteen years old, and he grew up in Petah Tikva. He got his nickname from the army. He was part of Unit 669, the military search and rescue team specializing in hostage rescue. They were silent, efficient, expert. As part of their operations, they routinely dropped from helicopters, climbed buildings and rooftops, rappelled down cliffs, and sneaked into homes and offices equipped with ropes, tactical axes, stun grenades, and suppressor pistols. At night, they calculated the trajectory of the electric lighting so they wouldn't cast a visible shadow. They always climbed very quickly, without making a sound, because the slightest noise could mean certain death.

"I was always the quickest climber," Monkey says. "And I never take unnecessary risk."

"Why are you called Gecko?" Sroch asks.

"I like the color green," she says, and takes off one shoe, then a sock, and massages her bare foot. Her nails are perfect half-moons. There are bits of fluff from the dark socks between her toes. Her foot is pale and long, like a swan. This must be what the famous ballerina Franceska's feet looked like before they were mangled from hours and hours of practicing. Sroch wishes he could slip the dancer's high heels on Gecko's feet, to see if they fit, like some strange, new Cinderella story.

They end up talking for hours, as the horizon is washed in faded sheets of yellow and orange, and Sroch admires the light bathing Gecko's face, her dark blue lipstick, and her slightly smudged eyeshadow. By the time they say goodbye, they've already set a date for the next climb, and he's back down on the ground, it's almost six-thirty in the morning. He's exhausted but also wired, fizzing with nervous energy. As he makes his way home, he can't stop thinking of Gecko's dark lipstick, the smudged shadow around her eyelids, her pale foot. All he wants is to sleep for hours and hours, but he needs to go to school, then work at the shop. At three the next morning, he knows he'll go climbing again. His body aches from the exertion of the climb, and his head throbs from lack of sleep, but no matter how tired he feels, he always goes climbing, to feel weightless again.

After practice at the School of Gymnastics and Artistic Dance, Franceska is utterly exhausted, but she keeps dancing, just as he keeps climbing. He imagines her slick with sweat, muscles burning. Her head hangs heavy, her stomach clings to her spine. She's eaten five almonds today, drunk a cup of dark coffee, and smoked two Gauloises. When she first joined the company, the entire dance troupe rehearsed on the shores of Druskininkai Lake in Lithuania. The sky was the color of wet cement. Standing on the tips of her toes, reaching for the sky, she sank into the sand. The troupe raised their black stockinged limbs in unison, ruffled their feathery white tutus, then stood resolutely still, propped up on one leg, a sedge of snow cranes.

When Sroch was a boy, his father taught him that shoes could be made from anything. To prove his point, he constructed a pair of sandals from plaited grass and made Sroch wear them all day. After he learned that lesson, Sroch slowly acquired more and more responsibilities around the shop. His first official role was to measure the customers' feet and then mark the length on a piece of leather. He grew accustomed to having a stranger's foot very close to his face, and he knew all the different kinds of unfortunate smells that a human heel could emit, from the sharp stench of the marbled rind of a Camembert to the vinegary odor of pickled purple onions.

He studied feet very closely under the tutelage of his father, a process that involved pop quizzes about the twenty-six bones, thirty-three joints, and more than a hundred muscles, tendons, and ligaments of the human foot. He learned that the foot is divided into three parts: the hindfoot, the midfoot, and the forefoot. The human foot has two longitudinal arches that curve above the ground, from the heel bones over the keystone ankle bone to the three metatarsals. His father also insisted he study ancient cobbling techniques, including shoes that were German-sewn, Bolognese-stitched, and English-welted. He learned about Chinese foot-binding and Silk Road shoes, Kampskatcha slippers *à la Turque,* and the Duke of Wellington's boots.

Sroch meets Monkey and Gecko, as they planned, at a construction site in Ramat Aviv, a northern suburb of the city, which they have scouted out beforehand. It's half an hour north from his home by bike, an area where new high-rise apartments are popping up all the time. They climb the red and white hammerhead tower crane to the top of the mast, pass the turntable and operator's cab, then head down the counterjib to the main winch and motors section. Sitting on the steel-trussed beam, Gecko lights a cigarette, reciting the many names she has for cranes: *sky beasts, robot arms, steel trees, playgrounds in the clouds.* And for those who climb them: *night crawlers, crane scalers, sky walkers, height addicts, idiots.*

"I like you," Monkey says, perched like a stone gargoyle. "You don't say much."

Sroch doesn't say anything, to not break the spell.

The three of them sit on the crane, their feet dangling, sharing a cigarette.

"What do you do?" Gecko asks. "Besides climb cranes at night?"

"I'm in school, mostly. And I work at my father's shop."

"What kind of establishment?" Monkey asks.

"We sell shoes."

Sroch starts telling them about his childhood at Sandelmann's. The shop smelled of old leather and the inside of a shoe. It was so small, like a shoebox. They are buried in shoes, in a catacomb of footwear. It's embarrassing, really, the way he talks about it, and he notices the way they exchange smiles when he tells them about the high heels above the register. As he begins the story of the Polish dancer, he can see in their eyes that they aren't sure whether to believe him. His father could tell it better, probably. He's never told anyone else Franceska's story. It's always been a kind of family secret. It sounds dumb when he tells it out loud, but he just wants to impress them.

Gecko takes a deep drag of her cigarette and looks at him through narrowed eyes. She begs to come to the shop and see the dancer's heels. "I want to try them on," she says.

"A dancer's shoes?" Monkey says. "They'll never fit you, Bigfoot."

Sroch has always been climbing, first trees and chain-link fences, then bouldering in Hayarkon Park, and finally he began leaping from rooftop to rooftop, striding across an endless grid of solar water heaters. He remembers the first time he climbed at night, when he scaled the water tower on his street, next to the Bauhaus building with its round white balconies. It was a barrel-shaped Eretz Israeli water tower, with a seven-branched menorah on its roof. He sat at the very top, one hand clutching the menorah, his feet hanging down and swinging, watching from above as one car after another passed by. A group of girls stumbled around in search of a midnight snack, oblivious to his presence. He enjoyed being invisible. To watch but not to be seen. That first night he stayed up on the water tower almost until morning, watching the city spewing the leftover drunks, the dregs of the night.

Now he meets Monkey and Gecko almost every Saturday night. They explore different parts of the city, climb cranes in construction sites, and share cigarettes at the top. Even though they're at least ten years older than Sroch, in their mid- to late twenties, they feel like true friends. They've adopted him into their small circle, and he feels part of something.

Then one afternoon about a month after they all first met, Monkey and Gecko show up at the shop. The place is empty, even though normally there are customers around at this time. When they walk in, Gecko greets Sroch too enthusiastically, her laughter echoing in the empty shop. She's wearing big tortoiseshell sunglasses and a green spaghetti-strap floral dress. Her flowing, glossy hair is dark blue in the daylight. She looks like a different person, an actress or a game show presenter, her smile effortless.

Monkey nods at Sroch, alert and suspicious, as if he were a KGB agent on a covert and deadly reconnaissance mission. He wears muted colors, a gray cotton shirt, dark blue pants, and Beluga-caviar-black boots. His head is shaved to the quick, chest square, shoulders wide, cheekbones high, knuckles decorated with white scars, and his eyes are the palest glacier blue.

Sroch imagines seeing the shop with a stranger's eyes: rows of shelves with old-fashioned and ugly shoes that no one wears anymore, a musty and stifling smell, like leather left out in the sun, his mother in the back, looking shabby with her tousled gray hair, his father scratching his scraggly beard, the bald dome of his head bent over the accounts, a stub of a pencil in his mouth—and the high heels above the register, a bizarre homemade shrine.

Shmulik asks how they know his son. He isn't suspicious, just curious. He must be glad that his son finally has friends, even though they look much older.

"We're teachers from Sroch's school," Gecko says. "I'm a drama teacher." She flicks her gorgeous hair back.

"I instruct gymnastics," Monkey deadpans.

Sroch struggles not to laugh, imagining Gecko doing improv classes or Monkey blowing a gym teacher's whistle, asking for three more laps around the schoolyard. Only his father would believe such blatantly made-up identities. They don't look like any teachers Sroch has ever had.

"Would you like to try on shoes?" his father says. "For my son's teachers, we can do a very good price."

"Actually," Gecko says, "Sroch has been telling us about Franceska's heels."

"Oh," Shmulik says. He looks at Sroch quickly, unsure what to make of the interaction. They've never told anyone about Franceska. It's kept within the family. Shmulik smiles at Gecko politely, scratches his beard, and doesn't say anything more.

"Do you think I could try them on?" Gecko says.

"Well, they're very old and delicate," Shmulik says.

"I'll be extra careful."

His father can't say no to anyone. But Sroch can see the pain in his face as he tugs at his beard and sighs. On the one hand, he feels loyal to the long-dead Franceska, to the story of her heels, but on the other hand, here is a living woman, one of his son's teachers, a potential customer, asking to try them on.

"Actually, I don't think it's a good idea," Sroch says.

Gecko looks annoyed but also slightly impressed. With her beautiful smile, she probably isn't used to people saying no to her. A part of him wants Gecko to try on the shoes. If she fits perfectly in them, it has to mean something, but Sroch knows his father doesn't want anyone trying the shoes on—the heels have never come off the shelf. As far as he knows, no one has ever worn them except Franceska. They belong to the dancer. They'll always belong only to her. Sometimes Sroch wishes his father could be tougher. He's too kindhearted and gentle. Sroch looks at the pain in his father's eyes, because he's unable to refuse anyone, so Sroch has to say no for him.

One night they sit in the empty operator's cab of a silver fixed crane in Montefiore, in the center of Tel Aviv, its floor littered with plastic Diet Sprite bottles and Bamba wrappers. Monkey sprawls in the corner, puts on his headphones, closes his eyes, and plays AC/DC's *Back in Black* at full volume, so loud that the reverberations make Sroch's head throb. Gecko's wearing the shortest shorts imaginable, leaving nothing to Sroch's imagination. Her legs are tucked to her chest, ending in ankle-high Blundstone boots. She's drawing little green hearts on the operator's cab walls with a Sharpie.

She leans in close and whispers in his ear, "Do you know the real reason I'm called Gecko?"

She tells him that when she was a little girl, she'd chase geckos around the yard all the time. They'd lie still in the grass, slowing their heartbeat. But she could be still, too. She could be patient. She waited and waited, until the geckos felt secure again and confident enough to leave their hiding place, and then she pounced, grabbing them. They wriggled and squirmed in her hands, detaching their tails and scampering away. She always let them escape, but she kept their tails as souvenirs, tied together with a rubber band, corkscrewed and stiff like Twizzlers.

Sroch sits quietly next to her, his own heart pounding like a frightened gecko in hiding.

She punches his arm. "I'm joking, Mr. Shoelace."

Sroch blushes. Gecko leans her head against his shoulder. He can feel her warm breath in his ear. Her hair tickles his cheek.

"Hey, I want to ask you for a favor," she says.

She wants him to make her a pair of shoes. She doesn't need climbing shoes. She already owns a pair. She wants comfortable ergonomic sandals. Lightweight and supportive. Long and thin—just like you, she adds.

"You could pattern them with a lizard. And I'd think of you whenever I put them on."

The following week Gecko glides into Sandelmann's in flimsy flip-flops, a velvet camisole, and a ruffled pale green miniskirt that shows off her long legs. Not for the first time, Sroch is at a loss for words in her presence, so he fills a cardboard box with cream-colored slurry alginate jelly, to create a mold of her feet. He wants the shoes to be exactly right for her. Gecko sits down on the wooden try-on bench and lifts her skirt slightly, revealing glorious shining legs. She places both her feet inside, shrieking at the shock of cold gelatin against her bare skin, wriggling her toes for a moment like a floundering flatfish before settling under the surface. They wait for the material to harden and solidify, so the imprint will remain fixed. For twenty minutes, Sroch enjoys the company of her bare legs: her pale thighs, the reddish skin of her knees, the tiny stubble of dark hairs on her shins where she neglected to shave.

"We should go climbing, just the two of us, next week," Gecko says.

"Where will Monkey be?"

"He's working. We can go to a crane in Neve Tzedek. Meet me Wednesday night at Suzanne Dellal."

Sroch wonders if Monkey is going to be jealous. It's hard to tell how he feels most of the time. He agrees to meet Gecko and tells her he'll bring her lizard sandals. She claps her hands and kisses him on the cheek. After she leaves, he can still feel her lips there.

Once the mold is complete, he pours plaster casting material into the negative, to make a three-dimensional model of Gecko's feet. The wet plaster dries overnight, after which he covers it with tape, then takes all the measurements down. He sketches a concept on graph paper. He draws several versions of a lizard twisting around the sandals, settling on a design where its tail snakes around to meet its mouth and it eats itself.

Sroch works for hours and hours on Gecko's sandals, with a care and dedication for shoemaking he hasn't known before, and wonders if this is how his father feels every day. He models the design on Tanakhi sandals, famously found in archaeological digs in the ancient fortifications of Masada, with two leather straps across the foot and one around the heel. As he puts the finishing touches on the lizard snaking its way across the sandals, he imagines Gecko hugging him with gratitude, her arms around him, her body pressed against his own, the firmness of her breasts against his chest, the up-and-down of her rib cage with each breath, and her lips, almost imperceptibly soft, tenderly kissing his neck.

At three in the morning on Wednesday, Sroch meets Gecko in Neve Tzedek, outside the Suzanne Dellal Center for Dance. She isn't wearing any makeup except for jade-green mascara. She's fully lizard-like tonight, with an artichoke-colored backpack, skintight lime leather pants, and a crop top, decorated with a sequined praying mantis, that reveals her flat, toned stomach, the diamond glint of her pierced bellybutton. They walk around the deserted neighborhood, with its old pastel-colored buildings, cafés, and wine bars on Shabazi Street, the ice cream parlor with the pale green window frames and huge glass vitrines, where all the colorful flavors are arranged like a collection of rare butterflies. Even though it's the middle of the night, he feels as if they are a couple on a date, on their way to sit at an outdoor patio, under the shade of the city's oldest ficus tree, to share a chocolate mousse garnished with strawberries and the filigree of a golden leaf. They make their way down tiny side streets and alleyways, to the crane, next to the beachfront Panorama Hotel, the salty smell of the sea caught in the breeze, the splash of waves on the cliffs.

Sroch bashfully shows her the plaster mold of her foot and

then, with a small flourish, the sandals he has made. She traces the lizard with her pinky, then, retrieving a Sharpie from her backpack, she draws a green heart on the plaster mold of her foot.

"They're beautiful," she says, shoving the sandals rather roughly into her backpack. "You keep my plaster foot." She turns, looks up at the crane by the vast Panorama Hotel, a beehive structure of little balconies overlooking the dark sea. "Come on, let's go up."

Gecko climbs ahead, quick and steady, finding purchase easily on the rungs of the ladder, just like her namesake, the sticky webbed-foot reptile. Sroch follows more slowly. When he reaches the operator's cab, he pulls himself up to a crouching position, hanging on to the rusted beams, catching his breath and looking out at the sea below, frothing. Gecko, serene and unflustered by the climb, winks at him, then keeps climbing to the apex. She doesn't mention the sandals again, and Sroch wonders if she actually hates them. Maybe she expected more expensive materials or a factory finish.

They reach the tower peak and stand side by side on the steel-trussed beam, looking down at the swelling, rippling waves.

"Have you heard of Silent Disco?" she asks, taking earbuds from her backpack.

"Aren't those Monkey's?" Sroch says.

She shushes him, puts one earbud in her own ear, the other in his. They're connected by a cord, so close he can see the jade-green mascara smudged around her eyes. She's an otherworldly fairy, leading him astray down a dark, swampy forest path, like the ghostly, floating light of a will-o'-the-wisp. He wants to kiss her. He imagines running his hand through her hair.

She puts on a song by Regina Spektor, something sad and acoustic, and starts swaying. "You are my sweetest downfall," Regina Spektor sings.

Sroch grabs the overhead beam, the skyline tilts, he's terrified he's going to slip.

"Hey, you have to move with me, or the headphones are gonna fall."

Sroch starts swaying just as she is. They shuffle their feet awkwardly. She takes his arms and puts them around her bare waist. He can feel her hip bone, the warmth of her skin.

"Now watch my feet."

He mimics her movement, back and forth, back and forth, being careful not to step on her toes. She lifts his chin with one finger. He can't stop looking at the way her mascara has escaped, smudged at the creases of her eyelids. Maybe she applied it in a hurry, or perhaps she just didn't care that much. He wants to wet his finger and fix it.

"What are you staring at?" she says. "Have you never danced with a girl before?"

Dancing with Gecko, Sroch thinks of Franceska. The dancer is wearing her stiletto heels when she works at Adria, Warsaw's most notorious nightclub. She wears an extravagant white fur coat. Her friend, also from the same company, is wearing a black fur coat. With their graceful movements across the dance floor, their fur and pretty blue eyes, they are two Siamese cats. No one dares grab their slim waists, with the owner watching. He's an enormous man at two hundred and three kilos, dressed in a white suit, a red silk flower folded in his lapel, with a forehead as wide and empty as a field of potatoes, fleshy cheeks, and delicate, sensual lips. A pair of golden spectacles hang from a chain around his neck. He's widely known for being able to chug a liter of vodka in one swig, for crushing a man's skull with his bare hands, and for being able to play Chopin's Nocturnes opus 9 on the club's wax-polished Steinway. He's smoking a fat cigar, his pudgy fingers curled around the stem of a martini glass. He could just as easily snap a neck as break the stem of the glass.

Sroch imagines Monkey could do the same to anyone who danced with Gecko. But when Gecko invites him to meet her and Monkey the following week at a crane in Shapira, he promises he's going to be there. On his way back home, Sroch thinks of Gecko up on the crane, of the two of them dancing, held together by the umbilical cord of the earbuds, and how beautiful she looked all in green. He's so happy, he feels like he's floating. Filled with helium, he can't get back down. Stuck in the kingdom of air, up, up, up.

Franceska is at home, standing in front of the mirror in her high heels. Her room is filled with ribbons, medals, and trophies from various competitions. She's used to strangers throwing flowers at her feet. She's met her future husband, the son of a wealthy merchant, a boy with two left feet, kind and handsome, who most importantly loves watching her dance. They attend banquets and society balls at the Savoy, where industrialists and diplomats dance to ragtime jazz. Franceska is young and glamorous, she wants to bite into the world like a ripe peach.

The following week Monkey and Gecko don't show up at the construction site in Shapira as they'd planned. Sroch climbs the crane anyway, intending to wait for them in case they're running late, but they never arrive. It no longer feels the same to be up there by himself, and after a short while, he heads back down and goes home. The following week he returns to the same site, wondering if he got the day mixed up, but they don't show. He misses Gecko. Why would she just abandon him? Maybe Monkey got jealous. Or maybe she never cared about him in the first place. He keeps thinking of the two of them, dancing above the entire world.

In the shop, his father is talking about heels again. He tells Sroch that in English, in America, a *heel* is someone untrustworthy, who treats others badly. Monkey and Gecko are heels, they're also wolves in sheep's clothing. His father is a sheep in sheep's clothing. Your Achilles' heel is your weak spot. His father's Achilles' heel is his kindness and natural good-hearted nature, and maybe Sroch is more similar to him than he wants to admit.

He must look particularly miserable, because his father tells him to smile, that no one will buy shoes from someone who's frowning all the time. He stares at the mold of Gecko's feet, which he keeps hidden in the back, in one of the boxes of spare shoelaces. He shouldn't have made her those shoes. When they leave for the day, his father's hand trembles slightly as he locks the shop. He's getting old. Those tremors have become more and more frequent. "It's caffeine, nothing more," Shmulik says, and refuses to discuss it. He looks old and insubstantial: the bald dome of his head, the dark creases on the back of his neck, the stoop of his back like a question mark.

The next morning they find the store completely trashed. One of the windows is shattered. The latch on the door is broken. Carcasses of shoes are scattered everywhere, entrails of laces and thread in heaps, ripped pieces of leather like scraps of bloody meat. The cash register is untouched. Sroch runs to the back of the shop, almost slipping on an overturned shelf of Teva Naot sandals, to the box of shoelaces where he keeps Gecko's mold cast. Something new is written on the pale plaster, but in the same green Sharpie. MEIR PARK, 20:00.

"Why would someone break in and leave the money?" his father asks.

"Who cares why?" his mother says. "Just be grateful, don't ask questions."

Sroch can feel the betrayal in his stomach. For the first time in his life, he feels vertigo. He has the sensation of falling, falling, falling, and he can't stop. He looks up at the shelf, above the cash register, then catches his father's eye.

"Franceska's heels," Shmulik says. "They're gone."

Ultimately, Franceska is betrayed by her friend, ensnared by an elaborate ruse concocted by German agents and Jewish collaborators. The scheme lured Jews into believing they could purchase fake foreign passports and leave the territories occupied by Nazi Germany. In reality, they were taken on an expensive train straight to the camps and led to their deaths. In her fur coat and high heels, Franceska goes to meet her friend, a fellow dancer, who is also her contact at the Polski Hotel on Dulga Street. Her friend helps supply fake foreign passports for other Jews—she's promised Franceska this will save many lives. Franceska has already secured passports for herself and her husband and her family. If everything works according to plan, they will be starting a new life in Argentina. Franceska's already imagining starting her own ballet school in Buenos Aires. She pictures her students, little girls with ribbons in their hair, standing all in a row, wearing light blue skirts. After class, she will buy them all lemon Popsicles. They will sit in the sun and enjoy the feeling of the ice melting on their tongues.

Monkey and Gecko are easy enough to find. They're waiting for him at the construction site where they first met, in Meir Park. He's early—it's not yet eight o'clock. The shops are all still open on King George Street, bustling with customers carrying shopping bags, the dog walkers are out in the park, there's a long line of people waiting to buy *sabich* on Tchernikhovski Street, and the construction workers have already left the site. He spots Monkey and Gecko sitting at the foot of the crane, smoking. Her bored expression doesn't change when she sees him, but she nudges Monkey, who waves the high heels in the air.

"You can have these high heels back, Shoelace, but only if you catch me."

Monkey stuffs the high heels in his backpack, climbs onto the base of the crane, then starts heading up the rungs, higher and higher, despite the fact that it's still light out, and there are many people around who can easily see him and call the police. He's very quick, almost unnaturally nimble. Sroch watches Monkey scale the crane without stopping, just as if he were running on solid ground, unnerved by how effortless it seems for him. Monkey has said he doesn't take unnecessary risks, but what is this if not an unnecessary risk? Sroch knows he shouldn't follow him. His father wouldn't want him to go up the crane and chase the heels. They aren't worth it. But Sroch can't stop his feet from moving, as if they have a life of their own, separate from his thoughts. He reaches Gecko, who flicks away her cigarette. "So, are you going after him or what?"

But Sroch is already climbing, shooting up the crane in pursuit of Monkey, feeling the city pulsing below through the vibrations in the rungs. Sounds become fainter and more distant, but he can't get Gecko out of his head: dark blue lipstick, smudged eyeshadow, her naked foot wriggling in cold jelly. His hands on her waist, warm skin, hip bone. He can't focus, his grip is slack, sloppy. He stops for a moment and takes a deep breath, but it doesn't help, he's lost all his confidence and struggles with the rungs. Once or twice his feet slip, he's holding on, barely, with the desperate strength of his arms. Sweat runs down his forehead and into his eyes, stinging and blurring. He can hardly see anything, relies on muscle memory. He's terrified, tries not to look down, but when he does, the ground tilts and sways, as if he were the last man on board a doomed ship, in the toothless mouth of a storm, about to be swallowed whole.

The high heels are probably fake, anyway. They never belonged to Franceska, they're just ordinary old shoes. Maybe Sroch has known that all along but never wanted to admit it. The fantasy is just too tempting. There never was any footwear collector named Zalman Lauterpacht, no auction house for stolen Jewish possessions. It's just a story his father made up, because otherwise life in the shoe shop would be too dull and meaningless to bear. His father has been lying to him for years, how can he not have seen it before? It's a ridiculous tale, without a hint of truth. It's the worst betrayal Sroch can imagine.

Together with the wealthiest Jews in Poland, Franceska

boards a real train, gleaming and expensive. This gives the ruse credibility. They aren't stuffed on a cattle train like the rest of the Jews—the men wear their finest suits, the women silk dresses and furs. Franceska wears high heels. Like everyone else, she wants to believe in the promise of a new life far away. The Nazi officers divide the men and women on the train and take them to the showers. Some of the women undress immediately for the promise of a hot shower, while others are more hesitant. When a stooped elderly lady proudly refuses to undress, one of the soldiers slams the butt of his rifle into her delicate rib cage with the sharp snap of metal on bone.

Now Franceska knows this is the end. There is no escape, no dance school in Argentina, there never was. She loops a finger around the mother-of-pearl button of her shirt, flicks it open. She sways her hips, flutters her eyelashes, and gets so close to the officer with the pistol in his holster that she can see the blond hairs on his youthful cheek. The pistol is within reach, so very close. The young Aryan officer is overjoyed at his luck, as the beautiful Jewish ballerina lifts her skirt, stretching her leg skyward, and removes her heel, slowly, pouting. Then with remarkable quickness, she stabs him in the left eye with the tip, the stiletto dagger, puncturing it like a grape. She grabs his pistol and fires two shots into his abdomen, then fires another round, wounding a second officer and causing him to limp for life. The other women take this as a signal to fight back with their bare hands, clawing and scratching at the soldiers, but more officers storm the showers, firing indiscriminately. The women don't stand a chance; not a single one survives. Franceska is killed by a bullet to the temple. The bodies are all carted to the crematorium to be burned.

The story went that Franceska's high heels were confiscated by the soldiers, along with the rest of the Jewish women's valuable possessions—pearl necklaces, fur coats. But now Sroch knows better—the shoes were doubtless incinerated together with her body.

When Sroch finally reaches the top of the mast, his knees are wobbly. He has no sense of how much time it has taken him to get there. His palms are sweaty, he wipes them on his pants. For a moment, everything is blurry. Indistinct shapes blend into one another. Metal beams double and triple, a smear of bright city lights against a dark sky. His ears are ringing. He feels a terrible nausea, his stomach is doing somersaults. When his eyes refocus, he can see Monkey standing on the jib's metal beam, dangling the heels off the edge of the crane. He pretends to almost drop them, then, laughing, sighs in mock relief.

"Do you know that story of the golden slippers?" Monkey says. "It is a Russian Cinderella. Evil stepmother, poor stepdaughter, handsome tsar prince. It is a well-known tale."

"Give them back," Sroch says. His voice sounds weak, whiny.

"What if you plummet?" Monkey says. "It is the common misfortune of night climbers. It won't be just a leg you break."

Sroch feels dizzy, the vertigo makes his entire world spin, his life hangs balanced on a string. The way down is long. One wrong step, one lapse in concentration, one push, and he will tumble down. A gust of wind shakes the crane. A police siren blares in the distance, so far away it could be on a different planet. On this strange moon, people walk on air. They don't feel anything down on Earth, so they climb higher and higher, and now they don't want to go back down. They are stuck between the sky and the earth, unhappy above and miserable below.

Sroch feels the metal beams of the crane lurch beneath his feet. Far below, the city stretches out in every direction, skyscrapers of glass and metal, rows of apartment buildings, the green of parks, the blue of the sea. The luminescent glare of speeding cars whooshing by, one after another, in a steady stream of color. Somewhere, among the bright lights down there, his father is tossing and turning in his bed, thinking of the lost shoes of a doomed dancer.

"If you are a man," Monkey says, "put on your most favorite dancer's shoes. If you walk on this crane with high heels, I shall reinstate them to you. My promise."

Sroch doesn't allow himself to think of anything except what's right in front of him. A metal beam, five centimeters wide. He needs to concentrate now. He takes off one shoe, then the other. He doesn't know if he should wear the heels barefoot or not. His foot is way too big, with or without socks. It won't fit, there's no way. He pushes his foot harder and harder into the shoe, feeling his skin tearing. He manages to fit partly, with his heel still sticking out. He can hardly stand, let alone walk in a straight line eighty meters up in the air. When he tries to stand up on the balls of his feet, he nearly loses his balance but steadies himself. He closes his eyes and thinks of Franceska, anxious and afraid, moments before her last dance begins. The lights come on, the curtains open. The audience is a sea of darkness. He takes a breath and prepares to walk in the air.

Jellyfish in Gaza

W‍e made a deal that every time we had a bad thought about Aba, we went into the water hole. It was a rule that my brother and I created to keep our father safe, while he was in Gaza. If we kept doing the rituals, he would stay alive. The water hole was a well, covered in rusted sheet metal. Aba used to take us there. He was the monster in the well, a creature that lived in the dark, waiting for curious children to fall in. He would submerge himself in the water, lie in wait. We took turns sticking our heads in and shouting, our voices echoing back at us, and then he jumped out and chased us, dripping wet.

Eyal told me he had pictured Aba's uniform buttoned up to the collar. It was a bad omen. Only dead soldiers were buttoned up to the collar. In order to counterbalance the bad thought, he needed to spend one minute in the water hole. The well was deep and narrow, the space just wide enough to fit a grown man. My brother grasped the rim with his thin wrists, hanging like a fish off a hook. He lowered himself slowly into the cold water, arching his back, howling and shivering, blue-lipped. Once he was inside, I pushed the sheet metal shut on him with a clang. "Let me out," he begged. "Please, this was a dumb idea." "Never," I said, and sat on the metal, pressing it down with my weight. I felt his hands clawing from the other side, trying to escape.

My bad thought was ongoing. It never really stopped, but I didn't tell Eyal that, otherwise he would have kept me in the well forever. I saw Aba shot, strangled, stabbed, crushed. Once he even choked on the canned food the army gave out as provisions. When it was my turn to go into the water hole, I couldn't stop thinking of Aba drowning. I closed my eyes. I heard the metal sheet slide shut above me, and I panicked. I pounded the walls, kicked my feet until they slipped on a jagged edge and bled. I was going under, water rushed up my nose, stung my eyes. My fingers grasped for a handhold, clutching at the grooves in the stone. Every time I tried to shout, water filled my mouth. Light came in, and I caught my brother's hand, and he pulled me up out of the hole. I spat and heaved, puking water until I felt empty.

At home, we tallied our cuts and bruises. A bluish-yellow bruise below the right knee. A small cut in the shape of a half-moon above the left eyebrow. Cracked, dry knuckles. Split lip. A hairline fracture of the shin. Two scratches on the left shoulder blade. It didn't matter whose injuries they were. They could have been mine or my brother's. Eyal and I looked very similar. We were fraternal twins. We looked almost the same, except he had a mole on his chin, my eyes were farther apart, his hair was slightly darker, and one of my front teeth was chipped from a fall. We closed our eyes and imagined each other's pain. It was part of our ritual, to lessen Aba's pain.

We lived in Zikim, a kibbutz in the Negev, close to the border with Gaza. Our village grew mangoes and avocadoes. Yellow wildflowers bloomed on the hills. We used to pick the flowers with Aba, rub them all over our bodies, run around and flap our hands, pretending we were yellowhammer birds. Along the sand, houses reared up, as bleached and splintered as fragments of bones. We collected shrapnel from fallen Qassam rockets. Aba drilled holes in the metal pieces and looped lengths of string through them to make necklaces for us.

We shared the same beach with Gaza. Before he left, Aba told us that if we wanted to talk to him, we could just ask the jellyfish to pass on a message. We used our sticks to interrogate them, demanding answers and poking them in their soft bellies. "Tell us where our Aba is!" We didn't know where it hurt the most if you were a jellyfish, since they were soft all over. Maybe they couldn't feel anything. Sometimes the jellyfish were our enemies, other times they were our friends. We jerked them around on sticks, like puppeteers. We made them march across the sand, glide in the air, swim in the sea. We took no prisoners. We whispered our secrets to them and leaned in to hear their answer, knowing they couldn't talk but hoping they would anyway.

When the Code Red sirens blared, we knew rockets were being fired at us. We went to hide in the bomb shelter. We heard the Iron Dome missiles intercept the barrage of rockets. Some of the rockets fell into the sea or destroyed fields and homes. We didn't leave the shelter because the rockets kept coming, filling the air with bursts of smoke and flame. When the sirens stopped ringing, it was safe again. We went out to the beach and stood next to the barbed-wire fence separating our shore from Gaza. Weeping white broom bushes spilled out from the sand. Two palm trees stood tall by the water. Looking out at the border, we heard the *whoosh* of fighter jets streaking across the sky, then the *boom boom boom* of explosions. We saw dark pillars of smoke curling on the horizon. There were no air-raid sirens or bomb shelters in Gaza.

We went to the abandoned Arab villa, alone on the hill, by the entrance to the kibbutz. It was overgrown with cacti, the tousled hair of dry grass, a few red poppies. The villa was made of white stone. The roof was held up by columns and arches, broken in places, showing rusted metal bars. The names and dates of the fallen were carved on the walls. The painted floor tiles had all been stolen. We went inside, tiptoeing over rubble. In our favorite room, the walls used to be blue. We sat on the dusty floor and looked up at the ceiling. We saw Aba in the chipped blue paint, the dark wet stains, and the cracks.

We did most of our rituals in the yard, where Aba used to take us camping. After he left, we refused to sleep in our beds. We set up a tent in the yard. We cast shadow shapes with our hands and a flashlight. We made rabbits run so fast they were a blur, birds fly away into the night, snails crawl across slow and steady, a swan raise its long neck. We opened cans of tuna, as if we were camping out in the desert. We stuck a piece of toilet paper in the tin, lit it on fire, and watched as it burned until all the oil was gone. We slept close together, as if we were one person.

We wore our shrapnel necklaces and ate salted crackers

until our mouths dried and cracked. We were parched, but to drink water was to admit defeat. We tore up grass and stuffed camouflage shirts, hung them up on tree branches, and watched them billow in the wind, assuming the form of hunters. We propped up a pair of military boots by the trunk. We made copies of Aba, wooden soldiers standing in a row. We smashed pomegranates against the tree, watched them shatter like grenades. We dipped our fingers into the juice and pips, painted the soldier's shirt red. Our fingers were sweet, sticky. We licked them clean. Still, he did not return.

The night before he left, we sat on the bed, all four of us. Ima had her arms around Eyal—she was blowing in his ear, trying to make him laugh. I rested my head against Aba's shoulder. Our room was small, with space for a desk on which rested our most recent birthday present, an ant farm. It was a transparent box made of glass, filled with soil and sawdust, through which we could see tunnels and cavities, the pathways of the ants.

"Why do you have to leave?" Eyal asked him.

"See the ant farm?" Aba pointed to the ant farm. "That's why."

He explained to us how Hamas had built tunnels all the way from Gaza into Israel. Some underground passageways led right into people's living rooms. "We could be in the kitchen one day," Aba said, "making eggs for breakfast and suddenly"—he clapped his hands—"gone!"

That night, I dreamed of thousands of ants scurrying into our kitchen from a hidden tunnel. They kept coming and coming, a huge swarm carrying off everything we owned, including pieces of us. Aba's ear floated by, and Ima's nose. A pair of worker ants carried around my thumb, struggling under its weight. They stole all our bodies and grew and grew, until they were regular size, walking among us, looking just like anybody.

The heat turned the grass yellow, and the broken pomegranates rotted in the yard. We decided to bury the remains of the fruit. We dug holes in the earth. At first we made many small ones, as if a giant woodpecker had come and pecked everywhere, without any kind of design. Then we connected the dirt holes to make one big dirt hole, one grave. We threw the pomegranate skins in, one by one, like stars being sucked up by a black hole. Eyal dared me to go into the hole, to lie there on top of them.

I crawled inside. A small rectangle of blue hovered above my head, the earth surrounded me, dark and moist.

"As long as you're down there," Eyal said, "Aba won't be buried alive."

We returned home from camping in the yard, silent and hungry. We found Ima sitting in front of the television. The news was on. Gaza was greener than we expected it to be. There were fields and olive trees. We saw cows and ducks. Rows of houses with several stories, laundry hanging from the line. A moment later everything changed. We saw soldiers blasting walls, armored bulldozers smashing homes. Broken concrete everywhere, orchards dug up, tanks parked in backyards. Sheds taken down, trees uprooted. Rooftop water tanks peppered with bullet holes. Crumbling balconies and toppled mosque minarets. Everything was flattened—the area looked like a massive sandbox. We looked for Aba on the screen, but couldn't find him.

Planes dropped hundreds of thousands of notes, little white paper birds fluttering down from the sky. For a moment, Gaza was a snow globe. The leaflets spiraled in the blue sky, carried by air currents, falling on Beit Lahia and Jabaliya and the al-Shati refugee camp, on dilapidated hospitals and industrial zones and playgrounds, and on the tiny sand-swept fishermen's boats off the coast, as thousands of Palestinians fled their ravaged neighborhoods and homes, driving pickup trucks, riding carts pulled by donkeys, or walking down dusty rubble-strewn roads, mothers with small children crying in their arms, boys and girls carrying mattresses and their belongings in plastic bags, going to shelter at UNRWA schools.

"They're warnings," Ima said, "to leave, to evacuate homes. After the notes come the explosions."

Bright volcanic orange eruptions, huge billowing clouds of thick, black smoke. The buildings were gone. The ones that were still standing looked like scrapyard junk, blasted with huge holes. The ground was littered with fallen debris and twisted metal, fields of craters. When the dust cleared, only rubble and ash remained. The TV showed an old man with a white beard climbing through the rubble, standing on a pile of dusty pale bricks. All around him, the city was destroyed, the sky was smoldering. My heart pounded. I felt my throat closing up. I was back in the water hole, drowning.

And then, in the middle of the destruction of toppled buildings and devastated homes in the Shujaiya neighborhood, I saw a father giving his two daughters a bath. Somehow the bathtub had remained perfectly intact during the bombings, while the entire house around it crumbled, its walls and roof nothing but fallen debris. The two girls were washing in the oval bathtub, dresses clinging to their skin, wet hair soapy with shampoo, laughing, while their father stood over them with a green water-spurting hose, against the backdrop of the skeletal remains of the ruined city.

We cut up blank pieces of paper confetti and rained them down on each other. We burned an offering in the yard, a bundle of wildflowers and dry thorns, bougainvillea and hibiscus petals, onion grass. In the bundle, we put our warnings. We wrote on yellow sticky notes, things that Aba should watch out for: bullets, big knives and small knives, men in large coats hiding suicide vests, land mines, indigestion, tunnels, jellyfish. We lit the warning and watched the smoke curl up and escape, drifting, we hoped, in his direction. When the ashes grew cold, we rubbed them on our faces like war paint, drawing lines along our eyebrows and cheeks, above our lips.

We hid in Aba's closet, touching our noses to his coats and pants, to his boots and sandals, his string of ties hanging like tongues. He was everywhere in the closet with us. When we closed the door and it was dark, we felt him in the rustle of fabric. We found his dark shoe polish and painted our nails, then put our fingers to our nostrils and smelled Aba. We used to play hide-and-seek at home. Both of us would always go into the closet, every time, but he would pretend that to look for us was very hard. When he found us, he would sit down among the coats, in the dark, and tell us a story.

There was one story, about when we were born, that he told again and again. "When you were both babies in the womb together," he said, "you knew everything. You had all the knowledge in the world. You sat in Ima's belly and studied Torah day and night."

"Wasn't it too dark in there to study?" Eyal asked.

"How did the Torah fit in her belly?" I asked.

"You had a flashlight," Aba said. "And she had a big belly. Anyway, you came into this world knowing everything. But before you could speak, an angel came down and touched you here." He put his finger above Eyal's lips, then above mine, right on the indentation that bridged the mouth and the nose. "And you forgot it all."

When Aba returned from Gaza, a month after he left, he looked the same but acted different. He had the same sad, droopy bulldog eyes. He had the same nose, sharp as a cliff face, which arched down to his lips. He came out of the shower bare-chested, with a towel wrapped around his waist, and we saw the same birthmark above his belly button, shaped like an eye. He had the same half finger on his right hand, from the accident in the kibbutz. He even had the same breath in the morning when he shook us awake, like burnt rubber.

On the surface, everything was the same. Except he was different. We wondered if an angel had come to him to make him forget. We tried to test his memory, to ask him things only he would know. Eyal said it was possible that Aba had died and been reborn. If he was reborn knowing everything, then the angel would have had to come and wipe his memory. When he drove us to Ashkelon National Park, to see the oldest dog cemetery in the world, we started asking him all kinds of questions, to test him. We asked him if he remembered what he had done for our third birthday party. He didn't answer. The answer was that he had drawn enormous tigers and elephants, snakes and zebras on the walls of our house. The plan was to break down the walls a month later to renovate, so he convinced Ima to let him transform our home into a painted jungle. We asked him if he remembered how many ants came in the birthday present he had gotten us. We got a note with the purchase telling us the number. He said he didn't know. We also couldn't remember, but it was a bad sign that he had forgotten as well. We asked him if there were really jellyfish in Gaza. He started sweating and thumping the wheel, over and over, his face red. He stopped by the side of the road, breathing hard, his hands clenched on the wheel. He turned back without saying a word.

That night we watched him sleep, because we knew that people said all kinds of true things when they were dreaming that they wouldn't say when awake. We sat and waited on the floor by the door of our parents' bedroom. All we could hear was the hum of the ceiling fan as it spun and then the alarm of a car out on the street. Then Aba started screaming and shaking in bed, the covers pulled all the way to his nose, and Ima was getting up now, too, and holding him. He was too strong for her, but she kept putting her arms around him, wiping away his tears. We had never seen him cry this way before, even when the refrigerator fell on his big toe and it swelled to an enormous size.

"What if it's not him?" I asked. "Someone else could have come in from the tunnel. He could be wearing a disguise."

I imagined Aba peeling off his face, exposing a man with completely different features. The man inside Aba was thinner, with cruel, suspicious eyes. He stepped out of Aba's body, dusted himself off. He rubbed his wrists from where the skinsuit disguise had been pressed tight, and performed a series of stretches, cracking his back and neck. Below his collarbone, he had a tattoo of a large babushka doll, inside of which was another doll, and another, and another, getting smaller and smaller until they were just a dot of ink or a freckle.

We crawled onto Aba's lap, pulled his nostrils wide, and stretched the skin on his cheeks, to check if he was wearing a mask. We pinched his thighs and tickled his feet, to see if he still felt anything. He sat on the sofa, oblivious to our efforts, watching TV and eating sunflower seeds. He split open the seeds in his mouth and spat out the shells into a white bowl. We looked for rips and tears in the disguise, or obvious flaws in the design, like three ears. When we started pulling out the hairs on the top of his feet, to check if they were real, he told us to leave him alone. We sat by his feet. We searched for clues in the scattered shells Aba left in the white bowl. I put one of his discarded shells in my mouth, rolling its sharp edges around my tongue, hoping to find a hidden message from Aba.

"We have to find the tunnel," Eyal said.

We searched the house for any hidden entryways, passages, and trapdoors. We opened cupboards and drawers, checked under the sink and every bed. We ran our hands on the floorboards, making sure there were no surprises. We even tried to peer down the toilet, since that was a possible entry route. It was hard to see clearly, so we poked a stick in to check if the sewage pipe got wider, but the water ended up overflowing, spilling over the rim of the bowl, and splashing our feet. We carried the ant farm outside, picked up pieces of loose gravel, and smashed the glass, watching the insects escape in all directions. We destroyed it just in case the tunnels Aba was talking about were actually in the ant farm.

It was useless—we would never find the tunnel. "He's probably covered his tracks," Eyal said.

When we were younger, Aba taught us about SOS signals. If we ever needed him, he said, we should make a signal. The best signal attracts attention, he explained. Use whatever you can find. The point was to make it big, make it loud, make it bright and strange. You needed aliens and birds to be able to see it from above. He showed us pictures of crop circles and Mayan temples, aerial photographs of coral reefs the size of small towns. It made me sad to see the earth from above, the rows of checkered fields, landmasses, and oceans. We needed to devise our own signal. If he was so far away, this was the only way to bring him back to us. If he saw the signal, wherever he was, he would return home.

We took the trail to the beach, signposted with a marker nailed to an electrical post. *Hatzav* sea squills bloomed everywhere, long stalks of tiny white flowers. Bright dragonflies darted between the tall grass and sand dunes. On the beach we shared with Gaza, hundreds of jellyfish washed up on shore, looking like abandoned plastic bags. We tiptoed between their translucent bodies on the sand, playing hopscotch. We started collecting them, without telling each other our plan. We knew we were making something that would bring our old Aba back. He was going to be reborn, except this time with all his memories.

"I'll stab any angel who tries to make him forget," Eyal said.

We carried the jellyfish off on the tips of our sticks, ripping their soft, translucent flesh, and staked them in our yard, like scarecrows. We made rows of staked jellyfish, one after another, all along the yard. We tied a string of fairy lights around them, making them glow. The yard was filled with their mushroom-like caps, fluorescent bulbs trailing tentacles like strings of pearls. We sat in the yard, among the bright jellyfish, and waited for our SOS signal to work.

Walking Shiv'ah

_____

Never mind, it's good to die for one's country. Previously, when the messenger made the announcements, he attempted to console the grieving families with this line from Trumpeldor, to smile gently and maybe even place a comforting hand on a shoulder. But now he was tired and could not bring himself to say a thing to ease their pain, so he simply stood in silence. He arrived at the Friedman household early in the morning. In front of him stood a beautiful woman wearing men's work clothes, dirtied with plaster stains and paint-splattered. There were various woodworking tools sticking out of her front pocket: chisel, drawing knife, crosscut saw. This was already his fifth death of the day, one of countless deaths during his short-lived career as a messenger during the war, but this was the only time he gave the message to someone with such striking red hair. He handed her a thin manila envelope and watched her mouth move, sounding out the words slowly: _Aleph Friedman killed._

He noticed that her fingernails were bitten raw. Her *falach* peasant hands were rough, coarse, and calloused. He couldn't decipher her expression—she seemed to be confused rather than sorrowful. He paused for a moment and took a deep breath to make sure his voice was not going to break or falter. When he finally spoke, his tone was clipped and unemotional; he prided himself on his strict professionalism.

"That will be fifteen shekels," he said abruptly. "We charge five shekels per word, there are three words in the message, so fifteen shekels in total."

"Ah—"

"Even though *Aleph* is an initial, it counts as a word in this case, yes."

"No, you don't understand." Rachel's head was throbbing. She grabbed hold of the doorframe, to prevent herself from falling over. "Which Aleph Friedman? There are two."

"That's all it says. I have reached the Friedman household, right? This telegram came from the front. Is Aleph Friedman a soldier?"

"My brothers, Aharon and Avraham—they're both soldiers fighting in the war."

The messenger shifted around uncomfortably. "There's no way of knowing which one of them is the Aleph—"

Rachel shook her head. "Either one of them could be dead."

"Go to the Girls' School," said the messenger. "It's been repurposed as an infirmary for the wounded, and that is where they also keep the lists of all the dead. They may be able to help. I'm sorry for the confusion. Still, someone must pay for the telegram."

"We must pay?"

"With the costs of the war being so high, well, yes, you must pay for it."

Rachel paid the messenger and went to her mother, Leah, who was sitting on the sofa in a pale dress staring vaguely at the whitewashed limestone walls. Her mother, paralyzed from the waist down, was eating a persimmon—juice dribbled down her chin, trickled down her neck, dripping onto her lap.

When Leah heard the news, she tore the hem of her dress, covered her face in her wrinkled papyrus hands, and refused to look up. Rachel heard her mother mumbling the words to the blessing of the dead: *Barukh ata Adonai Eloheinu melech ha'olam, dayan ha'emet.* She stroked her mother's head in slow, circular movements.

"But who do we sit shiv'ah for?" Leah said. "Aharon or Avraham? Who do we grieve?"

"I don't know, Ima. The telegram was sent from this address, see? A school. That's where they record the names of the dead. I'm going to go there and find out."

"I'll go with you. Take me there, to the school. I have to know which one of my sons is dead."

"Ima, no, no. I mean, how will you get there? You cannot walk. It will take us at least seven full days on the road. What if it rains? What if the soldiers stop us? It's too dangerous."

"If you die, Racheli, there will be no one to take care of me. So, you will take me, and that is final."

Rachel knew her mother was right. She couldn't in any case leave her on her own in the empty house. With the war going on, who would take care of her? She couldn't get by on her own. If anything happened to her on the way to the school, if she was delayed by soldiers or trapped behind blocked roads, hit by mortar shells, caught in a rainstorm or burst of hail, or even if she tripped and fell into a ditch and broke her legs, then she would be powerless, just like her mother—no help at all. Then her mother would be left all alone. Rachel couldn't bear thinking of her mother by herself, waiting for her uselessly, unable to move, staring at the wall, the persimmon juice sticking to her face, her body slowly rotting like an overripe fruit.

Rachel had been working on a contraption to transport her mother for the past several months, ever since her brothers left for the war. With just the two of them in the house, her brothers away fighting and her father long dead, she struggled to take care of her mother in the daily routines of life. Usually, Aharon or Avraham would lift her easily and carry her around the house. She ordered them around all the time. *Take me to the kitchen—no, wait, I forgot my comb in the bedroom. Actually, I would like to lie down on the sofa, but I need my cream, it's by the sink, next to the powders and Nabulsi soap.* On and on, all day long, it was exhausting. But with her brothers away, her mother was too heavy to carry around all the time, and so Rachel had begun working on the makeshift cart.

Now she was hurrying to finish it. As a base, she had used an old wheelbarrow, a steel rod, and bicycle wheels. She refashioned the barrow seat as a box with three sides, to which she fastened two long handles. She lined the seat for comfort, with a padding of leftover garments scavenged from the *shuk* and the trash heap, woolen blankets, and feathers from her bedside pillow. She worked all day and all night, hardly stopping to rest or eat, but she enjoyed the physical work. She no longer had the soft girlish hands of her youth, but she didn't mind. The homemade rickshaw cart was relatively comfortable, she thought, it

was balanced, and the wheels turned smoothly. When the contraption was complete, she was proud of what she had built.

Rachel packed a jug of water, a loaf of bread, jars of walnuts and cashews, and an assortment of dried fruit—her favorite was the leathery *mishmish* apricot. If the journey was
long, they would have to find food on the way. Perhaps they
could stop at the *shuk* for supplies. She packed a knife,
wrapped in cloth, and a pistol without any bullets for deterrence in case of emergencies. She put the pistol under the cushion for safekeeping and wrapped a scarf around her curly red
hair. She was used to the attention of men and wanted to avoid
it, if possible.

They left very early in the morning when it was dark out
and the neighbors were all still asleep. The narrow, cobblestoned alleyways were mostly deserted. A banner tied between
two palm trees read, YOUTH OF TODAY, THE NATION CALLS
YOU! Vendors from the *shuk* were setting out their wares:
crates of rotten pears, sacks of flour, and an emaciated goat
tied with a rope. An old man opened a large case, upon which
rows and rows of eyeballs were pinned like jewels. Each eyeball
was of a distinct hue; dozens of shades of blue, green, and
brown stared back at her. Many men had lost their eyes during
the war, she had heard, and it was a common practice to sub-
stitute a real eye with a fake one. A sign next to the eyes read
HAND-PAINTED. Rachel pulled her mother along the stalls,
and the rough-hewn men, sipping their coffee, hardly gave her
a second glance.

Rachel went to the vegetable stand, to the vendor with a
crescent moon tattooed on his knuckles and long white scars
running down his arms. She imagined those arms around her

neck if she got caught stealing, a cucumber slipping from her limp hand, and swallowed nervously. The vendor watched her absentmindedly, counting yesterday's change. He started flicking the coins, one by one, into a little pile and muttering under his breath, *Eser, esrim, shloshim, arbaim*. Rachel wheeled her mother right up against the stand and took off her scarf, smiling shyly at the vendor, noticing how his eyes changed once he got a good look at her, his voice rough and sweet as prickly pear. With practiced ease, she asked him about his produce: where he acquired his potatoes and eggplants, how fresh were the carrots and celery stalks, how was business during the war.

Her mother, with the most innocent expression on her face, pocketed a kohlrabi, completely unnoticed. Once they were out of sight, Rachel halved the kohlrabi, after peeling it with the knife, and handed a piece to her mother to chew on.

"Avraham always cuts the kohlrabi into small pieces for me, then dips them in lemon juice," Leah said.

Rachel tried not to scowl as she told her they didn't have any lemon juice. Once they crossed the market, she rested for a moment, because her shoulders and back ached, and the palms of her hands were already developing blisters. She spat on the palm of her left hand and rubbed it together with her right. Her wounds stung, as if, she wryly observed to herself, she had squeezed a lemon's juice over them.

They made their way along the city walls, overlooking the sea, where the air was cool and salty, which revived her slightly. She heard the waves crashing against the rocky boulders below, splashing white foam, like the saliva of a rabid beast. They stopped by the side of the wall, next to a pair of low bushes, because her mother needed to relieve herself. She lifted her from the cart, clutching her under her arms, and held her dress up, exposing thin veiny thighs.

"Hold me steady," Leah said. "You're too weak. Your brothers would have no problem."

Rachel heard a steady trickling sound; a pool of piss gathered at their feet, wetting her sandals. Rachel remembered how Aharon had once challenged her to a pissing contest when they were children. For the first time in her life, she'd been jealous of what was between her brother's legs. Aharon went first, of course, pulling out his pale penis, which made her shriek in fear and delight. He released a stream of urine that arced into the noonday sunlight, and the dry earth was stained dark and wet. Avraham, who was younger and of smaller stature and followed his brother around dutifully at that age, rose to the challenge eagerly. He could not reach as far as his brother with his modest stream, and she watched as his face reddened, heard the pitter-patter of the last drops as he shook himself and pulled up his pants. Rachel knew she could not compete with them at all, and she ran away, hiding her warm tears.

A group of young boys, dirty and barefoot, started jeering and making faces at Rachel and Ima, miming obscenities, sticking out their tongues and shoving their hands into their pants. They followed them around incessantly, peppering her mother with a stream of questions. "Were you born that way? Do you like being carried around? Are you a queen? Can I ride in your carriage? Do you have any money?" Leah reached under the folds of her blanket and brought out a loaf of bread, which they had been saving for dinner, and tore out small chunks with her hands and handed them around to the boys.

They whooped and cheered, pulling the cart eagerly. They even fought over who got to pull. The cart went fast, with a dozen young hands pulling. Ima laughed, holding on to the edge of the cart, and Rachel felt herself relax slightly. She let the boys do some of the work, since her muscles were so sore, and it was a relief to take a break for a while. She walked a little behind the cart, unable to keep pace with the frenzied boys. Her mother looked cheerful, surrounded by children, her hair was caught in the breeze, and Rachel could see her as she used to be, carefree.

Leah remembered what it was like to be able to walk around, to feel the earth under her feet, to wade in tall grass and yellow mustard flowers up to her knees, to swim in the river, the current dragging her dress across the smooth pebbles, the tiny fish darting here and there, nibbling on the dry skin of her toes. On the day she lost the ability to move, her younger son, Avraham, was beside her. They had gone to pick the hazelnuts that grew on cliffside bushes by their home. The drop was lethal, and the only thing standing between them and almost certain death were a pair of harness ropes tethered with a stake to the granite. It was Avraham's turn to watch the ropes, while she made her way down to pick the low hanging hazelnuts. Usually, he didn't let her do this part, because it was so dangerous, but she insisted. What had distracted him? It didn't matter. All she remembered was that one moment she was fumbling around in a mess of catkin flowers and fuzzy leaves, reaching for a branch of hazelnuts, and the next she was falling. He never left her side after that, not until the war. Avraham was her favorite son, she knew that, even though she would never say so aloud.

The boys stopped pulling abruptly and lifted the cart to stop it from moving, making the wheels spin uselessly in the air. One of the boys, with a splotch of dark purple birthmark on his neck, said they would not go any farther than the animal market that led to the tower. He was slightly taller than the rest and looked older. He was the leader of the small gang of boys.

"There's a sniper in the tower," he said. "Don't go there."

"Maybe we should go a different way, Ima."

"No," Leah said. "To find your brothers, we need to go past the tower."

"We must," Rachel told the boy. "The main road is patrolled by armed men. We can't go through the beach, either. I won't be able to pull this cart in the sand. The unmarked fields are too dangerous."

"You're slow," the boy said. "An easy target. The man in the tower has been picking people off like flies. He shoots anyone who goes by."

"We have no choice."

"Go after dark, then."

Rachel and her mother waited by the side of the road until night fell, watching as the limestone houses, broken in places by mortar shells, grew darker and darker, more indistinguishable, like peculiar deep-sea creatures lurking in shadowy corners. The sea, from above, appeared as a flat aluminum sheet. Every so often, dark water lapped the shore in black crescent waves. Then the wind picked up, blowing hard suddenly, and the agitated sea roared to life. They had to hurry to make their way past the tower. It would be their only chance, now that the streets were completely dark. Rachel hid Leah under a large tarp, and this made her think of the ritual of covering mirrors in the home of a mourner when sitting shiv'ah. If they had been sitting shiv'ah now at home for one of her brothers, they would have been covering all the mirrors.

"Can you breathe under there, Ima?" Rachel said. "Try not to move too much, or you will draw attention to yourself."

They made their way toward the tower, Rachel pulling the cart slowly, bowing her head and praying silently under her breath, *Please, please, let us pass, don't shoot down a woman wheeling her cart.* The wheels made squeaking noises as they turned, and she could hear her mother breathing loudly, and she was sure they would be discovered any moment. With every breath, the wooden base creaked. Then the wheels got stuck—they must have hit something. Rachel paused and stared at the ground, trying to decipher the obstacle, its large, fleshy proportions, in the dark. She squinted and bent over to peer at the thing. It looked like a body, but not a human one. A dead donkey, with a wreath of buzzing flies. She pulled the cart around it, trying to breathe through her mouth so as not to smell the carcass, gagging slightly as the stench penetrated her nostrils anyway.

Sewage ran through the street, dirtying her dress. They were close to the animal market, approaching the tower, and chicken feathers floated in the air, sticking to her sweaty face. Rusted metal beams were scattered around. She tripped on one, making a clattering sound. It cut her ankle. She bit her lower lip to stop herself from making a sound, as the warm blood dripped down to her foot.

Movement just to her left, sharp and sudden. A figure in the darkness. A man, carrying a sack slung across his shoulder, was running with long strides, his body leaning forward, like a desert predator. He barely made a sound. He made it to the tower, and she could see his figure lit up against the stone by a spotlight, the shine of his head and even the heaving of his rib cage underneath his sweat-soaked shirt. He ran past the tower now. He was going to make it. No sign of a sniper. Rachel breathed a sigh of relief. But then the man tripped, fell, and dropped the sack. Heads of lettuce scattered all around him, one rolling all the way to Rachel's feet. He stood up again but was unsure what to do. A shot rang out, and the man dropped to the ground immediately.

Rachel stayed absolutely still. The man was facedown in the mud. A spasm of movement made his legs jerk, and then he was still. She retreated slowly. In the cart, under the layers of blankets, her mother was shaking, but she didn't make a sound. Rachel put her hand on the moving pile of blankets. She felt around, until she grasped her mother's hand; she squeezed it, and the hand squeezed back.

"We'll sleep on the beach tonight," Rachel whispered. "Everything will be okay."

Lightning erupted, electric violet in the black sky. In the distance, Rachel saw the tower, illuminated suddenly. A low gathering rumble, then the sharp crack of thunder. Five large stone steps led down from the wall to the beach. At each step, Rachel had to lower the cart, and the going was torturous. Her mother complained that the bumps were hurting her back, and they argued over whose back hurt more, until they were both too sore to speak. When they finally went down the last step, Rachel was exhausted.

They started making their way on the beach, looking for a

sheltered place to set up their blankets to protect themselves from the night's cold wind and the unbearable sun in the morning. At first, it felt only slightly more difficult to move around in the sand, yet steadily the wheels turned slower and slower, until they stopped completely. Rachel tried to pull and pull, but they would not budge in the sand. She tried pushing from the back, hit the cart in frustration, and sighed. Another dead end. They had hardly made any progress toward the school; it was still a few days' walking distance.

"I guess we'll sleep here," Rachel said.

Rachel lifted her mother from the cart and laid her down on the sand. The wind was strong by the sea, and Rachel made sure her mother was tucked under the blankets. They slept close together for warmth.

Leah woke up from the glare of the sun. Her mouth tasted of sand. She looked at Rachel, inspecting her as if for the first time. Lying next to her daughter, she realized how extremely different they were. Rachel's long arms were like date honey in the sun, and her hair was the color of a ripe pomegranate, tumbling down her back. Leah looked down at herself—the skin on her arms hung in dry folds, like forgotten laundry on the line. Her thighs, unused for so long, had dwindled to nothing. She felt trapped inside a broken old body. She looked down at the sea, knowing that even though it was only a few meters away, she could not go there on her own. She could crawl, but Rachel would wake up if she did. All she could do was sit there, as if she were already taking part in an endless shiv'ah, for herself. She would never tell her daughter any of this. She closed her eyes, feeling the breeze against her face, and thought of her two sons, how she wished it had been her daughter who had been killed instead of one of them.

Rachel stirred, yawned, sat up, and looked over at her mother, who was staring out at the bright water, a strange expression on her face as if she were remembering something painful. The cart was still beside them. Rachel looked up at the five steps she'd descended, which she knew she had to now ascend. They had to go back up—there was no other way. Two fishermen, with faces like gnarled driftwood, walked past them carrying a bucket with wriggling fish, splashing in crimson-tainted water. They had already started their working day, oblivious to the war, following only the tides of the sea. The fish were still in the sea, people must still eat. There was also an octopus in the bucket, even though it was forbidden to eat by kosher law. One of the fishermen was descaling a fish, his knife glinting in the morning sun. His expression was tender as he attended to the body of the fish, like a member of the sacred burial society *chevra kadisha* who treated the corpses of the dead, cleansing them of dirt, immersing them in the ritual waters of the *tahara*, and wrapping them in white muslin shrouds.

Her older brother, Aharon, made friends with all the fishermen, sailors, and dockworkers in town. She thought of how he enjoyed accompanying them on their tasks, listening to their stories, and even absorbing some of the peculiarities of their speech, the little inflections of rough, drunk men. He knew all about their trade: what kind of bait to use, what rods were best, and how to scale a fish and prepare it for the grill. Aharon had a way of making anyone want to talk to him, to tell him their life story. He knew how many children each sailor had, and at which port they had lovers and mistresses, and what they enjoyed in bed, specifically the feel of a tongue on their bare toes, a nibble on an earlobe, and the kinds of sea glass they collected for their children to make bracelets. He would come home late at night, sometimes drunk, and tell Rachel their stories. She made him promise that he would write them all down one day, maybe make a book out of them, but he never did.

Several warships dotted the horizon in the early morning hours, and the line was so thin between sea and sky that they seemed to be floating in the air. Rachel began to climb, pulling the cart with her mother, one step at a time, sweating so much that her vision was blurred, and she could hardly see where she was going. At the top, she rested by a row of cacti. They were headed to the main road, which would no doubt be patrolled by armed men. They walked along the deserted highway, where, strewn around, were empty orange crates bearing the words JAFFA SPHINX ORANGES and IMPORTÉ DE PALES-TINE in bold letters, with a drawing of the pyramids. A convoy of military vehicles drove by in a long column like a colony of ants. A truck carrying supplies tipped over and blocked the road, and the drivers started shouting at each other, pushing and cursing. Rachel pulled the cart over to the tall grass by the roadside, and they were able to pass unnoticed by the men.

They'd been walking for no more than an hour when they spotted two men at a makeshift checkpoint that blocked the road with pieces of rubble. The men were brewing coffee over a camp stove, guns slung across their chests. Rachel stopped the cart.

"Where are you going?" asked one of the men.

"To see my brother."

"Do you have a permit to cross?"

"What permit?" Leah shouted from the back of the wheel-barrow. "She needs a permit to take her mother on a walk?"

"We are at war. Of course you need a permit, *zkena*. Go back to where you came from."

The men's blank expressions didn't waver, and it would be useless to try to argue with them, Rachel thought. The smell of their coffee, bitter and burnt, stung her nostrils. She turned the cart around and started walking, her steps heavy and her jaw clenched. The only other way was through the open countryside, on unmarked paths. The fields were dangerous. Outlaws and thieves roamed around and looked for easy prey. They reached a crossing, from which one road would take them back home, through the alleyways along the coast, and another would take them to the fields and eventually the school.

"Rachel," Leah said, "be brave. We need to know. We cannot go back."

They went in the direction of the fields, where the tall grass provided some cover. Yet Rachel could feel eyes watching them as they made their way through the unmarked land. She kept staring straight ahead, shuddering as blackbirds cawed on the skeletal trees, her spine tingling with all the strange eyes on her. Her mother answered the birds in a high-pitched voice. Every blade of grass against Rachel's thin dress felt like an unwanted hand. She heard the whisper of fallen leaves and the branches shuddering in the wind. It was so dark now that she could barely see her hands in front of her face. She stumbled with the cart over thick, sprawling roots.

By the time she saw the three men, it was too late, they were too close. They were dressed as farmers. They hung back slightly. It must have been a strange sight: a weary, young woman pulling a cart with an old crone inside. Rachel pulled the cart ahead, but they kept a steady pace behind them.

Finally, she stopped. "We have nothing for you to steal," she said.

She heard laughter. The men approached unhurriedly, swinging their arms, chests puffed out, shoulders wide.

"We don't want to steal from you," said one of the men in a deep growl, walking toward her. His movement was graceful and predatory, a natural hunter stalking his prey, with a disarming smile on his face, the glint of teeth. He looked strong from many moons spent working outside, and his hands were big. His pale, hungry eyes and dark beard reminded her of a wolf.

"Then what do you want?"

"To help you," said the Wolf.

"Who asked for your help, fool?" Leah said.

Rachel hushed her.

"What a big mouth you have, Grandma," the Wolf said, spitting out a wad of chewing tobacco.

"You don't know these men," Leah whispered.

"Maybe they can help. Ima, I don't want you to sleep outside tonight." Turning to the Wolf, she said, "Is there any place where we could stay for the night?"

The Wolf and the other two men led Rachel and her mother to a greenhouse, which looked abandoned, overrun with creeping vines. Inside there were slats of broken wood and scattered rubble, dead plants in ceramic pots with dry soil, and through

the gaps and holes in the shattered windows, held together between greenish-rusted steel beams, wild plants grew, threading
their way inside, like eager uninvited guests. The vines twisted
and curled on the broken beams and traveled up to the ceiling,
most of the leaves crumpled and torn, yet somehow, here and
there, amid the decay and rot, grew delicate purple wisteria,
hanging like bells.

The Wolf helped her with the cart, while the other two men
slid the door shut with a loud metal clang. The sound echoed
in the empty chamber, reminding Rachel just how alone and
exposed they were. There was no sign of a bed, nor any kind
of mattress or cushions, nothing but the hard floor. The broken glass panes let in the cold air, and Rachel shivered.

"Where will we sleep? My mother is tired, and so am I."

"Why don't you pick some flowers for Grandma?" the Wolf
chuckled. "You will sleep soon enough."

The men went to the corner of the greenhouse, clearing
away space, kicking aside the crawling vines and dry twigs,
and began preparing a meal over a portable cooking stove, ignoring her question. A cold gust of wind burst through the
broken ceiling, blowing away Rachel's scarf. Her long red hair
fell down her back. The men stopped peeling potatoes and
stared at her. She retied the scarf quickly, hiding her hair.

A light rain started, so the men moved the cooking stove
away from the exposed area, and they ate in silence, each alone
with their thoughts. The meal was made up of hard, boiled
potatoes that were tough to chew and made Rachel's mouth
ache with the effort. Her mother kept looking suspiciously at
the men, but Rachel managed to coax her into having half a
boiled potato. After they ate, the only sound was the Wolf's

disgusting spitting of tobacco every once in a while. She made sure her mother was comfortable in the cart, wrapping her up in all their blankets and watching her until she fell asleep. Rachel almost never went to sleep with a scarf still wrapped around her head, but she was wary of taking it off here.

She lay down on the floor. Her body ached—all she wanted was to rest. She took one last look at the men, who were sitting in the corner, then turned her back to them and closed her eyes. Moments later she felt a large, rough hand on her shoulder. The Wolf crouched over her.

"Now we'd like our payment," he said, and his grip tightened, digging into her flesh.

"What do you mean? We have nothing. My mother and I, we've brought nothing with us, no money—"

"I'm not talking about money."

"No," she said.

"You misunderstand me," said the Wolf. He chuckled. "I just want to see your hair. Take off that scarf."

Rachel untied her scarf. Her long red curls tumbled down. "There. Now I would like to go to sleep."

"Hold on," the Wolf said. "Let me feel your hair."

"No," Rachel said, standing up. "We're leaving. Ima!"

"Wait, wait. Don't wake Grandma up," the Wolf said. "She needs her rest."

The Wolf reached out his hand and stroked her hair. Rachel flinched. She picked up the scarf and tied it back over her hair.

The Wolf tore it from her head. "Now take off your dress," he said.

The Wolf's hands were rough and excited, clawing at the

straps on her shoulders, digging at her skin. She pushed him away, but he advanced, knocking over a potted plant, which shattered. Her mother woke up in her seat, confused and sleepy, calling for Rachel in a panic. The Wolf grabbed Rachel's dress and tried to pull it over her head, but they got wrapped up in the fabric as she struggled. The Wolf managed to take off her dress, leaving her standing in front of him in her underclothes, her skin covered in goose bumps.

The other two men advanced slowly, watching, waiting for their turn. The Wolf lunged toward her, and she knocked his hand away, but he reached again, roughly snapping the clasp of her brassiere with his hands, but it held. He grasped her waist, and she kicked him, screaming. The other two men laughed like hyenas. Rachel backed away, stepping on a shard of pottery. She picked up the jagged piece and swung it at the Wolf, leaving a jagged red line on his cheek. He grabbed her wrist, sharply pulled her toward him. His cheek was covered in blood from the cut, and his chest smelled of sweat and the sour, earthy scent of boiled potatoes. He turned her around, away from him, pushed her face down, and tugged at her hair.

"Get away from her, animal, *ya kelev!*"

Rachel turned to see her tiny mother sitting up in the cart, propped up by the cushion, with the pistol in her hand. She was breathing hard, and her eyes looked slightly crazed and out of focus.

The Wolf laughed, let go of Rachel, raised his hands in the air, and took a step toward her mother. "Come on, Grandma, no harm done. We were just having a little fun."

Her mother cocked the pistol. The men froze, their smiles gone. They started backing away, never taking their eyes off the pistol. The Wolf told her that she'd regret this. It was going to be way worse now. They would use Rachel, again and again, until she was raw. They would cut off her breasts and feed them to their dogs. When they were finished with her, they would make their dogs mount her.

"Get out," Leah said. "I'm not afraid to shoot all of you."

The Wolf backed away as he cursed her, disappearing into the night. Rachel shut the greenhouse door and dressed quickly, her cheeks and ears hot. She didn't look at her mother, she couldn't bear to.

"It doesn't even have any bullets," Leah whispered. "It's empty."

"We can't stay here tonight," Rachel said. "They may come back."

They set up camp in a field, under a large ficus tree. Rachel lifted her mother from the cart and rested her on the ground, covering her in blankets. She heard dogs howling in the distance, and the wind blew the rain sideways. Her dress was torn, and the blankets were soaked through. Rachel couldn't sleep. Her throat hurt, her body was bruised, and the palms of her hands were covered in blisters. Her mother's eyes were wide open, and her teeth chattered.

"I just thought we would get a good night's sleep," Rachel said. "Now we're out in the rain. The blankets are wet. And those men—"

Her mother's hand reached for her, cold against her wet face. She touched her fingers to Rachel's eyelids, to the tip of her nose, and finally to her lips.

Rachel shrugged Leah's hand away. "He wanted my hair. They were going to do things to me."

Her mother hushed her. "I know. I know."

"I want to get rid of my hair," Rachel said.

"You're strong. Stronger than your brothers. And so much more beautiful than your mother has ever been. Keep your hair, like the hero Samson."

"No. Cut it for me. Use the knife."

Her mother cast her eyes down. She clutched Rachel's long red locks in one hand and the knife in the other, tugging at her hair as she cut it, letting it fall in clumps all around them. Rachel's scalp was burning. She ran her hands over her scalp and felt her hair, short and uneven, like moss on a boulder. Her mother put her hand on Rachel's head, making circular motions. Rachel turned her back to her mother, pretending to be asleep, but her jaw was clenched, tears flowed down her face.

Watching her daughter sleep, Leah thought of the day the war broke out, and how she had had to cut both of her sons' hair, to shave it all off, each of them in turn, in preparation for their army service. She had spread old newspapers out on the kitchen floor and made them sit side by side as she snipped and snapped, watching their curls, red just like Rachel's, tumble to the ground, covering up the words in the articles, which she could neither read nor understand. She remembered one of the pictures in the newspaper the day she cut off their hair, it was of a felled tree, taller and thicker than any she had seen before. It had been blasted by explosives to clear a path for a wide road. Now she imagined Rachel's red curls instead on the bed of newspapers, like fallen red anemone flowers, and she wished she could have sent her daughter to war instead of her sons. Leah pictured her fierce daughter fighting the nation's enemies on the front lines, while her two sons stayed home taking care of her, drawing lavender-scented baths, cooking stews of cabbage, lentils, and spinach, and filling the house with their vitality and careless love.

For days, they walked through the fields. On the seventh day of their journey, broken-down homes began to appear. It was morning, and Rachel pulled the cart slowly, stumbling forward, her dress now covered with dirt. Her feet ached. Sometimes she stopped the cart to run her fingers through her short hair, scratch her tender, itchy scalp. The whitewashed houses around her were riddled with holes, and their roofs were caving in, exposing the steel framework. The air was filled with dust, and Leah began to cough. The skeletal husk of an abandoned bus lay by the side of the road, sniffed at by stray dogs. A large mutt with light blue eyes, its fur sticky with blood, walked alongside the cart, circling them warily and whining softly. Rachel shooed it away. She heard the thundering sound of an engine overhead and quickly pulled the cart to the side of the abandoned bus and crouched, hidden, as a propeller warplane flew by. They walked along a promenade where the trees had all been uprooted, their trunks severed into smaller pieces, probably to be used for firewood. Small, inedible fruits and pigeon droppings littered the ground.

If her mother ever asked her, she would deny having any preference, but Rachel knew in her heart that she loved her older brother Aharon more than she loved young Avraham. Aharon was the one who encouraged Rachel to work with her hands, who did not make her feel strange when she showed him what she had carved and crafted. He defended her from the meaner young women in the neighborhood, who whispered and giggled whenever she was around. They were all in love with Aharon, of course, because he was handsome and kind, but he didn't pay them any attention at all. Before the war, they spent many afternoons together tinkering with wood. She would carve little boats and tiny wooden whales for Aharon, and he would make up stories of shipwrecks and sea monsters. He could imitate the sound of the rushing fountain of air spouting out of a baleen whale's blowhole, and the clicking and whistling of bottlenose dolphins. His favorite deep-sea impersonation was the haunting, eerie songs of the humpback whales, whom he called underwater composers. He'd joke that a humpback whale would make the best cantor, leading the synagogue in songful prayer.

She smelled it before she saw it. In front of them, a man was pulling a cart with a body. She could see men pulling more carts, dozens of them, all wheeling the dead. They were dumping the bodies into a large mass grave, and the earth was buzzing with flies. The men with the carts waved their arms, swatting away scavenger birds picking at the bodies. A bonfire raged next to the mass grave, where the clothes of the dead were being burned. It was not allowed, to burn bodies. But Rachel had a strong sudden urge to push the cart with her mother into the flames or to jump in herself, to end this senseless journey. They continued down the promenade, heading toward a rundown building at the far end, surrounded by fencing. They had reached it at last—the Girls' School.

The facade of the repurposed school building had been painted a pale green color. The tall windows in front of the fenced-in garden were barricaded with strips of plywood. Framed photographs hung along the walls, of young girls in uniform, with pigtails and skirts and stockings, hands clasped behind their backs. Some of the photographs looked very old, and the faces of several girls were blurred, their features marred and indistinguishable. Rachel pulled her mother along the empty corridor, heard the moaning of the wounded coming from behind closed doors, faint and desperate. She wandered past a portrait of the remarkably handsome Joseph Trumpeldor, the one-armed Zionist hero. Underneath the painting was his famous quote, his last words, spoken when he lay mortally wounded in the battle of Tel-Hai: *Never mind, it's good to die for one's country.*

They reached a reception area at the end of the hallway. The only source of light was a naked bulb in the ceiling that flickered on and off, on and off, illuminating a tall man in wire-rimmed glasses who sat cramped behind a desk meant for a schoolchild. The desk was heaped with papers and folders, the lists of the dead. Rachel dragged her feet as she wheeled the cart toward him, her face burned red in embarrassment. She licked her dry lips.

"No vehicles allowed inside," the clerk said.

"This is not a vehicle. It's for my mother. She's crippled," Rachel said bitterly. "We must consult your records. We're looking for Aleph Friedman."

"First name?" The clerk positioned his glasses on the edge of his nose.

"Aleph."

"That is not a name, it's an initial."

"That is all we know."

"You don't know the person's name?"

"We do not know for sure."

"Why did you come here if you don't know for sure?"

"Listen, we have come from far away," Rachel said. "My brothers, Avraham and Aharon Friedman, both share that same initial, Aleph, and they share the same family name, Friedman. We received a telegram informing us that Aleph Friedman had been killed, but we don't know which one of them the letter meant. We were told to come here."

The clerk looked at them. The young woman with the short, messy red hair might have been beautiful once but looked tired and worn beyond her years, and next to her, a tiny woman with a shriveled prune face was sitting in some kind of makeshift cart that looked like it might fall apart at any moment. Their torn clothes suggested they were in mourning, but they could have just gotten into trouble—this area was not safe anymore. They were certainly not the first to come asking about their loved ones, nor would they be the last.

"Hold on," he sighed.

He looked through a thick folder, stacked with papers, on his small desk, rifling through each sheet, where lists of names and dates were printed in dark ink. Rachel watched him go through the lists slowly, as if he were memorizing each and every name, and she wanted to shout at him to hurry up but restrained herself. His finger hovered for a moment, caught in the act of pointing.

"There seems to be some mistake," said the clerk.

Rachel felt her knees start to buckle, she just wanted to lie down and sleep.

Leah looked up hopefully at the gaunt man in spectacles. A mistake? Maybe Avraham and Aharon had come home by now, she thought, only to find them gone. They must hurry back to catch them. She could make their favorite meal. Borscht with a dollop of *smetana* sour cream, or maybe goulash, with tender meat, roasted garlic, caraway seeds, and red wine if she could find it. Of course, meat would be hard to come by now, so she would have to bribe the butcher with a fine fabric for his wife. Maybe she would give him Rachel's scarf.

"There are two Aleph Friedmans listed here," the clerk said.

"Two? How is that possible?" Rachel said.

"Maybe you cannot read," Leah said. "Give it to my daughter. She can read."

"I assure you, *giveret*, I can read," said the clerk.

"You must be wrong," Rachel said. "This can't be."

"What kind of a system are you running here?" Leah said. "Making errors about the dead. You should be ashamed of yourself."

Rachel swallowed the lump in her throat.

The clerk was sweating heavily. He wiped his forehead with the sleeve of his shirt. "I am sorry, but I'm certain this is not a mistake. I remember it very clearly now—I thought it was odd receiving the same name, one day after another. But look, the dates are different. These are two different people listed here, but with the same name."

There was a heavy silence.

"So, what if the dates are different?" Leah said. "You made two mistakes then!"

"These are two different people, your sons, your brothers," said the clerk. "Avraham and Aharon, right?"

"Don't say their names!" Leah says. "No, no, you've made a mistake. And you cannot say their names!"

Rachel put her hand on her mother's shoulder. It was bony and frail, like the wing of a small bird.

"No, no mistake," said the clerk. "No mistake," he repeated. "I made no mistake."

"So, they are both dead?" Rachel asked. "Is that what you're saying?"

The clerk nodded, breathing out shakily. His hands were trembling on the desk so much that he hid them under his folder.

Leah appeared lost, as if she had forgotten where they were, looking around at the clerk, then at Rachel. She seemed not to recognize anyone.

"I would like a bath," Leah said. "Can you run the water?"

The clerk coughed nervously.

"Ima," Rachel said quietly, "I'll give you a bath later."

Leah shook her head. "Avraham can give me a bath. He always makes sure to check that the water is not too hot. When Avraham was small, I used to give him baths. He always stayed in for too long. His fingers would become wrinkled like a frog."

"Avraham isn't here to give you a bath," Rachel said.

"Do you know my sons, Avraham and Aharon?" Leah asked the clerk.

"He doesn't know them, Ima," Rachel said.

"How do you know? We need to go," her mother said. "Come on. Wheel me out of here."

"Where? Where do we need to go?"

"We must look for them," her mother said.

"There's nowhere left to look," Rachel said. "They're gone, Ima."

The clerk was busy stacking his papers. Rachel could tell he was still listening to them and only pretending to be occupied.

"Where would they be?" she asked him. "The bodies, I mean."

"I'm afraid we do not keep any of the dead here," the clerk said. "We're at war. There is no time for ceremonies. They have been buried where they fell."

"Shiv'ah," Leah says, weeping now. "For seven days, Rachel, we must sit shiv'ah."

This journey is a kind of shiv'ah, Rachel thought. *We walked seven days to come here, and now we will walk seven days back.* Seven days of shiv'ah for each brother, mourning both Avraham and Aharon, a walking shiv'ah.

Rachel turned the cart around, thinking how she would never share this peculiar thought with anyone, not even her mother. As she and Leah left the green building, the sun outside did not observe their sorrow—it shone like a bright lemon in the middle of the sky. The birds did not join their shiv'ah either, they flew from branch to branch lightly and with ease. The leaves fluttered, and the fat bumblebees settled on fragrant spring flowers. The smoke of the bonfires, where the clothes of the dead were being burned, wafted through the air.

Rachel pulled her mother along, away from the school, past the men carting the bodies along the boulevard to the mass grave site. Aharon and Avraham, she thought, were not merely an initial in a tired clerk's list of the dead. They were buried somewhere, where they fell, wherever that might be, she and her mother would never know. But they were mourned. The warm wind felt good on Rachel's tender scalp. She looked at her tiny mother sitting in the cart, gripped the handles tighter, and set off to walk for another seven days to complete the ritual.

The Miniaturist

I arrived at the Ma'abara refugee absorption camp set up in the newly established State of Israel in the winter of 1950, in the midst of the greatest snowstorm of the century. Together with my parents and four older brothers, I trudged through the thick, powdery snow, an endless flurry of white flakes, watching figures emerge from the pale mist, silhouettes misshapen by everything they carried, all their lifelong possessions rolled up in rags, bundled in wool and fur, tied together with strips of string, stuffed into worn leather valises. We were all wanderers, ghostly apparitions plucked out of thin air like black sunflowers, searching for a place to lay down roots.

My family came only with the clothes on our backs and a laissez-passer, a one-way travel document. Six of the seven suitcases we'd shipped got lost on the way. We were checked for lice, our bodies sprayed with insecticide to prevent the spread of malaria and typhus. Our congested tent city, housing thousands of immigrants, stretched across the coastal plain from

Mount Carmel to the east all the way to the sea in the west. We lived about one kilometer away from the water, but we could never visit the beach. A barbed-wire fence encircled the tent city, and we couldn't cross its perimeter without permission from the authorities. We were confined to a small patch of land and left to fend for ourselves.

Our canvas tent was hut-shaped, identical to all the others, except for a unique number painted in white on the front flap: 244. We unpacked our one remaining suitcase and arranged our meager possessions inside the tent. On the floor, we spread out a precious carpet, patterned with pomegranates and hummingbirds. On the tent flap wall, we hung a family photograph, all seven of us standing by the dome of Imamzadeh Esmaeil Mausoleum. My parents kept their *ketubah* marriage certificate under their straw mattress. We slept on metal-frame beds, our blankets crawling with fleas. We were never told exactly how long we would stay in the tent city, only that it was temporary. Our day-to-day was always the same: wandering listlessly between filthy puddles of sewage and waste, standing in line for food tokens, showers, and toilets, sitting on empty orange crates, waiting and waiting, forever waiting to leave.

It was in the beginning of spring that I first met Esther. The winter storms had finally passed, and a stifling humidity settled over the tent city. Rockrose and thorny broom covered the slope of Mount Carmel in the distance. Esther stood alone in a barren field, like a rare flower blooming in an empty landscape. She was without a doubt more beautiful than me. Her most distinctive feature was her huge bluish-green peacock feather eyes and long dark lashes. She was wearing a midnight-blue taffeta dress. The late afternoon light illuminated the blond hairs on her cheek, her graceful neck, and braided black hair. Her ears were pierced with tiny silver hoops.

I felt ugly and worthless by comparison. Instead of girls' clothing, I wore my older brothers' hand-me-downs. Dirt-brown shorts and a striped collared shirt. My ears were bare. My knees were scabby, my fingernails dirty. My skin was itchy, and my long hair hung in tangled clumps, unwashed for days. She was special, gemlike, gold-dusted. I was dull, ordinary as a handful of carob seeds.

Esther showed me half a walnut shell in the palm of her hand, like a tiny, wizened brain. "This is Thumbelina."

"Where did you get a walnut from?" I asked.

"I brought it from home," Esther said. "My family had a walnut tree in the garden."

"My family had a marble tree," I said. I showed her my lucky marble, translucent with swirls of blue and green.

"I'm waiting for a butterfly," Esther said, and stretched out her hand.

From the first moment I saw her, I wanted to be exactly like Esther, so I stood unmoving next to her and stretched out my hand, too. We were two scarecrows in a dusty, desolate land. Flies and gnats buzzed around my face. The sky was enormous and clear—occasionally a formation of birds flitted by. Stalks of dry grain swayed in the breeze, climbing my ankles, making me shiver. A tiny moth, white and faded, landed on my shoulder. I caught Esther's eye. A moment later, it flew away. Esther told me that it was a good sign the moth chose me. It meant I was trustworthy.

"Adinah!" my father called out. "Come here, now!"

My father stood at the edge of the field, a patch of dry

earth scattered with dying grass, one hand raised to shade his eyes from the sun's glare. I ran to him without looking back at Esther. He wore an elegant shirt, frayed at the collar, nearly half its buttons missing. He was completely out of place here, in this strange land where everyone wore shorts and khaki, and he liked to remind me of this all the time. Eretz Israel was not his home. He didn't belong here, and neither did I. *My heart is in the East, but I am in the West.*

"That girl isn't your friend," he said. "We don't talk to her family."

When we walked back to the tent together, my father was tense, wrapped in his own thoughts, ignoring greetings from our neighbors. My mother was hanging dripping clothes on the line. My brothers still had not returned from work, clearing rocks and planting trees. My father heaved himself down onto an old wooden stool, sighing, and I sat on his lap. I used to often sit on his lap outside our shop in Golbahar, the Jewish quarter of Isfahan, where we sold hand-woven rugs. Now, sitting by our tent, shoulders stooped, he rolled a cigarette, his nails stained yellow. He spread the tobacco onto the paper, evened it out with his thumb and forefinger, and licked it shut. He took a deep drag. Smoke curled and twisted from his cigarette, like vines of honeysuckle, as he began to weave together the threads of our families' history.

"Our families have always been in competition," my father said.

Our rivalry went back hundreds of years, to Spain in the early fourteenth century, to what my father called the Great Split between the two schools of Jewish miniaturists in Catalonia. Our ancestors, the miniaturists, sat in Barcelona's dusty scriptoriums and sun-drenched ateliers, decorating the borders of holy texts in gold filigree, painting tiny colorful pictures in the margins with the smallest of brushes.

My family belonged to the first school of miniaturists, who took the Second Commandment very seriously: *You shall not make yourself a carved image, or any likeness of anything that is in heaven above.* Our drawings were decorative, like arabesque patterns in Islam. But Esther's family illustrated the sacred stories, just as Christians did. Esther's ancestor was a man called Nissim ben-Tzemach Albargeloni, the Miniaturist of Catalonia. He became famous all over the world for his delicate and masterful illustrations. His most renowned work was the Alfonso Bible, commissioned by the King of Aragon, with an illumination of the fourth chapter of Genesis, the story of Cain slaying his brother Abel. He illustrated Cain standing over young Abel, grasping his little brother by the locks of his curly hair, raising his weapon, the bloodied jawbone of an animal of the field, prepared to strike. The Hebrew letters that adorned the illustrations were decorated with leaves of gold, bunches of blue-black grapes, and crimson pomegranates. *A restless wanderer shall you be on this earth.*

My ancestors were expelled from Spain in 1492, along with the rest of the Jews who refused to convert to Christianity. Esther's family became conversos and kept practicing their Jewish faith in secret. Our families parted for centuries, yet the story of our enmity was passed down from generation to generation, should we ever meet again. After many years, both Esther's family and mine settled in Isfahan, the third-largest city in Iran, famous for its carpets and textiles. Now, in the Ma'abara, our families lived in the same place again, side by side, in makeshift tents. We had lost everything, and all that remained was the memory of our rivalry.

One morning, a few days after I first saw her, I found Esther sitting on the ground, tracing a pattern in the sand with a thin stick. It made me think of what my father had told me, about her great forebear, the Miniaturist, illuminating a manuscript. She could've been hunched over a worktable in an atelier, painting the borders of a holy text just like her ancestors hundreds of years ago, tapping her foot on a mosaic floor patterned with octagons, light streaming in from the tall windows, golden dust motes floating in the air. Esther's brows were furrowed in concentration, and she was breathing loudly through her nose. She didn't notice me staring at her, or maybe she pretended not to care.

"My daddy told me not to talk to you," I said. Still, she didn't look up. I tried a different tactic. "What are you drawing?"

"It's my house," she said. "We lived next to the Grand Bazaar in Isfahan."

Esther traced the stick along the paths she outlined in the sand, showing me Abdolrazagh Street and Hakim Street, and together we remembered the thousand-year-old vaulted marketplace, the tiled archway adorned with lions and winged beasts, endless handicraft shops selling ornamental plates and copper teapots, kilim and carpets. I missed walking around the boulevards and gardens, eating sugared disks of *poolaki* and juicy melon slices, my fingers sticky, watching the haggling vendors, the jugglers and puppeteers and acrobats, trailing ribbons of bright fabric. Here in the tent city, there was nothing but dust and sand.

"We were neighbors," I said. "I lived by the Ali Gholi Agha bathhouse."

"We still are neighbors," Esther said.

Esther gave me my first scar. About a week later, on a warm, dull afternoon, we challenged each other to a race to the fence separating our tent city from the sea. We careened down the endless rows of dark tents, our bare feet scorching the hot earth, zigzagging past the boy pulling a wooden cart piled high with straw pillows, avoiding the women hanging laundry on a line, nearly colliding with the blind man groping for invisible treasure on the ground. Esther was ahead of me, her braided hair bouncing up and down. My lungs were burning. We barreled through a line of people waiting for their food tokens.

I was so close to Esther now that I could smell the talcum powder on her skin. She dodged a group of screaming children and a man gardening, planting a few sprigs of mint, and I was so close to her, I was about to pull ahead, when suddenly she bumped into me, slipping ahead, and I stumbled over a tent rope and fell on a rusty shovel. My scar was shaped like a sickle.

Even though Esther felt bad, she never apologized. But after that she did make more of an effort to be my friend. A few days after our race, she showed me what she called her secret spot, a tin shack, a kind of storage room where rows of mattresses were stacked one on top of another. There were piles of woolen blankets, worn and threadbare. She lifted one of the blankets, and we crawled inside, imagining our dream room. It was a tiny, fragile model world with walls made of pearled seashells, crawling with golden scarab beetles and lazy monarch butterflies, complete with an antique dollhouse. One side was exposed to reveal a dining room with a crystal chandelier, a kitchen with tiny pots and pans hanging off hooks, and a bedroom with spun-silk gossamer curtains. We were safe in our imaginary world.

We spent our days wandering together through the makeshift vegetable gardens of the tent city, talking to the plants to encourage them to grow. Many of the plants drooped, withered, and died under the harsh glare of the sun, despite our attempts to save them. But some survived, sprouting haphazardly from the dry earth. Sprigs of fresh green mint, a few bright red bell peppers. When a small kiosk opened up that sold sacks of flour, powdered eggs, and bubblegum, we went through the trash to find the gum wrappers whose comic strips, cartoons, and jokes in Hebrew we couldn't read. We liked drawing the cartoons on the sand with sticks, copying the strange letters, and waiting for someone to walk by and laugh at the joke, but no one ever bothered to look down.

Except for occasional Ivrit lessons with volunteers from the neighboring kibbutz, we had no school or structure of any kind. We did whatever we wanted: spent an entire day rolling a tire down a hill, kicking around a ball of wet rags, playing Five Stones, throwing one knucklebone into the air, and sweeping the other four off the ground, playing Three Sticks, jumping farther and farther as the distance between the sticks grew, playing Salted Fish, taking turns closing our eyes and leaning against a tree, counting one, two, three, *dag malooach*. Sometimes we played *machboim,* hide-and-seek, in the tent city. *Echad, shtaim, shalosh,* Esther counted, hiding her face in her hands. When she found me, we were silent for a moment, staring at each other, and I remember thinking I never wanted to be apart again.

Our favorite game was *julot,* marbles. I was the best sharp-shooter in the Ma'abara, even better than Esther. My marbles were precious and could be sold for a real profit, but I saved them in my pockets like secret trophies. I never played with my green and blue swirly marble from home because I couldn't bear to lose it. We played as a team against all the boys, flicking our marbles against theirs, winning them as our own. Our toughest game was against the Prince of Marbles. He was the reigning tent city champion, a nimble-fingered boy from Yemen, all skin and bones, who hated to lose.

It was Esther's turn. She concentrated, pursing her lips. She flicked her own marble, sending it spiraling in a whirl of bright color, to collide with the Prince's.

"I win." She swiped the Prince of Marbles' marble.

"You cheated," he said.

"She didn't cheat," I said. "You lost."

"Give it back!" The Prince of Marbles grabbed Esther's arm and tried to pry away the marble.

Esther's fingers were clenched tight, and he couldn't get her to open her hand. I kicked his shin, and he howled, jumping around on one leg. Esther giggled, imitating him. The Prince of Marbles hobbled away, promising revenge—"I'll steal all your marbles and tie you upside-down from a tree"—but as it turned out we never saw him again. He was one of the first boys who got sick. He was taken to the children's hospital and never came back. Other children began to disappear, swept away in the night. One moment they were playing with us, the next they were gone. Whenever we felt very scared of the sick, disappearing children, Esther and I went back to her secret spot, the storage shack lined with mattresses, crawled under the blanket, closed our eyes, and conjured up our dream room.

The sandy *khamsin* wind made living in the tent city unbearable. On blistering-hot summer days, Esther's mother would set up a bucket of precious water in front of their tent, painstakingly retrieved after waiting in line for hours at the communal tap. Esther would stand naked, completely oblivious to herself, and her mother would pour water over her body. She was small, even for her age, but never seemed childlike, but rather fully formed and compact. My mother began doing the same to me, bathing me in the open with the aid of a bucket. We stood, the two of us, in front of each other, naked, with our mothers pouring water over us in the midday sun.

Like her famous ancestor, Esther enjoyed illustrating stories. She made a little book of drawings with scenes from the story "Thumbelina." A dozen children sat around Esther in a semicircle, enraptured by the intricate pictures. I loved the little golden-haired girl emerging from the stalks of barleycorn, and the fat toad in a bow tie sitting on a lily pad. Soon I got tired of telling Esther just how talented she was all the time. She glowed with the attention—her bright eyes searched for my delighted expression as she turned the pages, even though I had seen her pictures a thousand times already. I drew the same images over and over again, two girls standing in a field, dozens of tent triangles poking up out of the earth like sharp teeth. But Esther never once told me she liked any of my drawings.

In the fall, Esther and I paraded our drawings past the small group of craftsmen and artisans, hoping they would notice our work. The men sat around Abu Shlomo's, an improvised café in the tent city, smoking, drinking palm wine *lagmi,* and playing *sheshbesh.* Abu Shlomo, the owner of the establishment, had built the shack himself using old Tnuvah packing crates. On the floor, he'd spread out a beautiful, worn carpet of green and gold. A cardboard sign hung above the door: ABU SHLOMO'S MAGIC CARPET CAFÉ. A small transistor radio played music by Farid al-Atrash, strumming his oud and singing his mournful songs. Usually the artists were too drunk to pay any attention to us. Back in Tripoli, Baghdad, Cairo, and Tehran, they were revered for their creations, they were respected sculptors, potters, and painters, but here, without the materials or the space to build, they were nothing but weary and despondent men, clinging to the past.

The most respected artist in the entire tent city, one of the regulars at Abu Shlomo's, was the photographer Shmuel Sassoon. We heard that back in Baghdad, Sassoon had been very close to the King of Iraq. One day Esther and I decided to follow Sassoon everywhere, without saying a word. He didn't seem to mind that we were trailing him. He was completely absorbed in his work, heedless of us, his two shadows. He wandered around the tent city, a sleek black and silver camera dangling from his neck. We liked watching him take pictures. We wanted to see what he saw, but we didn't understand his preoccupation with the dull, mundane images of life in the tent city. He photographed a stretch of dark tents against a pale sky, an old woman sitting on an empty crate of oranges, desolate fields and faraway hills powdered with flowers. Sometimes he took pictures of the sea, radiant in the distance, beyond the fence. He made strange clicking sounds with his tongue every time he looked through the lens.

After an hour of creeping around and spying, Esther decided to confront him. When he was down on one knee, framing a shot—a single yellow flower sprouting from cracked earth—she stepped right in front of him, hands on her hips. She blocked the view from his camera. "Can we see your pictures?"

"I'm afraid not," Sassoon said, speaking Farsi with a slight Iraqi accent. "I'd show you the pictures if I could. The truth is they don't exist yet."

Sassoon explained that he'd brought a 35mm Leica from home but couldn't afford any film. So instead of taking an actual photograph, he'd look through the lens, frame the scene, capture the composition, and click his tongue to indicate he'd taken a picture in his mind.

"Were you really friends with the King of Iraq?" Esther said.

"We weren't friends," he said quickly. "I worked for him."

"You were his photographer?" I asked.

"In a way. But not directly. I was the Assistant to the Assistant to the Photographer of the King of Iraq, Faisal I bin Al-Hussein bin Ali Al-Hashemi."

"But now you can't take any more pictures," Esther said.

Sassoon sighed and ran a hand through his curly hair, graying at the temples. "Oh, I can. And let me take your picture. Be still, please. No moving. Tell your friend to come stand next to you. When I leave the Ma'abara at last and get myself some film, we'll do this again. But for now—come girls."

While framing the shot, he told us how in Baghdad he'd

taken pictures of backgammon halls, cabarets, and taverns. His favorite haunt was the Shabandar Café on Al-Mutanabi Street in the Bookshop District, where poets and politicians sat on wooden benches with small glasses of sweet tea and bubbling hookah pipes. When he worked for the king, he took the official portrait of Faisal I in his ceremonial uniform with golden epaulets, sitting on a throne in Qasr al-Zuhur, the Palace of Flowers, under a ceiling inlaid with hundreds of thousands of hand-carved granite flowers.

We stood for our own portrait as he spoke, still as statues until Sassoon clicked his tongue. He told us how he had taken passport pictures of Baghdadi Jews to help them emigrate to Israel, where they eventually ended up in the Ma'abara. Eventually, he took a picture of himself and came too. Esther was so bored of his story that her eyes were closed. I wondered if she could have fallen asleep standing up.

"Open your eyes, child," Sassoon said.

"What if I want to keep them closed?" Esther said.

"You will get a photograph with your eyes closed."

"I don't mind."

"It's not a real photograph, anyway," I said.

Sassoon looked very sad at the mention of this, and I instantly regretted saying it. His cleft chin wobbled slightly, and he looked at the ground.

"When I was your age," he said, "I was already working for the King of Iraq."

"When I'm your age," Esther said, "I'm going to be the King of Iraq!"

A few days later Esther and I were both sitting on the ground by the table of craftsmen and artists, drawing with colored pencils. Sassoon sat on a rickety stool, smoking a cigarette, his face flushed with alcohol. Esther was deep in concentration, confidently shading the feathers of a small finch. I was absentmindedly drawing a tree, an ugly brown line for the trunk, a clumsy green halo of leaves, listening to the men's conversation. They sipped *lagmi* and spoke at length of the great artists of Jerusalem, the Armenians who renovated the tiles of the Dome of the Rock mosque and opened a ceramics workshop, on the Via Dolorosa in the Old City, that specialized in the depiction of birds of paradise. After several minutes, Sassoon got up shakily, stumbled, and nearly stepped on Esther, leaving an imprint of his shoe on her drawing.

"You ruined it!" Esther said.

He waved away Esther's accusation and requested to see the drawing he had nearly destroyed. Colorful birds intertwined together. Eye-spotted trains of peacocks' tails, necks of pale swans, plumage of yellow and blue parrots, outstretched wings of eagles, dark blur of ravens, coral twigs of pigeon feet. He didn't even ask to see my drawing.

"Birds of paradise," he said.

"It's just the pictures of a little girl," I said, but no one was listening to me.

"Show me your other drawings," Sassoon said. "Child, bring them to me."

"Adinah, can you go get them?" she asked.

I knew Esther kept all her drawings under her straw mattress, protected by a layer of onionskin paper and wrapped in old towels. I ran to her tent as fast as I could and gathered all her drawings. For a moment, I thought of throwing them away, pretending like they were gone, but I didn't. I returned with a bundle of them under my arm and laid them out on the table, pushing aside glasses of *lagmi*, and made a little exhibition.

Sassoon took his time, examining each and every picture, drawing the attention of all the other craftsmen and artists who looked over his shoulder, stroking their beards and nodding in approval.

"She may be little," he said to me, "but inside your friend there is a genius." He bent down to Esther, put his hands on her shoulders. "Who am I?"

"A photographer," Esther said.

"That's true," said Sassoon, "but it's not who I *am*. I preserve the history of my people. Who are your ancestors? You have an Old Master in your family, don't you?"

Esther didn't look up from her drawing. She bit her lip thoughtfully, before finally meeting his eyes. "Yes," she whispered. "The Miniaturist of Catalonia."

For some in the Ma'abara, hearing of the revered Sassoon's admiration for Esther was proof enough that she was the reincarnation of the Miniaturist's spirit, that she was destined for great things. With nothing to do and nowhere to go, the story gave people hope, or at least a distraction. Soon everyone was so enchanted by Esther that they pooled their limited resources and bought her a new set of colored pencils, a notebook lined with thick paper, two paintbrushes, and cheap watercolors. And yet they didn't let her enjoy her gifts for long—they began making all kinds of demands, ordering her to make them artwork and portraits and other painting projects. She barely had any time left for me. Whenever I wanted to play, she was always busy. Her parents gave her a little corner of the tent in which to work, and she sat there for hours with her tiny paintbrush, illustrating fairy tales for the other children, painting portraits of entire families, and patterning the hands of new brides with henna.

I was so jealous of Esther's drawings. Everyone was always praising her masterpieces—*how elaborate, how wondrous*—and no one said a word about my little sketches. I hated how much I wanted to be told I was good. In all her pictures, the fence separating our tent city from the sea never existed. To spite her, I drew only fences, tall and crude, dividing. Esther's illustrated world was vivid and particular but also boundless. Little black tents bloomed in the vast expanse of sand, massive wildebeests, Arabian camels, and snowy-maned lions roamed the earth, and in the depths of the sea swam ghostly transparent whales and mammoth medusae, while mermaids bathed on mossy boulders, holding up offerings of giant pearls.

Sassoon hired Esther to work for him. Every day she went to the studio of the former Assistant to the Assistant to the Photographer of the King of Iraq. It was a great honor for her family. Sassoon's studio was in a tin shack on the outskirts of the tent city, under the shadow of Mount Carmel. Esther painted backdrops for his photographs: a starry sky, its night peeling slightly at the edges, a desert landscape with cacti, a marble-floored palace with golden columns. She decorated the walls of Sassoon's studio with a crackling painted fireplace, a vase adorned with dragons and lilies, plush velvet stools, and heavy burgundy curtains. Behind the painted curtains, the room itself, of course, was empty. Nothing but dust.

I kept imagining a tiny man inside Esther, the Miniaturist, pulling her strings like a puppet master and controlling her every movement. In my mind, the Miniaturist had silver, shoulder-length hair and a waxed beard and wore a green-silk floral brocade patterned with roses and chestnuts. He sat on a red Spanish rug from Catalonia, in a fully furnished ornate living room inside Esther, complete with paintings hung in gilded golden frames, and within each painting, a miniature scene: a group of hunters disappearing in the snow without a trace. For some reason, this vision terrified me. I was afraid of the little genius inside her, of the never-ending miniatures. When she won a competition we held, to see who had the smallest handwriting—her letters so minuscule they were almost invisible and yet could be clearly deciphered with a magnifying glass—I was convinced it was true. Esther was the reincarnation of the famous Miniaturist, and I was nobody.

I found my father smoking outside, under a night sky as dark and smooth as velvet. I could see the deep lines of his face only by the glowing ember of his cigarette. I wanted to tell him that whatever I did, it was never good enough. I just wasn't a talented girl like Esther, nor the reincarnation of anybody important or famous, certainly not the Miniaturist. In my past life I was probably a snail with a humble shell, making its slow way in the world, leaving a trail behind that soon evaporated.

"Daddy, is Esther really the Mini-tsuris?" I asked.

"Do you want to hear a secret, Adinah?" My father flicked away his cigarette and began rolling another. "The Miniaturist never finished his most famous work."

My father told me the Miniaturist died of the plague before completing the Alfonso Bible commissioned by King Alfonso the Kind, and his most beautiful illumination, the rivalry between Cain and Abel. The Black Death also took the Miniaturist's eldest son and frequent studio collaborator, but his young daughter survived. Growing up, she had watched her father and older brother at work in their studio, creating tempera paint by mixing mineral pigments and plant dyes with egg yolk, outlining the drawing with lead point, and applying red clay and gold leaf to the manuscript. She took up the thankless task of finishing her father's work and preserving the family legacy, painting Abel's cloak with precious lapis lazuli, adding blush to Cain's lips with Phoenician purple, a pigment made by crushing the spiky shells of hundreds of predatory sea snails. But her contribution was never formally acknowledged, and she was mostly forgotten.

The days got shorter and darker and colder, and I was always alone. Esther never spent any time with me at all anymore, she was always busy with some project. I wandered around the tent city, sometimes going to Esther's secret spot, hoping she might be there, but she never was. She probably thought I would always wait for her, that I was a trustworthy friend, but I wanted her to miss me, to feel hurt and lonely, just as I did every day I spent without her.

But no matter how often she was praised or was told how extraordinarily gifted she was, Esther never went anywhere without her Thumbelina, her good luck charm. Only once, when her mother called her inside the tent urgently to finish working on the portrait of an important rabbi, she accidentally left the walnut out on the ground. I stole it, put it in my pocket, and ran my fingers over the wrinkly and hard shell. I walked toward the fence separating our tent city from the sea we never got to visit. I gripped the chain link, stuck my nose into the gap, breathing in the fresh sea air mixed with the slightly rotting scent of seaweed, and, my heart pounding, tossed the walnut shell away, outside the fence wall and down to the strip of sand that led to the water, where we could never go.

When Esther discovered Thumbelina was missing, she looked so anguished and alone that for a moment, I wanted to confess. We were standing in the field, here and there clumps of dry grass boldly grew in the desolate earth. Her body shook with sharp bursts, quick gasps.

"Where is she?" Esther said. "I can't find her."

She patted herself down over and over again, crawled around in the dust, pulled out grass like hair, and picked up small rocks and metal bottlecaps.

"Adinah, I'm scared."

"We'll find Thumbelina," I said.

For the first time in our friendship, I felt stronger, in control. But she looked so miserable, standing there, crying, that it was almost too much to bear. I felt so guilty. If I told her the truth, she'd hate me, never forgive me, whereas I just wanted her to need me.

Esther wiped her eyes, composed herself, and took a shaky breath. "You'll help me look for her, right?"

I promised to help her search for Thumbelina, and we called out her name, peering into the cracks in the dry earth, and the scattered clumps of grass. When we overturned stones, we were careful to avoid the *akrabuts*, yellow camel spiders as big as our fists. We saw plenty of white-spotted swallows flying around, and Esther pointed them out, gliding across the sky, relieved, nodding to them as if they had some secret pact to protect Thumbelina. We walked through the barren field and along the fence, encircled with barbed wire, separating our tent city from the rest of Israel, looking out at the clean, white houses of the kibbutzim, surrounded by fruit gardens, the sea sparkling in the distance. Esther peered closely at the stalks of barleycorn, whispering *Thumbelina, Thumbelina*, hoping she would appear, but she never did.

That night I couldn't sleep. As soon as it got dark, the jackals started howling. I heard them clawing and biting the tent. I shut my eyes tight. *Sniff, sniff,* went the jackal. *Scratch, scratch, scratch.* Was it looking for me? Or would it take Esther away, salivating jaws clamped around her dress, dragging her to its dark lair? Beside me, on the bed, my mother lay in her nightgown, her heavy bosom rising and falling. Next to her, my father was tossing and turning, moaning every once in a while. My brothers slept shirtless and sweaty, all in a row. I felt like everyone in the entire world was asleep except for me.

Winter brought cold winds and plagued us with endless rain and flooding. Sewage pits were overflowing, garbage hadn't been collected in weeks, tents were crowded with the sick and the dying. We slept on wet blankets, shivering, teeth chattering, listening to the *drip drip drip* from the tent roof. Rain fell as much inside the tent as it did outside, we had no protection at all from the storms. All our last remaining keepsakes from our previous life in Isfahan were destroyed: our family photograph taped on the tent wall, our precious rug patterned with pomegranates and hummingbirds, my parents' *ketubah* marriage certificate, everything was soggy, covered in creeping mold. It all fell apart in our hands. Many of Esther's drawings, even those protected by a layer of onionskin and rags, were ruined, their color washed away. Birds lost their shape, became blurred as if captured in midflight. All the animals she drew, lions, camels, and wildebeests, they all drowned.

It was early morning, and Esther was drying the remains of her drawings in the sun, weighing them down with small rocks to keep them from flying away in the gales. Some drawings were ripped and crumpled, unrecognizable, and others were so wet they seemed to seep into the earth. Esther looked defeated, sapped of her glow, her light slowly fading. Her face was sickly and pale, her mouth set in a thin, trembling line. She wandered between her drawings, whispering to herself and to them, her flimsy dress clinging to her rib cage, placing pebbles on their paper corpses before the burial.

Secretly, I was happy her drawings were ruined. I hated seeing her so upset, but without her drawings to distract her, she could go back to playing with me. It would be just the two of us again, without the spirit of the Miniaturist getting in our way. We could focus on playing marbles or hide-and-seek. We could go to our secret spot, crawl under the blanket, and share our secrets. But there was no going back. Esther was devastated. She kicked the ground, wild-eyed, tearing her drawings up, stomping again and again, until all the colorful paper fluttered away and scattered to the wind.

A few days later Esther got sick. She was infected with the measles virus. I wasn't allowed to visit her at all, since the disease was so contagious, so I sat outside her tent and watched her through the fluttering tent flap. I felt so guilty and ashamed, I could hardly breathe. She lay swaddled in blankets, tiny and powerless, in a small bed. Shivering uncontrollably, eyes swollen and inflamed. Mucus dribbled from her nose. Her skin, speckled like those spotted leopard mollusks she loved to draw so much, was marked with ruin. She was taken to a children's hospital outside the Ma'abara in the middle of the night. I was asleep and didn't get to even say goodbye.

The hospital, I found out, was only an hour's bus ride away. A ticket cost sixty prutoth cents. I sold all my marbles, the ones I had won in countless games of *julot*, for one prutah each, so I could afford a ticket, but kept only one bluish-green marble, the color of Esther's eyes. I had enough prutoth for one journey. I would have to walk back, or find some other way to get home, but I promised myself I wouldn't leave the hospital without Esther.

I sneaked out of the tent city early the next morning, blending in with the crowd of children going to study Ivrit at a neighboring kibbutz, sixty-three prutoth jangling in my pocket. We weren't allowed to leave without permission, but no one noticed me. It was my first time on a bus. I counted out the change slowly, giving the exasperated ticket seller in the back one cent at a time. Most of the seats on the old wooden benches were unoccupied—there were only a handful of people on the bus: two farmers in khaki shorts, and one old woman holding a birdcage with a chattering songbird. I sat by the cloudy cataract window, the countryside blurring past: flat, asbestos-roofed houses, sheets of yellow wildflowers, and spots of limestone, pine trees, and brambles.

Down a winding path, I saw the hospital building with its white-latticed shades. Two doctors, smoking by the entrance, hardly glanced at me as I slipped inside. Children walked around the fluorescent-lit hospital corridors in mismatched pajamas and ill-fitting stockings of different colors, like sleepwalkers under an electric moon. Nurses wandered around in bulky shoes and gowns, swishing and clicking wherever they went, pushing metal trolleys, clutching spoiled linen and bedpans, checking charts, and handing out brightly colored pills.

I wandered into one of the rooms, smelling of antiseptic and bleach, where the children were sleeping on gurneys. I stared at all the sleeping faces, one by one. Many of the children had red spots like Esther, and some had swollen necks. A single bed, stripped bare, was empty. There was a drawing of a spiral on the wall next to it, made with a blue pencil, Esther's favorite color. I couldn't be sure, but I imagined Esther, lonely and afraid, weak from her illness, slipping out of bed to draw the spiral, creating a magic portal and stepping through it, emerging who knows where. I imagined her shrinking to miniature dimensions, a thimble-size Esther I could slip into my pocket and keep with me forever.

A nurse stepped into the room, shoes clacking loudly. She took my hand and began asking me questions I couldn't understand. I struggled against her grip, but she was strong. She dragged me out, down the hallway, talking the entire time, her asparagus breath in my face. I tried to grab on to anything on the way, my fingers scraping against the walls, but the nurse kept pulling me. When we were close to the entrance, I bit her arm, hard. She shrieked and let go of me, and I ran outside, past the smoking doctors, down the winding dirt path, through a field of yellow wildflowers, until I could hardly breathe anymore, and I crumpled to the ground, pressed my knees to my chest, and closed my eyes.

I walked toward the main road, the one the bus drove down. The grass was very tall, filled with brambles and little thorns that cut my bare legs. Every so often I glanced over my shoulder, to see if the nurse or one of the smoking doctors had followed me, but I was alone. A spitting drizzle started. My feet ached, several times I slipped on the mud. I kept rubbing at my eyes. Wet hair plastered my forehead. Here and there small olive trees, twisted and withered, sprang out of the ground, like the twisted hands of an ancient people buried under the earth. I reached the road, spent and empty, and stood there in the rain for a very long time. When the bus finally arrived, I cried so hard that my entire body was shaking, and the driver waved me inside, and let me sit near him, even though I only had three prutoth left.

For weeks I stayed in bed with a high fever. I had caught the measles, just like Esther. My parents were terrified of sending me to the hospital. They hid my illness from everyone and tried to take care of me as best as they could, pressing cold towels to my forehead and praying for my health. When I was strong enough to keep my eyes open, I saw the world through the tent flap, a slice of blue, and imagined Esther on the other side, watching over me. Mostly I was in the dark. I couldn't tell if it was day or night. I wanted only to be with Esther. She had left a sign for me to find in the hospital, that spiral. In my bed, I traced small spirals on the sweat-soaked sheets. I thought of the spiral now as a doorway through which she could return to our world, if she wanted to. *Come back,* I thought. *Show yourself, Esther, please, stop hiding.*

But Esther never came back from the hospital, and her family soon left the tent city. Perhaps they were finally given real housing. I had already forgotten what it was like to have a real home. Eventually, I began to feel better, my fever was gone, and the sheets were no longer damp with sweat. The weakness in my limbs stayed, but I felt more awake and alert. I left my bedside for the first time, stepped outside. It was spring again, except this time, walking through the budding mint and thyme plants, I didn't have Esther next to me. I was all alone. The sun was bright, so bright I had to shut my eyes. Dancing red sparks. A dull throbbing pain under my lids. My skin crawling with goose bumps, a thousand hungry ants. I stumbled around, raw and hazy, covering my eyes, like I was playing a game of hide-and-seek with Esther. I walked past the storage room, where we used to crawl under the scratchy blanket whenever we felt scared. I was terrified all the time, but I couldn't go there without her.

I walked toward the fence separating our tent city from the sea. Esther and I always dreamed about going to the sea, shedding our old clothes like snakeskin, letting ourselves be carried away with the tide, far, far away. We liked looking out at the earth and sky and sea neatly divided, breathing it all in behind the chain-link fence, feeling the cold spray on our faces on particularly windy days. As I walked by myself along the fence, barefoot on the dry earth, I wished my family had stayed in Iran. We should never have left everything behind, I thought, to come to Eretz Israel in the middle of a great snowstorm to live in a miserable tent in this land of refugees. If we had stayed in Isfahan, selling carpets in the Golbahar neighborhood, I might never have met Esther.

Sixty-three years later, it's snowing again in Eretz Israel. Not since 1950, the year I arrived in the country, has the snow been so thick and heavy. They're calling it a highly unusual weather event, a Middle Eastern cold snap. An endless stream of white flakes falls on Jerusalem, enshrouding the streets of Nachlaot in a white tomb.

As the years went by, the bright bloom of Esther's memory slowly faded, buried under the mundane and relentless topsoil of everyday life, but a part of her always stayed deep within me, patiently growing roots. I'm a professor at the Hebrew University, specializing in illuminated medieval manuscripts. I have devoted my life to the study of the Miniaturist, perhaps in the hope that it would lead me back, somehow, to Esther. Even though I'm old and I wear loose-fitting, dark dresses and long silver necklaces, and my hair has lost its color and thickness, I feel as if I am still a girl, running barefoot after Esther in the dusty tents of the Ma'abara.

My family finally left the Ma'abara, after three years of living in the tent city, and we relocated to Jaffa, and eventually my father opened a carpet shop on Olei Tzion Street. I studied very hard in school, and after my military service, I got a scholarship to study history at Tel Aviv University. While my classmates divided their time between Café Kasit and Eden Cinema, I committed myself to studying, reading and writing until my eyes were weary, my fingers ink-stained and blistered. My professors were pleased with my work, and in my final year they sponsored a trip to Barcelona, to the birthplace of the Miniaturist, to the home of my ancestors and Esther's family, to examine the illuminated manuscripts of calfskin parchment or vellum, lavishly decorated with gold leaf and pigments, held together by glues of egg or gum arabic. Sitting in the empty basement of the library's rare books room with my white-cotton gloves, handling the tissue-thin manuscript pages of the Megillah, the Book of Esther, painted by Nissim ben-Tzemach

Albargeloni, the Miniaturist of Catalonia, I expected some kind of revelation. I admired the calligraphy of the square Sephardi script and searched for the hidden face of my childhood friend and rival in the form of the beautiful Jewish Persian queen, but I couldn't find her.

The snow falls heavier now as the sky darkens, a whooshing whirlwind of flakes that obscures the road signs and limestone homes and synagogues, little cobblestoned alleyways and artisan shops. Jerusalem is frozen silent, preserved as pale white ivory. Out of habit, I trace a spiral in the condensation on the cold glass windowpane. On Agripas Street, two Haredi men are pushing a cart of bread down the gray slushy sidewalk. Boys are hurling snowballs at each other. A little girl with braided hair, wearing a dark duffle coat, is skipping in the snow. She's graceful and confident in the way she moves, and for a moment I think it's Esther, as I knew her so many years ago, finally coming back to me. The girl skips past my window and continues down the white-blanketed road. Snow keeps tumbling down, blowing thick under the glow of streetlamps, and I watch her figure get smaller and fainter in the distance until finally she disappears.

Acknowledgments

Enormous thank-yous to: My agent, Janet Silver, for her stead-fast support, wisdom, and guidance, and for believing in these stories from the very beginning. My editor, Robin Desser, for her brilliance, kindness, and devotion, and for reading these stories with such incredible care and generosity; if the Minia-turist of Catalonia had illuminated my acknowledgments page, then their names would be inscribed in gold leaf and the most precious lapis lazuli. My teachers over the years at the University of Cambridge, Boston University, New York University, Bread Loaf, and Tin House. My very first mentors, Ha Jin and Sigrid Nunez, for their boundless encouragement and faith. My inspiring teachers at NYU, for their openness and insightfulness: Kiran Desai, Katie Kitamura, David Lip-sky, Julie Orringer, Darin Strauss, and Hannah Tinti. My friends and family in Tel Aviv, Jerusalem, Paris, Berlin, Los

Angeles, and New York, for your stories and your love, one thousand and one other things.

Thank you to the amazing team at Random House: Rachel Ake, Avideh Bashirrad, Rebecca Berlant, Ayelet Durantt, Tangela Mitchell, Carrie Neill, Clio Seraphim, Noa Shapiro, Robert Siek, Andy Ward, and Samuel Wetzler, whose enthusiasm and dedication helped me overcome my vertigo and scale the terrifying peaks of Mt. Publication.

I found the following books, films, and documentary series particularly helpful in my research: Adam LeBor's *City of Oranges: An Intimate History of Arabs and Jews in Jaffa,* Tom Segev's *One Palestine, Complete: Jews and Arabs Under the British Mandate,* Meron Benvenisti's *Sacred Landscape: The Buried History of the Holy Land Since 1948,* Rashid Khalidi's *The Hundred Years' War on Palestine,* Thomas L. Friedman's *From Beirut to Jerusalem,* Duki Dror's *Lebanon: Borders of Blood,* Dina Zvi-Riklis's *Ma'abarot,* Samuel Maoz's *Foxtrot,* and David Grossman's *To the End of the Land.* I am also indebted to Marc Michael Epstein, Sara Offenberg, Yair Bunzel, Tuly Flint, Itamar Radai, and Ronny Perlman for sharing their invaluable experience and expertise with me.

In the words of Israeli writer and peace activist David Grossman: "Every one of us has a kind of official story that we present to others, to strangers we meet, or even to people we know. . . . But if we are lucky enough to find a good listener, a sympathetic witness, then they will make us tell not only our official story but the story underneath it. . . . This will force us to give up on the protection of the official story that has become like a trap and even a prison for us. . . . The power of a good story is that it does not protect us but instead exposes us and brings us into closer contact with our own life." In this collection, I wanted to unearth the hidden stories of individuals beneath the fossilized official narrative. I hope I've been a sympathetic listener to my characters, and my final thank-you is to them, for telling me their tales.

About the Author

Omer Friedlander was born in Jerusalem in 1994 and grew up in Tel Aviv. He earned a BA in English literature from the University of Cambridge, England, and an MFA from Boston University, where he was supported by the Saul Bellow Fellowship. His short stories have won numerous awards and have been published in the United States, Canada, France, and Israel. A Starworks Fellow in Fiction at New York University, he has earned a Bread Loaf Work-Study Scholarship as well as a fellowship from the Vermont Studio Center. He currently lives in New York City.

omerfriedlander.com

About the Type

This book was set in Sabon, a typeface designed by the well-known German typographer Jan Tschichold (1902–74). Sabon's design is based upon the original letterforms of sixteenth-century French type designer Claude Garamond and was created specifically to be used for three sources: foundry type for hand composition, Linotype, and Monotype. Tschichold named his typeface for the famous Frankfurt typefounder Jacques Sabon (c. 1520–80).